Praise for *City of Dis*

'What ghostly eyes chart our hesitancies in this beautiful unknowable Dantesque prison we call the world? David Butler's compelling, mythic, metaphysical X-ray is beautifully written and ought to cement his already growing reputation.' – *Patrick McCabe*

Praise for *The Judas Kiss*

'Malcolm Little is among the more outlandishly repulsive creations of recent Irish fiction [...] That does not detract from the strength of Butler's remarkable characterisation.' – *Alan Murdoch, The Sunday Times*

'Several darkly comic characters share narrative duty in this affecting, tightly controlled story that's never dull.' – *Publishers Weekly (USA)*

'Searing.' – *Alison Walsh, The Sunday Independent*

City of Dis

City of Dis

DAVID BUTLER

NEW ISLAND

CITY OF DIS

First published 2014
by New Island Books,
16 Priory Hall Office Park,
Stillorgan,
County Dublin.
Republic of Ireland.

www.newisland.ie

PRINT ISBN: 978-1-84840-364-2
EPUB ISBN: 978-1-84840-365-9
MOBI ISBN: 978-1-84840-366-6

British Library Cataloguing Data.
A CIP catalogue record for this book is available from the British
Library.

Typeset by JVR Creative India
Cover design by Jim Butler, www.jimbutlerartist.com
Printed by ScandBook AB, Sweden

New Island received financial assistance from The Arts Council (*An
Chomhairle Ealaíon*), 70 Merrion Square, Dublin 2, Ireland.

10 9 8 7 6 5 4 3 2 1

About the Author

A former lecturer on English and Spanish literature, David Butler has been writing full-time since 2010. His first novel, *The Last European,* was published in 2005, while his debut poetry collection, *Via Crucis,* came out in 2011. Writing in *The Sunday Times* of his second novel, *The Judas Kiss* (New Island, 2012), the reviewer Alan Murdoch commended Butler's remarkable ability for characterisation, singling out the predatory Malcolm as 'one of the most outlandlishly repulsive creations of recent Irish fiction.' His short-story collection, *No Greater Love,* was brought out in 2013 by London publisher Ward Wood, while a one-act play, *'Twas the Night Before Xmas,* was the winner of the 2013 Scottish Community Drama Award, and is published by Spotlight Publications. Other literary awards include the Brendan Kennelly and Féile Filíochta prizes for poetry, and the Maria Edgeworth and Fish International awards for the short story. He lives in Bray.

Acknowledgements

*T*hanks are especially due to Sean O'Reilly for his inspired tutoring while I was organising the text, and to Pat McCabe for his generous comments. Also, hats off to my brother, Jim, for the cover design (http://www.jimbutlerartist.com). I am grateful to have received a bursary from The Arts Council of Ireland.

I ndilchuimhne ar mo mháthair.

Contents

PART ONE

I

The circles of hell are the circles we make for ourselves. The acquaintances. The routes daily walked. The routines. The rings left by coffee cups.

I'll describe my room. It's quite large, large enough for my requirements in any case. But it's misshapen, a poorly thought-out rectangle. From the doorway one can imagine this imprecision is a simple trick of perspective. Not so. I've had no shortage of opportunity to pace it out. The foot of the room is almost a full pace wider than the head.

To the left-hand side there's a single bed with a wrought-iron frame. Above it is a diminutive window, though I tend to keep the blind pulled, even during the day. The point is, the window looks directly at another window across the back lane. At some juncture the window opposite was whitewashed on the inside. This glaucoma induces an altogether unpleasant feeling; no more than three or four yards separate my room from its eternally blank scrutiny. Besides, my window won't open. I don't mean that it refuses to open, that its hinges have become stiff, over time. What I mean is, there's no hinge. The pane was never intended to be opened.

The bed beneath it is quite the antique. Its joints groan and rattle at the slightest change in distribution. But it's moderately serviceable. My landlady changes the sheets every month, and even provides extra blankets in winter. In this season, sporadic heat emanates from the bulk of an ancient radiator whose intestinal pipes tick throughout the night. But the bedside table is so small and low as to appear a child's toy. There's scarcely room for both notebook and bottle on its surface. Can it be trusted to take the typewriter I've long intended to buy so that all this can be finished? When my notes are in order. Sometimes, when the mocking humour is on me, I see a parody of my pretensions in this midget's bedside table.

The only decoration on the walls is a black-framed mirror that hangs above the wash-hand basin. I've no use for pictures. If I were to decorate the walls, I'd undoubtedly cut some images from the newspaper. Perhaps some advertisements, or topical cartoons. But the landlady wouldn't approve of such levity. It's true there's a single nail protruding from the wall above the bed. At night, a shadow that stretches beneath it makes its presence more apparent. Sometimes I imagine that a previous tenant was a priest; that this nail used to support a crucifix. But I'm probably mistaken. It's more likely that somebody's photograph, a loved one, as they say, once looked out from the empty space above the bed.

From the ceiling there hangs a single, naked light bulb. Like an inquisitor's eye, this light bulb sees everything in the room. You might say it's the room's presiding deity. Once, I tried to cover it with coloured paper to give the place a more festive atmosphere. But the shadows it threw about the walls were clumsy, and what's more, I was no longer able to depend upon its light to shave by.

There's a tomb-sized wardrobe at the foot of the bed. This sombre piece is so large it's difficult to imagine how it ever passed through the doorway. It dominates the room, so to speak. But there's also an easy chair, and it's on this, for preference, that I stack my clothes. In any case, half the interior is taken up with an old telly the landlady stuck up in the room after she got a newer model for downstairs. No use my telling her I never bothered with a telly. When I came back that evening, there it was, lording it over the only table in the room. I couldn't get her to remove it. I couldn't get her to credit that, all my life, I've hated the damn things.

I didn't want to insist. Bad enough I was a jailbird; I didn't want her thinking her lodger was somehow soft in the head. Bad enough that I persisted in paying my rent in ready cash rather than 'electronically', as she quaintly put it. Bad enough I hadn't a mobile phone, in case she ever needed to 'text' me. I'd had such a phone, once. Was I expected to explain to her its treachery? So, after a few weeks, I bundled the contraption inside the wardrobe, and I rescued the table for my bedside. I told her there was something wrong with the tubes. Above its bulk, only an old greatcoat hangs inside the wardrobe. To the rear there's an empty travelling case, a pair of patent leather shoes that I wore to Mother's funeral and a shoebox with various items I've collected over the years. The second shoebox, in which I keep my notes, such as they are, I keep under the bed.

So much for where I live. I'd describe it as a modest dwelling. And yet, every month, this room consumes the greater part of my ready cash. More and more, this town appears to me a great termite-mound. If it is a capital city, that's because the cells are mouths whose hunger must be fed, night and day, with capital.

I've lived all my life in this termites' capital. I was born not a half-mile from the room in which I now reside. The school I attended was just to the far side of the lying-in hospital, although its classrooms have been bricked up for several years now. It was run by what at one time we called 'the religious', before their fall from grace.

Of course, this half-mile has not been the full compass of my career. For a while I lived on the south side, on a busy street close to the canal. I remained there for almost three years. At another time, along another canal, I rented an attic over a butcher's shop that was so far from the city centre you could no longer walk the distance. But I despised having to depend on public transport, its whims, its inconsistencies. The arrangement did not work out. I've never again consented to live so far from the centre.

I had another, less pleasant, address. It too was hard by that squalid moat they call the Royal Canal. Royal! But I'll have cause enough to talk of that dismal prison, when the time comes.

One event stands out in my childhood. When I was twelve, my mother went blind. There was a mutiny in her blood which a daily charge of pigs' insulin, in dubious battle with Cork Dry Gin, singularly failed to quell. In any case, in the space of two months, cataracts of opaque wax filmed over both her pupils until she could see nothing beyond shadows. 'You're my eyes,' she used to say then. 'You won't ever leave me, Willy. You're my eyes now. You're all I have in this world.' I was all Mother had in the world for almost twenty years. And even that sightless world began to shrink in on her in the end as her mind deteriorated. By the time she died she no longer knew who I was.

Would I have moved away if I'd had the chance? If opportunity had knocked, as they say? Idle question. Once, in a bar on the quays, I overheard a sailor, a Norwegian I think he was, holding forth to a group of dockers. 'You've the life,' they said, 'one day here, one day there, seeing the world.' Our friend was having none of it. 'What you learn, miles from land with nothing but sky and ocean about you, is that no matter how far you travel, you always drag with you a circle of ten miles' radius. You never escape that circle,' he said, and slapped the table three times to stress the point.

The figure made a deep impression on me. I've never been in a boat, let alone to sea, but it was as if I could have described that circle, bounded only by the slowly shifting horizon, the Norwegian sailor tied to its centre as though to a mast. *A ten-mile radius*. It's not a bad approximation for the bounds of the city.

I'd been working for several years as a copying clerk at the legal firm of Doherty and Fitzgibbon. Then my only uncle died, quite unexpectedly, in a house fire. He'd been solitary, irascible, a bit of a drinker by all accounts. Mother told me that at one time he'd been a seminarian, and I imagine that in his youth he'd cherished certain ideals. In any event, he'd never forgiven her for becoming pregnant so young, and so carelessly. I don't know if that was at the root of his drinking. What it did mean was that he'd scarcely spoken a solitary word to me. As far as he was concerned, I must have borne the same guilt as Mother. You might even say that, in his eyes, I was that guilt made flesh. I imagine he saw Mother's blindness in much the same light.

But the point is, James Patrick Regan died intestate, and so his entire worldly estate, such as it was, devolved to my mother. This largely consisted of the insurance money for the burned-out house, once they were finally satisfied there'd been no criminal hand behind the conflagration. Still, it gave a boost to her disability pension. I left the legal company at Mother's behest, and returned to looking after her on a full-time basis.

From the age of twelve I'd acted as her guide through the city. 'What street are we on?' she would ask. 'How do the trees in the square look? Oh describe them for me, Willy.' Or 'What clothes do they have?' in such-and-such a window. We must have made quite a sight, the pair of us, year after year passing so slowly in front of the windows of the department stores that you'd have imagined the displays were set out in Braille. Sometimes, looking back on those times, it seems to me that it was Mother who acted as guide, not I.

Would I have married early if I'd had the chance? If I'd met the right girl? Another idle question. The more Mother became dependent on me, the more suspicious she became of my infrequent absences, my occasional conversations on a street corner. Oh, I had several liaisons. Several brief affairs. But they all foundered on the same sandbank. It was impossible that the girl be introduced to Mother, to her invalid's jealousy. I don't resent her for this; I merely state it. To round out the picture, as they say.

Mother's mind got so bad in the last few months that I'd little choice but to have her institutionalised. At length, I secured a bed in Swift's hospital. By this time she'd begun to think she was a young girl again, and barely slept or rested. Her eating, too, had become a problem. I'm quite satisfied that the decision to commit her was for the best, and besides, she didn't seem to be aware of the move. Up to a point, you might say we were simply swapping one dark interior for another. By the time of the confinement she no longer recognised voices. Whenever I visited her, in a public ward of the institution, she used to call me Jim. Jim was the name of the brother who'd died in the fire. Perhaps – who knows? – it was also the name of my father. Or perhaps his name was Willy after all.

Mother didn't last long in St Patrick's. Within four months she caught influenza. There was an epidemic of it doing the rounds that year, a particularly virulent Asian strain. Later it complicated into pleurisy. Or pneumonia, I'm unsure which. They never took the time to explain to me the precise mechanism of her drowning. In any event, even though she'd grown visibly feeble, at all hours she'd drag up great gouts of phlegm, tearing them out of her lungs in inconsolable coughs. Her only words were 'Dear God', repeated as an exhalation each time she lay back from the spittoon, her newborn baby's hair stuck damply to her forehead. This torture lasted the best part of a fortnight. To tell the truth, it came as a relief when, as the too-youthful chaplain glossed it during the burial, 'Moll Regan's spirit has finally been released from the rack of her body.'

You might imagine that this would have been a period of great liberation for me. I was still moderately young, midway along life's journey as the saying goes. And the small annuity deriving from the inheritance meant I didn't have to look to return to Doherty and Fitzgibbon, validating their interminable counterparts. Also, I was finally free to have a proper liaison, always supposing I chanced upon the right girl.

It was at this time that I took the room on the south side, not far from the canal. A south-facing room, too, which squinted past a great green dome towards the mountains. True, it was noisy, being above a public house and on a main thoroughfare. Not infrequently I was kept awake into the small hours, and at great length would slip into uneasy dreams, only to be woken by the sound of the morning rush hour snarling across the ceiling of the room. Yet, imagining this was life, I tolerated such inconveniences.

I fancied, that if I put my mind to it, I could be a writer. Or perhaps an artist. The smoke-rings of late youth. In one way or another I felt drawn to be a 'chronicler of the city'. Over the years that I'd accompanied Mother on her rounds of the streets, I'd kept a sort of daybook, a few words or thoughts, a sketch or two in pen and ink, passably executed. These I'd mainly done on our return home in the evenings, relying on my memory of the day while Mother dozed in front of the telly. On occasion I'd enliven these sketches with a quote from one of the books that Mother would have me read to her. Or, more likely, I'd transcribe a line from one of the library books I surreptitiously read, after she'd nodded off. For twenty years these guilty novels were all the subjects of my education. *Now she is dead,* smiled my soul, *you'll have the time to perfect your journals.*

Looking back, I barely recognise that youth. On occasion, I take out the daybook from the box in the wardrobe, and I entertain myself at his expense. Even the handwriting seems filled with self-importance. But it's the quotes accompanying the sketches which continually surprise. One reads: 'Now the city draws near which is called Dis / With its great garrison and grave citizens.' In the margins, a later hand had scribbled: 'Disdain; Disgrace; Disillusionment.' Another goes: 'The red belly of evening gleams at Baal / The great cities kneel around him.' Beside that quote I'd jotted the initials 'G. M.' *G. M.*! I should have been more attentive. I have an idea G. M. may have been a German poet, but I can't be certain.

These days I can't so much as look at a poem. Poets are charlatans. It took a woman to make me see that; a woman poet, to be precise. As for Mr William Butler Yeats, I would confine him to the blackest pit of hell! Poetry, it seems to me now, is nothing more than that branch of astrology which takes itself most seriously.

At the time I was living between the Grand Canal and the South Circular, I hadn't yet come to such felicitous conclusions. At that juncture I still had the notion that I might amount to something. A curious expression! Who could tally, as the clay dribbled onto Mother's coffin, to how much her shadow-life had amounted? Or the grave adjacent, with its three generations of stockbrokers? Had their lives amounted to more or less than that of the girl in the next plot but one, a twin who'd drowned at the age of thirteen? What sort of angelic or diabolic scales would be needed for such mensuration?

But I had the idea, at this time, that if only I applied myself correctly I could become someone in the city. A name. Someone who's known by people he doesn't himself know. I won't say a celebrity. But a personality. An observer. Someone whose opinion counts for something, whose opinion is on occasion solicited. It's not so much that I accounted myself more talented than the next man – which one of us isn't guilty of that sin? But I believed that chance or destiny had singled out Will Regan to escape the casual tyrannies of salary and advancement. While others were trading daylight for such securities, I had been Mother's eyes. That apprenticeship must count for something.

A chronicler, then, of the close of the old millennium, the birth of the new. Whether it would be in poetry, or in art, or in some as yet unclear combination of the two that I would make my mark I could not divine. But now, at last, my time was entirely my own, and since my material wants have always been modest, I couldn't foresee a time when I'd be forced into a career. You will become the city's chronicler, I said to my soul as it emerged from long pupation. What precisely I meant by 'chronicler' I'm not sure. But that I must first learn my craft ... of that I had little doubt.

I enrolled in the public library in Rathmines. Andrew Carnegie Esq., AD 1913. Every morning, before I set out for the city centre, I put in an hour in the reading room, poring over the national newspapers. But ambition as yet knew no restraints. I'd emerged from the dark chrysalis of Mother so recently that I'd not yet tried the wet membrane of wings. So in the afternoons I took to visiting museums and galleries. On Tuesday evenings I enrolled in a life-drawing course in a reputable college, half-price for the unwaged. I joined a poetry circle that met every second Thursday in a Fleet Street pub, I studied the rudiments of chess, and I began to be seen in the public galleries of the Four Courts during some of the more notorious trials. The press-hounds had not yet begun to bay and whimper about the heels of the interminable MacMurrough Tribunal, or I'd surely have haunted the Castle itself. But for the present the Four Courts were circus enough for me.

This is living, I told my soul.

II

*T*hree relationships stand out from this period. 'Relationships'. I use the word in its loosest sense. There were three, nevertheless, and all struck within the span of several months. I've never been so prodigal with my affections, before or since. All ended badly, for them, for me.

This coincidence gives the epoch a symmetry I could scarcely have expected to find. Perhaps, in spite of all, there is a rough logic that pushes our footsteps down the crooked byways. How Mother must be cackling from beyond the grave! This new intercourse I was so bent upon, this foison of intimacies, this pilgrim's progress of the personality led inexorably to gaol. It was scarcely a descent anyone could have foreseen. Even now, sifting through notes and memories, it's hard to see precisely when or where the die was cast, as the saying goes. Still less could I have guessed which particular entanglement would land me in prison.

At which step did it all become inevitable? That question obsesses me, as I imagine it obsesses the animal caught in a trap. It's a question these pages must try to answer. And of what sin precisely was the defendant guilty? Not as charged, that much I can say. Oh, I can hardly deny that the dutiful son had locked up his lunatic mother. Then, on the very eve of a new millennium, he was in turn locked up, immured inside those

Victorian walls that the inmates call, with lowbrow irony, 'the Joy'. Is there a moral here? Damned if I can find one. Damned if I can't.

My account begins with the slightest, the final one of my three relationships, though for all that, it was the one that you might say left the deepest mark. It's the casual engagement that wreaks the greatest havoc in the end. When the accounts are settled.

I arrived into the atrium of the Four Courts one day after about a fortnight's absence, just as a trial was drawing to an end. There was a considerable buzz about the place. I'd counted two television crews waiting outside on the quays as I made my way across the bridge from Christ Church.

The river was at low ebb. I don't know why such details stick in my head. In this instance I remember looking at the green carcass of a pram sunk into the river's dregs as I hurried towards the imperturbable chambers of the Law. I was working, no doubt, on the imagery of a poem, like some T. Malone Chandler of the late twentieth century. Thank God that's all done with anyway.

From what a porter said, I knew it was too late to catch much beyond the verdict. The final word. So, as I waited for the doors to open, I tried to get into conversation with the press-hounds and paparazzi idling about the atrium like so many carrion crows. They were hoarse and aggressive with their words. No doubt they'd smelt a rival.

It became clear all the same that there were charges of breaking and entering and of aggravated assault levelled against the defendant, a repeat offender. But it seemed likely that the whole case would collapse because of procedural irregularities. Nothing extraordinary here. The media interest lay in the fact that, months on, the pensioner who'd been assaulted was still in a coma. If she were to die, the status of the case that was about to be dismissed would alter dramatically.

'Then this is the trial of Joe Danaher?'

Croak.

'I thought that wasn't due up for another six weeks.'
Croak. Croak.
'You're sure it's his hearing?'
'It was brought forward.'
'I see.'

I'd chanced upon the case in a back-issue of a newspaper some weeks previously. It had stuck in my mind because I'd been at school with a boy whose name was Joseph Mary Danaher. 'I'll wait and see if it's him,' says I to myself. 'Just for a laugh.' Having no further need of begrudging cameramen, I turned my back on the lot of them and stepped into the uncertain April sunlight.

Some twenty minutes later the doors were opened, and a figure with a jacket pulled up over his head was hurried down the steps by a trio of court officials. The paparazzi had been stung to activity, and they began to flock their apparatuses about him, so many gulls squabbling over the river's refuse. I could see it was all the accused could do not to lash out at their impudent beaks.

I followed the frenzy at several yards' remove as it pushed up the stinking quay at a semi-trot. I'd had no more than the briefest contact with two eyes that peered from the makeshift cowl, too little evidence to be certain. But in that same instant, Joseph Mary Danaher's schoolyard nickname leaped into my mind. 'Danger!' I called out twice, once the media scrum had begun to tail off.

It transpired that Danger Danaher was in sore need of a floor to sleep on, a temporary address away from what he called 'prying eyes'. He was no longer referring to the press, and as for the guards, what could they do but glower impotently after the free man? 'But there's them all the same,' he winked, later, enjoying the confidence from beneath the peak of a baseball cap, 'there's them who'd take a rare pleasure in putting this Jackeen permanently on top of a pair of crutches.' So he jumped at the offer to lie low for a few weeks, south of the river.

The offer? I'd made no offer. For reasons that will become abundantly clear, I *couldn't have* made an offer. Not then. And yet, he accepted my offer.

There must be a precise point, when a lobster is in the mouth of a lobsterpot, up to which it could still reverse out. Once it passes that point, it's done for. I couldn't have known it at the time, but this 'offer' marked my point of no return.

Why didn't I simply tell the man to piss off? Was I afraid of him? In awe of him? Just too plain useless, or inexperienced, or solitary? Idle questions. But looking back, it seems to me that my dismay as we set out for Portobello was tinged with a contrary emotion. Somewhere, there was a dark thrill that this schoolyard tyrant, this latter-day criminal, had selected Will Regan as confidant.

Danger remembered me only as the boy whose mother had gone blind. But that was scarcely a surprise. I wasn't much given to mixing in school. I remembered him as a first-class bully. Someone who, despite his small stature, exerted a gravitational pull within his own circle; someone whom the peripheral ones among us dreaded. He laughed without mirth as I reminded him of his schoolyard exploits. One story had it that, the same year I was withdrawn, Tubby Roche, the classroom snitch, had received such a drubbing at the hands of Danger and his cronies that from that day to this he spoke with an insurmountable stammer. Father an auctioneer. But from the expression in Danaher's lifeless eyes, I might have been remembering a stranger to him.

They say that schooldays are our happiest. Mine were neither happier nor more miserable than any other days. If anxieties were smaller then, it seems to me that they were largely in proportion. During break times, Danaher and a half-dozen of his heavies used enact a casual tyranny they dubbed 'the ring'. 'We're giving you the ring!' It was a whispered taunt that filled our bellies with dread as lunch hour approached. Once out in the yard, they would form an unbreakable circuit about one or another of us. From about its circumference, nonsense questions were fired into the interior. As the victim turned to answer, tearfully, imploringly, he was pushed and buffeted and kneed from behind so that he collided with the inquisitor, who responded with great viciousness. The fun might endure for a full quarter of an hour.

More than twenty years had passed since such merriment.

'I want you to come with me, Regan,' said Danaher one fine morning. He'd been staying about a week, and the flat reeked of tracksuits and deodorant. My guest had the peculiar habit of discharging the aerosol in great circles about his body, as if he were trying to douse a flame. Today, in baby-blue hoody, green tracksuit pants, white runners and red baseball cap, he was the last word in inner-city fashion.

'Where to?'

'I've people I need to talk to, never mind where. All you're to do is to stand around outside looking hard, right? Don't open your gab, d'you understand me?' I nodded, but he wasn't reassured. 'Look, just keep your hands shoved into your pockets, Regan. Make out you might be holding something. D'you get me? Anyone says anything to you, you don't hear them. You just look the other way.'

I shrugged. 'Sure.'

The playground must cast a very long shadow indeed. Danger's circle had been so aloof, so indifferent to my kind, I could never have dreamed of such a charge. Twenty years on, my heart was suddenly pounding at the thrill of inclusion in one of his capers.

For the best part of an hour I hung around outside an oriental food store on Moore Street, trying, as he put it, to look hard. I imagine I looked laughable. But I probably passed unnoticed. I hadn't been in the vicinity for a number of years, not since the onset of Mother's dementia, and the degree to which the old market had changed blew me away. In her blindness, Mother used to sniff every sort of produce set out on the prams in advance of haggling over its price. This insolence was one of her keenest pleasures. But she was well known, and the fishwives and fruit-sellers tolerated her fads. 'Poor Willy,' they'd say, tousling my hair, 'sure he'd be lost without his mother.' Momentarily, I saw her nose pass inches above the white-eyed bream and mackerel that glinted like foil in the sunlight.

Under Mother's tutelage my own sense of smell must have grown very acute. It was now being assaulted by scents and spices many times more exotic than the Chinese and Cyrillic alphabets that had sprung up on all sides. My nostrils were all at sea! The events I'm describing took place in the last years of the last century. An entire millennium was drawing to a close. It was a time before we became acclimatised to change, as you might say, safe inside our Fortress Europe of fifteen flags and fifteen national currencies. And my nose was put out of joint by a cacophony of novel smells.

'Come on, we're going.' Danger dug an elbow into my side and was already pushing through the crowd ahead of me, hands deep in pockets and head angled forwards. Things evidently hadn't gone well.

Turning onto Parnell Street, his way was temporarily blocked by two monumental women in colourful costumes. Nigerian, I'd hazard. In any event, they were arguing in an indecipherable tongue. But it was as if Danger took the impasse as a personal affront. He parted them with such violence that he upset a pushchair cowering between their robes.

From the abuse that pursued him all the way past the Rotunda you'd have thought a child had been tipped out onto the street. In point of fact the pram had been heavy with nothing more than those fat bananas they call plantains, green and black and pungent. These were now splayed out like great dismembered hands over the pavement. All apologies, I made haste to reassemble them.

I finally caught up with Danger at the foot of the Parnell monument. 'This city has gone to the dogs, d'you know that?' He stared at me with eyes that were indignant splinters of ice. 'And do you know what the cause of it is?' I shook my head. But the lights changed before he had time to answer. We moved on, I about two paces behind. I was watching him, taking his measure, as they say.

Danaher was of slight build, even as a schoolboy, but ferocious as a bantam. I could sense in his clenched shoulders that he was working over the answer to his own question. When he was satisfied, he stopped, his head scarlet and jerking like a cock's above a protruding Adam's apple. 'Bucking… foddeners!' His hand swept out a great circle of the north inner city.

My gut was struck forcibly by the expletive. *Give us your buckin' lunch money*! The change in first letter stapled the adult immediately to the schoolyard bully. Anxiety gripped me. *We're giving you the bucking ring!* How was it I hadn't noticed, all the time we were in the flat? Had he said 'fucking' while there? Or had Moore Steet's associations with Mother's nose somehow readied the soil of memory?

'All about the city centre, the old neighbourhoods is destroyed with them. Bucking… he searched again for the elusive word, '… *foddeners!*' We had come to a halt not ten yards from a call centre, and I looked warily at a trio of Africans who were loafing about the door. Their lozenge eyes scarcely registered us.

'Destroyed, they have the place. They're letting all kinds in. Anyone and everyone.' His eyes darted about the shopfronts and hesitated on an ethnic hairdressers across the way. He gestured at it with a forearm that was tattooed like a comic strip: a flag, a dagger, a dark rose. 'But do you know the worst of it? They're doing it deliberately so they are.'

'Who is?' I was losing the thread of Danaher's pronouns.

'The politicians, man! The political classes!' He leaned towards me as though he were about to impart a great secret. My nose was invaded by the bouquet of cheap deodorant. 'And where are they from? Will I tell you, bro? They're from Castleknock and Killiney and Howth so they are. They're not from the centre. That's why the political classes don't give a damn. They want to see the centre destroyed, and that's the truth of it.' His jaw had a disconcerting habit of working the words before he spoke them while his Adam's apple operated up and down like a plunger. It distracted attention from the argument. His eyes did too, for they hadn't blinked once since Parnell's *non plus ultra*. 'Once the centre's destroyed and they've pushed the likes of you and me to the outskirts, then they can sell it on in chunks to big business. That's your bucking Celtic Tiger for you. When did you say your ma died?'

'Two years ago next month.'

'Mine too, this long time. But not the old man. The old man lives out in Finglas. Only the mind's gone. He knows nothing this nine year. Alzheimer's. But d'you know what it is? Maybe he's lucky. D'you know what I'm trying to say? He never had to see the whole bucking city flushed down the toilet, man. It'd break his heart to see it so it would.'

Here he broke off, paled, stared past me at the trio. I smiled vaguely, having no wish to challenge anyone. I was trying to imagine a Danaher parent.

He touched my elbow and we were again moving. 'Once the centre is broke, you see, that's when the immigrants come flooding in. You saw it over in England after the war, bro. Indians. Jamaicans. You name it. That's how England went to the dogs.'

Immigration must have been something of a hobbyhorse with Joseph Mary Danaher. An hour later, as we sat on the back seat of a lurching 15A, he picked up the thread as though it had been bare minutes since the previous. 'D'you know what else? They come over here with their gangs already formed so they do. I'm not telling you a word of a lie, already formed. Drugs. Whores. You name it, bro. I'm not saying there was no crime beforehand. Of course there was crime beforehand. But it was our own crime.' His cap's visor surveyed the top deck of the bus as though he were the first mate on a yacht. 'And d'you know who the worst of them is?'

I shook my head, bored, irritated. Whatever childish excitement had come when he'd first charged me with a confidence had long since gone flat.

'The Russians.'

'The *Russians?*'

'The Russians.'

I looked out the graffiti-scratched window.

'Did you never see them, Regan, on their mobile phones and everything? And of course they don't bother their arse learning English. Why would they? Everything is laid on for them here. Russian shops. Russian supermarkets. And their own bars, too, that'll be the next thing. You mark my words. I'll say that for the blacks and the chinks. At least they make some effort to learn the lingo.'

I was now examining the hairs on my hand and ignoring his unblinking scrutiny of me. But my heart was clattering. The unexpected turn to the East his diatribe had just taken was making my skin burn, because by this time I was already very much involved with a lady named Yelena Zamorska. If 'involved' is the word. If 'lady' is the word. But patience, my soul. We shall speak Of that lady in due course.

'D'you know what else?' Here he leaned towards me and touched my forearm. The upper saloon of the bus was by now empty, but his eyes shifted as though to ensure we were not being overheard. 'It's on account of the Russians that I had to do the last job. Know what I'm saying? I was short a few bob to pay them the interest on what I owed, but there was no way they were going to wait a few days. Not them fellas. You mess around with the Rooskies, you can end up navigating the canal from the inside of a suitcase, know what I mean? That's why I had to do a couple of flats about the place. No choice, bro.'

Deftly, I removed his finger from my arm. I wanted to put distance between us. All the same, my curiosity was disturbed. 'But Danger, is it true what they say?'

'Is what true?'

'That you beat the old woman into a coma?'

His Adam's apple bobbed up and down as though he were priming an airgun. 'Listen. You know nothing about it, man.' He gazed furiously into the convex mirror to the front of the upper deck. In its pupil, the hat was distorted to a great beak replacing his head, while my body ballooned away from him. Silence. At first I thought he was finished. Then he shook his head at his own distorted reflection. 'I'm there inside the place, it must be three in the morning, and I've lifted everything that's worth taking, which doesn't amount to bollocks anyway. The next thing, she's bucking standing there behind me, with her white hair down around her shoulders and her white nightdress, looking just as bony as bucking death itself. It frightened the life out of me so it did. I don't even remember hitting her, if you want to know the truth of it.'

'And so now her grandkids want to see you on crutches?'

'Her grandkids?' He rounded on me, indignant. 'What grandkids? The hell with her grandkids!'

I shook my head, baffled.

'It's the bucking Russians!'

'I don't follow you.'

'Let me put it this way. I wasn't going to be the only one that was going down, was I? So I gave them a few names down in Store Street. Plea bargain, you know how it is. Probably false bucking names anyway, so I don't know what their problem is.' His eyes narrowed. The thought that he himself had turned snitch made him suspicious. 'Listen. Anyone asks after me, anyone at all, you know nothing. You got it? You never so much as heard of Joe Danaher.'

I was starting to wish I'd never so much as heard of Joe Danaher.

One evening soon after this, as I was heading home along the canal, I saw a group of figures under one of the bridges. There were perhaps three, in cheap leather coats, ranged about a fourth, whose back was pressed to the brick arch. Normally I'd have hurried past. It was getting on for dark. But something in the arrangement held me. I was too distant for their faces to be anything more than livid thumbprints, but close enough to make out the Slavic gutturals in their speech.

As I hunkered down to watch, I must have taken a step too close to the bank. My left foot slipped and sank up to the shin in the reeds, startling a moorhen. The nearest figure turned about to investigate, and the one who'd been pressed to the wall seized the opportunity to struggle from the grip of the others. A grappling match ensued, a free-for-all in which the jacket was torn over his head. The third figure, returning abruptly to the affray, succeeded in getting him in a headlock. Whether or not some taunt or expletive reached my ear, I realised that the victim of the attack was Danger.

I can't say if I'm brave or a coward. I've had very little occasion to test my mettle, as the saying goes. Of course, from the age of twelve I'd to inject Mother's insulin. But did those daily episodes bespeak courage, cruelty or curiosity? In any case, on this one occasion, whether from bravado or from a sense of the ludicrous, I stood up to full height and began to rant and whistle at the assailants! It was enough to sow a moment's doubt. Danger, alert to the lapse, slipped fully out of his jacket, gave the nearest one a shove that set him teetering on the bank's edge, and ran for it.

One or both of the others must have nudged against their companion. As I turned to flee them I saw his arms windmilling just before he crashed through the surface of the canal. From the howls that followed, you'd have thought it was boiling pitch he'd fallen into. The other pair soon called off their pursuit to recover their accomplice.

Twenty minutes later, in the sanctuary of a snug, Danger looked at me as though I were a dog that had performed an outlandish trick. 'You done all right, bro,' he said, then later, as we were leaving, 'I owe you one, right?'

Several days after this incident he decided it was time to move on from the flat. As he packed away the overpowering bouquet of sweat and deodorant into his holdall, he reaffirmed the debt. 'I owe you one, Regan. Listen, keep an eye out for them foreign bastards. If you see any of them hanging around, you let me know.'

I said I would. He closed one eye and wagged a finger. And I knew damn well, for all his thanks, he was letting me know it was I who stood in his debt.

III

I mentioned three relationships. Joseph Mary, 'Danger', was not the first among them. Chronologically, I mean. In fact he was the third, if we discount the tyrant of the schoolyard. And I soon would have forgotten him, if Fate or chance or Mother's malevolent ghost hadn't intended our paths to recross.

In chronological order, Yelena Zamorska was the first. Yelena, who taught me all the miseries of love.

Later, I tried to square up Danger's views with everything I knew of her. She was not in fact Russian. She was from Eastern Europe though. I'd met her about a year before the canal incident through the poetry circle that used to meet in the Fleet Street bar on every other Thursday. By one of those coincidences that seem to have marked these times, it transpired her mother was an invalid who required constant minding. At quite a young age, a series of strokes had left Madam Zamorska partly paralysed, and entirely embittered. This gave me the pretext to arrange a drink with Yelena during a week in which there was no poetry session.

There was nothing particularly sexual in my eagerness to meet up with her. Not to begin with. She was a woman in her mid to late thirties, thick blonde hair touched with ash, and with glasses whose magnifying lenses seemed to place anguish in the corners of her eyes. When she removed these glasses, her pupils appeared to have difficulty in focusing, and two half-moons beneath marked her for an insomniac. I hadn't yet decided if the fragile edge to her voice was a result of anxiety or the effort of having to speak outside of her mother tongue.

The poetry circle itself had been a farce. I'm not sure what I'd expected, but the lack of anything resembling talent astonished me. At least with the life drawing you had something at the end of each session that approximated the human form. These poets, by contrast, did little besides deride and declaim. In proportion to the successes that any had actually enjoyed, their jealousies, their vanities and their propensity for the denigration of established poets knew no bounds. As Yelena would later describe it, 'Their circle has no gravity to it but *schadenfreude*.' That was her gorgeous word, and it was far from the only term I learned from her. Thinking of Mother, I scribbled it onto my arm. 'These little poets,' smirked Yelena, 'fondle one other's failures'.

If I'd expected discussions about poetry and its many techniques, I was soon disabused. Such pieces of their own work as they circulated on occasional photocopies were met with superior silence. Raised eyebrows, that sort of lark. I wondered what drove them to tolerate each other.

Yelena continued to attend only in order to improve her English. This she confided to me almost at once when we were alone. I smiled. Her eagerness to share this secret told me that my own disdain for the group must be poorly disguised. She had no difficulty in understanding my smile, and she returned it.

In the course of the evening, I also found out that, so far as poetry went, she had little need of them. She was a published poet in her own country. She had even won prizes. I asked her if she'd show me a poem, but she shook her head. 'Oh no, they are written in Polish of course.' Then she asked me had I ever read any Polish poets. Suddenly, I had an idea. 'You teach me about poetry,' I said, 'and I'll help you with your English.'

On the first night she stayed over in my room, I had very little idea of what to do. Oh, I don't mean the mechanics. Everyone has an idea of the mechanics. But the fact remains that I'd never been with a woman before, not for more than several hours, never in the intimacy of a bedsit. How the sequence of events might pan out, what whispered words and movements might help in the preparation, and at what precise moment to pull on the artefact that she'd slipped into my hand ... these were beyond my ken.

That afternoon we'd been to the zoo. This had been her suggestion. 'You can teach me the names of the animals,' she said. 'Everyone writes poems about animals, because they are elemental. An animal has no doubts.' I said fine. I hadn't been to the zoo for years, and besides, I was beginning to enjoy her company. I'd even begun to fantasise about her, if that's the word. In these fantasies, Yelena's face and gestures became superimposed upon the naked bodies that were becoming familiar from life drawing.

We met in a little cake shop on Parkgate Street. She was wearing a tweed coat with a fur collar from which dangled a jet-coloured muff. The muff was presumably for her hands, which were cold when I touched them, but since it was so high up the arrangement made me think of a cat with a dead mouse. It must have already been October, because I can see the leaves rusting on the chestnuts that mark Chesterfield Avenue. October. Too late, in any case, for our passage between the animal enclosures to have to contend with child-hoards.

Mother had no love for children. A natural antipathy, as you might say. On one memorable day, when she had me escort her around the zoo, we'd had to weave through any number of shrill school outings. With each new cage I watched her glower darken behind the dark glasses. Her mouth was already working tight circles. It would only be so long, I knew of old, before the charge was fired. We were standing outside the chimpanzee enclosure, and I'd begun to describe their antics to her. A group of little girls, enchanted, were gaping over their ice pops at us. A teacher smiled on. Somehow, Mother became aware of the adulation. 'They say in captivity,' her voice was hoarse and deliberate, 'they do kill their own young. They do kill them and eat them. That's right! Did you never hear that?'

I told that story to Yelena, just as I was paying our entry. She laughed like a schoolgirl at it.

I imagine it was on account of the bare October sky that most of the animals seemed to be hibernating in straw-filled corners, curled up into coils of their own animal scent. I had the impression that they, too, were reluctant exiles. The reptiles within their incubators were lifeless fossils, the hippo a snout in the steaming water. Only the wolves seemed in perpetual motion, animated by ancestral hunger. I was transfixed by their restlessness until Yelena pulled me away. Then we passed through an interior that smelled of the great cats. 'Do you know Rilke?' she asked. I didn't. So she recited from memory a poem about a panther, and then another about a gazelle. 'Which are you?' I asked. She forced a laugh as she examined me.

We stopped for a hot whiskey at a pub I knew to the rear of the great hulk of the Four Courts, and another closer to the Ha'penny Bridge. By this time it was all but dark, the rush-hour traffic still trickling thickly along either quay.

The half-light and the fur that rose to her cheekbones made Yelena seem younger.

'Look at the tail-lights,' she said when we were on the arch of the bridge, 'they stream away like magma, westward.' I wasn't used to spirits, and the whiskeys had brought a pleasant flush to my head. 'Or like streams of red blood-cells,' I heard my soul answer. Soul, for want of a better word. 'And look, Yelena, them is the white cells behind us. They must be flowing in to clean out the night-time city, once the red ones have left.' She looked at me, closely, quizzically. She'd withdrawn one hand from the muff, and she now laid it on my forearm. That was when we began to kiss.

That night, or very early the next morning, after I'd lain with her in any case, she recited to me her credo, such as it was. She must remain free to act as she pleased. I must never be jealous of her. Back there, she said – she'd never referred to Poland by name – back there, she'd been married from the age of nineteen. This hadn't been unusual in those days, and to begin with she'd imagined

27

herself happy. But her husband, a mechanic or an engineer, had turned into a drunkard. He was monstrously jealous of her. He used to beat her just for talking too long to the neighbours.

So I must promise never to be possessive.

I too was free to do as I pleased. After all, here she laid her hand on my chest and propped herself up magnificently into the dawn, man is not by nature monogamous. By 'man' she understood woman. By 'woman', Yelena.

I didn't argue with her as I might have. So far as I knew, I was no more looking for commitment than she was. At this time, I understood nothing of the rack of jealousy. I smiled, rolled over, and slept.

She must have had her doubts as to whether I'd understood her. Twice, before she left the following afternoon, she repeated her position. 'This cannot be relationship.' She stared hard into my eyes as she spoke, once with her glasses on, once without. To impress her statement onto my retinas, as you might say.

This cannot be relationship. What a world of misery lay coiled inside those four words.

Whatever else you could say about them, and I suspect you could say a great deal, one thing I can affirm about the three acquaintances who dominate these notes is that from each of them I learned something invaluable. You might even say that together they completed my education. Of course, my early education had been sporadic, to say the least. At the Christian Brothers I'd been at best a middling student, with little interest in any of the three Rs beyond reading. 'Riting and 'rithmetic were all very well in their place. Reading fascinated me. It's as well it did, or I'd have been fit for nothing that a guide dog couldn't perform with better grace.

The first three years after Mother withdrew me from the schoolroom amounted to a continual game of hide and seek with Marlborough Street – with the social worker, the truant officer, the occasional itinerant tutor. Mother was more than a match for any of them. I arrived at my Inter-Cert exams, at the

ripe old age of fifteen, with little to show for my home studies
beyond long division, a list of the principal rivers of Ireland, a
working knowledge of Boyle's Law, and the curious idea that
it was impossible for a camel to enter the Kingdom of Heaven.
Irish history was a long litany of failures, each one of which
might've won out if there wasn't always some tout to sell out
his country. Only in English did I have a passable knowledge
of the curriculum, and what I didn't know I made up for with
my fettered imagination. In English I got the honour. The other
seven grades that mark the culmination of my formal schooling
are best forgotten.

I remember Yelena once staring hard at me. 'You know you
speak exactly like a book?' she frowned.

'So? You speak exactly like a Pole.'

She punched my arm so hard it bruised. I took her bruise in
silence. How to explain that, for the better part of twenty years,
my books had been my boon companions? Her world of whim
and entanglement was new to me.

The world I learned from Chester Maher, the inestimable
Chester Maher, will reveal itself in due course. Regarding
Danaher's world, I daresay I was in the position of a gardener
who'd never peeked beneath the stones and planks at the white
life that scuttled about there. Years of guiding Mother had made
me more than intimate with the geography of the streets, with
the argot of its beggars and buskers, hawkers and hucksters. But
here was a parallel world of winks, threats, averted eyes. Here
was an entire ecology in which bags, packets and unmarked
envelopes circulated, in which the mobile phone was king, and
whatever you said, you said nothing.

It's to Yelena, though, that I owe what you might call my
sentimental education. It goes without saying, I learned a good
deal more than that. For one thing, she shamed me into learning
the bones of the history of the city. For another, she left me
with an abiding distaste for the poetry of Mr William Yeats. But
I don't want to get ahead of myself. Everything in its place, as
they say.

This cannot be relationship. She'd enunciated these words in the manner of a judge passing sentence. After each, her fist fell like a gavel. Here's the point. I wasn't ready to believe her. Over the months that followed, I, the eternal defendant, lodged appeal after appeal to ever higher circuits, midnight courts where I alone played judge and jury. She would make no excuse for her behaviour, so, in the absence of hard evidence to the contrary, I concocted entire defences for her. It was of course for my own peace of mind that I was concocting these excuses.

But in any case, the turn of events had taken me entirely by surprise. Prior to our day at the zoo, I'd have thought risible the idea that I might come to be obsessed by a middle-aged Polish woman. We laughed together, I don't deny it! We were comfortable in each other's presence. But I think we were considerably more so in each other's absence. And what is absence? The imagined presence of the other, so delicious, so soon short-circuited by reality.

On the morning after the zoo, with its unexpected denouement, I walked from Portobello to Kilmainham like someone who'd become detached from himself. It was as though I could observe this character, Willy Regan, this comic man already tumbling through his thirties, slipping into rotundity, this ludicrous figure, whose body-hair still retained the sweet brine of a first encounter with sex. I can't say there was any sensation other than that of unreality. So that's what all the fuss is about! I called to Soul, who walked at two paces remove. I was beside myself, as you might say. But Soul was scarcely able to conjure the image of the woman that I'd lain with. The lover, for want of a precise term.

Three days passed before I saw Yelena again. We'd made a vague arrangement to go to the cinema – there was a festival of French film on somewhere in Temple Bar – and I went to confirm the date from a phone-box. In those days you relied on phone-boxes, with their mechanical pips and whimsical 'A' buttons. Body and Soul were still wallowing in the light-headed luxury of absence as I pressed it in and heard the cascade of coins. But when her foreign accent lacked any warmth, or even recognition as it seemed, I felt it like a dig to the solar plexus. This first gut-wrench came as a surprise.

Later, I was aware of a slower turmoil in the gut. This torture intensified as I waited outside the gates of Trinity College, where Grattan sings his eternal aria to the impassive clock-face. She was of course late. Very late. We had to run to make the cinema. But the film didn't inspire either of us to talk, and that night she was not of a mind to come back to the flat. I sat by my desk for over an hour, but I made just a single entry into the journal. I underscored it three times: 'Still much to learn about women.'

Still much to learn about women! As if I understood even the first thing! I thought I knew all about them because I'd read a few novels? Give me a break.

Two days later, the degree of my ignorance was confirmed. Yelena appeared a different creature entirely. We held hands walking through St Stephen's Green. She led me laughing into an enclosure of stone curves. So many Greek theatres, I thought. There was an unusual statue in its centre, a thorax of verdigris, which she told me represented our national poet. News to me. For all the years that I'd wandered the city with Mother, it was the first time I'd set eyes on the place, or the statue. Amid a place of stone, be secret and exult. Over the months to follow it would become our enchanted space.

We sat beside each other and she began to give me little bird-pecks about the cheek and neck. Oh, today she was all affection.

'I have a proposition to make,' she said at length.

'Go on.'

'Well, I was thinking that…' and she interrupted her speech to tickle my ear with feline tongue.

'Thinking that what?'

'Well, I was thinking that maybe…' she squeezed my knee, nibbled at my jaw.

'That maybe what?' I laughed.

'That maybe, if you're so interested in learn poetry…' and now a hand began to creep furtively between my thighs. I was… I'm not sure what. Scandalised is the wrong word. But I was acutely aware of the sound of a child wailing, of a figure in a dishevelled parka who was hovering by the entrance.

'In learning poetry. Go on.'

'So if you're so interested in learning poetry, Mister, how do you feel about translate one of mine?'

I shook my head, more in disbelief than in dismissal. 'What do I know about Polish? Or poetry, for that matter?'

'Well, I will help you of course.'

'I see.' I didn't see. 'So do you have something with you?'

But she shook her head and pulled me up onto my feet.

'No. No. This is for another day. Today is for enjoy ourselves.'

And so, in haste, we went back to the flat.

It's not the place to talk of her predilections. Her flair. What is to the point is that this evening was to be the first of an endless succession in which she left as soon as she'd showered. Scarcely had the sun gone down when she sat on the edge of the bed, towelling her hair. 'So now I leave you.'

'You're not going?'

'Yes, I go.'

'But why? Where?'

'I'm going to see Polish film with friend. I'm fed up of always speak English.'

'But where can you see a Polish film in this town, for God's sake?'

She stood and threw the towel over my head. I tossed it aside. Yelena was already half-dressed. 'Where can you see a Polish film in this town?'

She looked at me with the narrow eyes of a tabby. 'My friend, he have videos.'

I looked at her with the eyes of a fool. 'He?' The pronoun was a rock dropped into a pond. She cursed quietly in her own language. *Ha!* cried Soul.

If it's a date she's going to, I argued, to quell the ripples, then she'd hardly be so brazen as to tell you about it. She zipped up her jacket, shook out her blonde hair and tripped to the door. 'He! He! Is man!' She stuck out her tongue.

'He's a friend you know from Poland...?'

She laughed, and was gone.

'Wait!' I cried, a minute later. 'Hold on a second!' I cried, jumping naked from the bedclothes. But I was too late by a decade to have a hope of catching her.

IV

When Danger Danaher began his rant about immigrants, I had a foreboding that sooner or later the two would meet. Sometimes on the street you spot a buffoon at thirty paces, and no matter what you do to avoid him you know he'll collide into you. There's always something inevitable about the encounters we dread the most. But Danger faded from my mind as rapidly as the waft of aerosols he'd sprayed so liberally about the flat.

Let me try to align chronologies.

By the time of the collapse of the Danaher court case, I'd been seeing Yelena for some six months. At this time, there was a visa requirement that meant she had to return, every so often, to Krakow. The Pope's town. Her visa had something to do with a study-abroad programme, and its periodic renewals depended on the university there apparently. The events I'm describing all occurred long before the so-called accession, with its wide-open doors. Europe was a rich man's club in those days. And Paddy was the court jester in cap and bells. We even had our own currency of watery smiles.

When she'd return to Krakow, Yelena tended to remain away for five or six weeks at a time. This was to relieve her older sister from the burden of permanently having to look after the invalid mother. I've an idea there was also a brother, but he was married or something. In Germany, I seem to recall. Yelena was never very forthcoming about family or homeland. One way or another, this brother returned as rarely as possible.

But to return to the chronology, the choreography, providence had determined that Danger came to stay on the floor of my bedsit precisely during one of Yelena's absences. He packed his bags and aerosols two days before her return.

I mentioned a third notable acquaintance; a third thread that would join the merry braid that Fate was blindly winding. Or perhaps it was Mother's handiwork. In fact, he was the second acquaintance I met. Or collided with. Met seems too tame a verb. It's of Chester Maher, the remarkable, the impossible Chester Maher, that my notes must now speak.

One evening, when I was in the Phoenix Park…

But first let me set the context.

I don't think Yelena's visa gave her any work entitlement per se. All the same, she had no shortage of translation jobs, and I rarely saw her on two consecutive weekdays. For some reason, these jobs were all from a clutch of real-estate firms that were putting out feelers behind the tatters of the iron curtain, and who weren't too scrupulous about RSI numbers. Payments may have been casually passed under the desk in brown envelopes, but she was anything but casual when it came to the hours she put in. 'Too many deadlines,' she said.

By and large, she didn't tolerate me hanging around any of these establishments, waiting for the moment she knocked off work. But one of them, located in Arbour Hill, was for some reason okay. I never fathomed what was so special about the Arbour Hill address, or what was so off-limits about the others. But then, I never fathomed most of Yelena's whims and figaries.

In any case, to kill the time before she finished, I'd got into the habit of taking long walks. Mostly these took me as far as the Phoenix Park, so empty as the short evenings drew to a close. Didn't someone once say that every trouble on this earth is caused by a man's inability to stay quietly at home?

Looking back, it seems strange that, with Mother, I'd ventured so seldom into the great park. But I think, in her blindness, wide-open spaces made her edgy. On one notable occasion, however, she'd taken a whim to retrace the route to the Pope's Cross. In the days leading up to the Papal visit, Mother still had hopes of recovering her eyesight. Her store of memories all dated from those earlier years when she could still see. It was a curious thing: on our walks through the city it was as if she could quite literally see the absences that marked its heart. In particular, she used to talk of the Pillar. *I'll meet you at the Pillar!* No doubt she was remembering some liaison from happier days.

But the Pillar was long since gone, with its clamour of trams.

'I want to go out and see the Pope's Cross, son,' she croaked at me one morning out of the blue. See it! Very well, Mother. So Mother and I had taken a bus as far as Infirmary Road. Then we'd eaten our egg sandwiches at the base of Wellington's obelisk. She had a thing about eggs. Eggs were the filling for special occasions. Always, though, with too much salt and pepper. You'd be thirsty for a week after eating them. I've little doubt it made her 'sup of gin' go down easier. Once the sandwiches were dispatched, Mother placed her arm through mine and folded away her stick. Behind her dark glasses, I saw she'd closed her eyes. She did that every once in a while. At such times you'd swear the blindness was no more than the caprice of a child.

Some sprite must've got into me with all the pepper on the eggs. I suggested, out of devilment, that we take a diversion around by the old Magazine Fort. At once I saw her scowl. Months earlier, I'd seen her turn sour when a neighbour had mentioned the place, giving me a significant glance that Mother had somehow intuited. And that hadn't been the first time, either. But I was too subtle to broach the subject directly. I may be mistaken, but over the years, from hints, from nuances, I've become convinced it was within these weedy recesses, somewhere in the moat beneath the ruined walls, that I'd been inadvertently conceived.

We never got next or near the Fort, or the Pope's Cross, or anywhere else for that matter. It seems the pepper had given her a sudden dose of heartburn. We returned home, and for a week she wouldn't talk to me.

The Irishman loves his girlfriend the best, his wife the most, but his mother the longest. With Mother dead, there was no longer any restraint on visiting the old Magazine Fort. I'd quite a *grá* for those battlements, so Euclidean and so gone to seed. It was late winter, some three months after the zoo episode. With the trees still bare, it was one of my pleasures to identify the landmarks to the other side of the valley: the Royal Hospital, no longer a hospital; Lutyens' Memorial Gardens, no longer forgotten; and the green copula of Mary's, which dominated my flat. Behind them loomed the mountains, near or far depending on the weather. Sometimes, I'd estimate if they might mark the circumference of the circle the Norwegian sailor said we are eternally condemned to drag with us.

I'd been giving some thought to an ugly dispute that I'd had with Yelena on the previous evening. It was an open spat about commitment, our first such. But it's not the moment to talk about infidelities. There'll be plenty of time and paper for that. It was late afternoon, and beginning to turn cold. I hadn't been paying much attention to my steps. Looking about me to get my bearings, I found that I'd strayed from my customary route. I was now standing at the edge of a copse of winter trees.

Some movement, some scandal or activity drew my attention. But it was difficult to make out the source. The sun, a huge white aspirin, had sunk low behind the boughs. It was caught in their lattice, as one of our Fleet Street poets might have put it. It was in old age, and it flecked my sight with liver spots. That was more my kind of poetry. So I began to grope blindly towards the noise, towards the motion, the commotion, pussyfooting, careful not to lose my footing in the undergrowth.

Then, all at once, my steps were urgent. The hubbub was of someone struggling. I thought I glimpsed in the solar disc a pair of legs, kicking out wildly against its perimeter. I hurried closer, and a most extraordinary scene began to take shape. There, like an outsized bell, a figure in a ballooning mackintosh was suspended by a belt from the bough of an oak.

The bough was slowly undulating in a sort of figure of eight. All this meant that the shoes, pedalling eccentrically, hovered between a foot and three above the uneven ground. Bellows and moans burst at each pass from the red swollen face. I could see the fingers of both hands had somehow insinuated themselves between belt and throat. 'Christ almighty!' I shouted. Or maybe I just thought it. Then I rushed to get my arms about the hips, to take the weight off the makeshift noose.

Granting the bulk the leeway to allow the man to slip the belt past his jaw turned into a music-hall routine. It took me a full five minutes to master its ludicrous repetitions. All the while, the hanged man was pedalling madly and blowing like a grampus. Worse, each setback set his legs flailing at me, as if he thought I was trying to assault him. And every time I lost my footing, I wound up on all fours and' before 'I took at least a blow to the head I took at least one blow to the head from the side of a shoe.

But a sense of the ridiculous kept me from panicking. At each failure, I called up to him a few words intended to calm him. Some hope! He'd no sooner saw in a ratchet of air than foam and gutturals would come streaming between his teeth, and he'd struggle like a jack-pike on a line. Then, when it seemed impossible that my arms could muster a single effort more, the belt buckle gave and we tumbled into the undergrowth together.

He lay unmoving, but drawing in great lungfuls of air. Long, lusty gulps, as if he were a shipwrecked man whom a surge had tossed to shore. For some minutes I watched him, my limbs too heavy to move. I began to notice, in the darkening distance beyond his gasping, that the central avenue of the park was already slow with traffic. It was the red flow of magma westward that Yelena had described. In the sky there flittered the suspicion of a bat.

'Jesus!' Suddenly the man was rolling, sitting up, rubbing vigorously. 'Jesus!' All about his flanks and head I made out a thicket of nettles, gone to wood. 'Jesus Christ!' he gasped a third time. But I began to laugh. I couldn't help it. He stared at me, indignant as hellfire, and I laughed as helplessly as a child being tickled. Now it was I who struggled for breath.

He was now on his feet, rubbing and patting wildly. Then he loomed huge and the red face with its mad eyes leaned in to mine. It was too funny. I couldn't help myself. A finger wagged at me.

'I know you.'

My laughter subsided. I mustered my forces and propped myself up to examine him, though in the copse it was already dark.

'I know you,' he repeated. His huge head was within a foot of my own. He was still breathing heavily through the nose, and his face loomed crimson, bloated and wild. The greyed hair was storm-tossed, the eyes outraged and mismatched. An angry white rash down one side of the jaw marked where the nettles had stung him. The fingers of the left hand continuously massaged the throat. Beneath them, I could just make out two violet furrows which marked how the belt had dug into the skin.

I peered at him for some time. Then I shook my head and lay back. 'Don't think so,' I said.

It wasn't that he appeared a stranger. Not as such. He was like a figure out of a dream or a fairy story. But the features, strangely familiar, wouldn't cohere into a definitive memory.

I shook my head again. 'I'm sorry.'

'You're Moll Regan's boy.'

Moll Regan! I sat up. The features all at once came together to form a picture. It was of a figure who'd hovered in the background during Mother's burial. There'd been so few mourners in the chapel, a bare dozen, that the extra figure in the graveyard had remained with me. I nodded, smiling towards him, though the memory disconcerted me.

'You knew Mother?'

'I did. She was… a very fine woman.'

Chester Maher's neck must have been every bit as stubborn as his disposition. Three times I suggested we call an ambulance, three times he growled that all he needed was a drink. Perhaps the fingers, trapped inside the belt, had cushioned his trachea. Perhaps the bough's wild undulations had set his feet dancing across the ground as often as through the air. Perhaps, no more than myself, he was in a state of shock. Whatever the pathology, his recovery from the bungled hanging was nothing short of remarkable.

A short time later, we were walking together in the direction of the Wellington Monument. By this time it was a black blade, thrust up into a blue twilight in which the evening star was as bright as the landing light on a plane. We'd said hardly a word. So to break the silence, as you might say, I tried: 'Would you look at the pair of us, the two wise men following a star to the East!'

'That's no star,' he spat.

'No?'

'That's a planet,' said he, very deliberately. 'A planet.'

I shrugged. 'Venus,' he went on, as though he were talking to a child or a simpleton, 'is a planet.'

'And the *morning* star?'

He stopped. The stupidity had stunned him. 'The morning star *is* the evening star. Venus! Lucifer!'

'Lucifer?'

'It's the same bloody thing!' he cried. I turned about. His eyes were staring in apoplexy at my chest. It was all I could do not to burst out laughing again. Here was a figure who not ten minutes since had been dangling by his belt from a tree, the life breath nearly out of him, and now he was arguing the toss about whether a star was a planet or a planet was a star as if his honour depended on it!

The standoff lasted maybe a half-minute, and then we set off again in silence. I knew the time was fast approaching when Yelena would be released from the Arbour Hill premises. I'd have to pick up the pace if I was to be sure to be there on time. But something held me back, something delicious. It was like the very first time I'd pulled faces at Mother's blindness.

'I remember you at the funeral,' I began after a while, when no other topic emerged. No other topic! It's hard to credit, looking back, that the circumstance in which I'd found the man never raised itself. All I can say is, it didn't. After all, when you think about it, it's hardly the easiest subject to bring up. 'How come you were trying to hang yourself anyhow?' It's just not asked. Perhaps I might have observed how a trousers-belt still held his pants from falling about his ankles, to ease into the topic. Evidently, the man had come prepared.

'A remarkable woman, your mother,' he repeated, when at length we were within sight of the end of the park. 'It came as a hell of a shock when I heard Moll Regan was dead, I can tell you that. Moll Regan! She can't have been more than…?'

I had to think. To tally it up. 'Fifty. She was fifty when she died.'

'Fifty!'

He had stopped again, and was staring hard at me with an expression that could only have been taken for outrage. I could've told him she'd looked closer to seventy, but I remained mute.

'Yes, I suppose she would have been fifty. Fifty!' He began to walk. 'But answer me this. Had she really been institutionalised?'

Was he accusing me? 'Her mind was very bad, towards the end.'

'Do you tell me so? Moll Regan? Good God!'

He stopped again. At this rate we'd never be out of the park! We were standing near a gas lamp, and in its halo I found I was at the end of a stare that was the very image of an accusation. It would take me months to realise that this face had only two configurations: haughty affront and hunted guilt. Neither mapped well the emotional convolutions of Chester Maher.

The yellow light and pools of shadow had made a gargoyle of his features. I daresay I was staring. In particular, I remember wondering at what point the symptoms of the bungled suicide would begin to subside. They never did. Throughout the year and a half that I knew him, the mismatched eyes continued to protrude, the face and neck retained their apoplectic volume, and the complexion, dusted with eczema, never dimmed below a vivid shade of madder. Only the rash of nettles and the violet furrow that gripped either side of his throat subsided, over time.

He shook his head, and the pools of blackness sloshed in his sockets. 'And of course the eyesight! The poor unfortunate.'

'I still can't really place you. Was it before she went blind you knew her?'

He ignored the question, if he'd heard it at all.

'The diabetes was it? Shocking the way it can do that to a body! How long ago did you say it was, son?'

'That Mother's eyes…? Twenty years. More. I would've been twelve.'

'Twenty years. Good God! Where do the years go?' Then he suddenly gripped my shoulder. 'She'd never have laid eyes on Stephanie, would she? What I mean is, all that would have been long before Stephanie's time.' He squinted at me. 'What I mean to say is, your mother would never have *seen* Stephanie Dujardin.'

'Stephanie…?'

'My wife.' He looked up and down the dark avenue. 'My… *ex*-wife.'

He took a step backwards, and exhaled heavily. For a third time, he fixed his exasperated gaze on mine. 'Don't,' he declared, 'ever marry a woman with a harpy for a mother!'

I guffawed. He wasn't expecting this. Then all at once he threw his own head back and laughed. 'Don't ever,' he slapped his thigh, bellowing into the night air, 'marry… a woman with… a harpy… for a mother!'

I was getting anxious, all butterflies, as they say. The hour was all but upon us when it would be no longer possible to catch Yelena Zamorska. And yet here was the thing. In the three months I'd been seeing her, if, as I say, that's the word for it,

I'd never once been late, nor stood her up. She, on the other hand…! Let's just say, with Yelena, you never knew where you stood. Was there a little sprite, frittering around the gas lamp, whispering into my ear to for once repay her in kind?

We'd walked perhaps another fifty yards and were on the crux of leaving the park when all at once he stopped and slapped his forehead.

'The case!' he cried.

'What case?'

'The case! The briefcase!'

I shook my head. He seized my arm and shook it. 'I had a briefcase with me.'

'I'm not sure I remember seeing…'

'Brown! So big!'

'I saw no case,' I stated. But he had already turned about and was marching back in the direction of the copse.

For a while I watched his figure recede. The mackintosh, which was torn at the shoulder, reached so far to the ground that only the heels of his shoes protruded. Although bulky, he was not a tall man. Somewhere just out of sight of consciousness, I calculated that if I left right now and trotted all the way, I could just arrive in time for Yelena. To go after the man would lead to my abandoning the rendezvous entirely. Two emotions surged like crossing tides, one anxious, one rebellious.

'There was no case,' I muttered to the sprite, or to the night. And I set off in the direction of the dark wood.

V

*M*other was a great one for the platitude. If, of an evening, I'd saved up a tabloid article on someone's downfall or disgrace, no better woman to dig out some old saw to fit the bill precisely. *She's fur coat and no knickers that one; Penny wise and pound foolish, that's what that is;* or, *They do say it's the old dog for the hard road.* She might sit in brood for a quarter-hour, clacking her teeth, rifling the dark combs of her brain for the ancient wisdom to set her cackling. On the rare occasion that these failed her, she'd withdraw into silence under a tactical: *Well it's the price of him* or *That'll soften his cough!* I often wonder what she would have made of my bestiary: the gloomy old circus lion in torn mackintosh; the bantam-cock strutting the inner-city tenements; the girl with cat's eyes and retractable claws.

And what would she say of me, her only begotten, if I were to read her my story? My inconclusive scribblings? *I knew bloody well it'd come to a bad end!*

But why did it end so badly, Mother? At what step did it all become inevitable? Some nights, when my task seems beyond me and the white page jeers, when the radiator ticks and tuts and the old shoebox of notes seems no less chaotic than the neon graffiti of the city, I console myself on another of Mother's adages: *They do say destiny delights in symmetry.* After Mother

44

dies, I chance upon a woman. Her mother is an invalid, and on that basis we take up together. Three months after our famous tryst at the zoo, I wander the ramparts where I may have been conceived. There or thereabouts I encounter a ghost who knew Mother in those days, and I fail that date with Yelena. Three months after that, with Yelena away to renew a visa, a schoolyard ghost returns to haunt me. He has a parent who is also an invalid. And he begins a rant against immigrants!

Symmetry, or blind chance?

And then there's this: on that first night I meet Chester Maher, knowing nothing of the man's plight nor he of mine, with a whole host of possible topics of conversation, not least his bungled attempt to hang himself, if that's what it was, he hits on the very subject that is fast becoming dear to me, though I scarcely understand its torments.

Blind chance, or symmetry?

Laughter lurks in the shadows behind such chances.

Moll Regan always fancied herself a fine judge of character. Whatever her fingers felt out as they ran over the Braille of the face, she swore they could trace the rough contours of a soul there. No plumber, doctor or social worker was allowed to enter our flat without first submitting to their scrutiny. But would you have fared any better, Mother, in judging between my trio of associates?

The three chronologies have finally been aligned. Providence can begin to juggle the triad of rings, whose trajectories she'll cross and recross with never a collision. Or better, she can begin to shuffle the three shells of the old shyster's trick, with me the patsy. Oh, Providence had me well fooled, right enough. But Mother, Mother. I ask again, would you have fared better? Would your weasel fingers have guessed under which shell the danger lay concealed? Under which, the trick that led to prison? Under which lurked murder?

Murder, Mother. It was my word.

I failed spectacularly to do it. How many times have I replayed the game in my head! *I knew bloody well it'd come to a bad end!* Well Willy Regan didn't. He could no more see it coming than the three could have guessed in which circle of hell each would end: in disfigurement; in banishment; in madness.

Back to the dark wood…

The briefcase, when at great length I stumbled upon it, was wedged between the bared roots of an ancient tree. It turned out to be every bit as dishevelled as its owner. What I unearthed was a contraption of scuffed leather, like something that schoolteachers used to carry in a more innocent age. One of the roots had snagged it, and as I tugged it free its mouth vomited a great quantity of papers. These were foolscap, unbound, typewritten, and variously crossed with pencil. But it was too dark to read their contents. Chester Maher swept them from me and rammed them into his satchel, jealous that I might read e'er a one of them. All the while we returned towards the lights of the Liffey, he clung to that case with such determination it might have been a developer's entire fortune in deeds and bonds.

'The world is everything that's the case!' For the present, that was the limit of what he'd reveal to me about its contents. 'The world is everything that's the case, hee–hee!' Over the space of a half–hour he declared it numerous times without altering a single syllable. So it must've been a quote. He seemed to find it amusing, at any rate.

It was by now quite dark. Venus, or Lucifer, was in the ascendant and was now clear of Wellington's gnomon. Time had moved on. Back in the copse the man had argued over everything from the nettles to the configuration of the trees, and it was only when I'd pointed to where his struggle had stripped bark from the knotted limb that he'd conceded it was the very oak. The de-buckled belt lay beneath, a snake in the grass. I might have lost my temper. I might have wept at the pointless delay. But as said, somewhere inside me, there was a delicious foreboding such as I hadn't felt since I was a schoolkid. Transgression! The taste of that dark fruit made the blood course to my throat and filled my stomach with delicate fluttering. No power on earth could now deliver me in time for the rendezvous with Ms Zamorska. And I damn well loved it!

It's a curious thing: that night, Guinness's must've been roasting their hops. As we made our way down towards St James's Gate, the air became thick with the bitter, nutty tang of it. Grow up in the Liberties, and its taste is as familiar as the trick of a voice or a song. But to this day, I can't catch that whiff without my heart beginning to skip, and my stomach to tumble like a naughty schoolboy's.

'Don't ever marry a woman with a harpy for a mother!' Chester Maher repeated as we made our way inside Walsh's of Parkgate Street. He said it once more as the first pints of porter arrived. It seemed he was a great man altogether for the repetitions. The cold had entered our bones by now, and I daresay the waft of hops helped us towards the yellow allure of the first bar to hand.

'Don't ever marry a woman with a harpy for a mother!' The woman, the wife or *ex*-wife, as Chester so nicely insisted, was one Stephanie Maher. Stephanie *Dujardin* Maher. The mother was a nameless harpy who persisted in speaking French before her detested son-in-law. Someone once said that all happy families are alike; every unhappy family is unhappy after its own manner. Over the pints that followed, I became acquainted, in fits and starts, with the rudiments of the Mahers' particular genus of domestic bliss. Or better: I was put in the position of the archaeologist who's come across the minimal quantity of bones to be able to guess at the shape of the skeleton. All that's required is the time and the patience to examine, to conjecture, to arrange.

In the order that the fossils were unearthed, then, I was allowed to glimpse: a failed marriage, a half-dozen affairs (hers), a tumour that turned out to be benign (his), a legal separation (theirs), a hostile family (hers), a daughter (on balance, his), a failed business (indisputably his), one house repossessed (no longer theirs), another in imminent danger (whose?), disdain, pathological jealousy, clinical depression, and, I think, love, that opportunist word.

A man, then: a hominid biped; middle-aged, and wearing horns.

The other topic of conversation, the other partial skeleton whose bones intruded sporadically into the grave of their marriage, was the curiosity he kept inside the old, battered satchel. Up to the first pint or two, he'd guarded this as if it were a reliquary. My one attempt to find out more was dismissed with a gruff 'Never you mind what that is!' Judge, then, of my surprise when, on my first return from the loo, I found the tabletop thick with yellowing foolscaps.

'Your masterpiece?'

He wasn't impressed. In fact, he began to gather in the pages as if he'd never intended me to see them. I apologised. He continued to sweep the table clear. 'Please,' I said, 'I'd be very interested…' He gawped at me, surprised to see anyone standing before him. I nodded in encouragement. I even smiled. And so it was that the chief subject of our conversation on that first night, after the prelude of the less than faithful Stephanie Maher, was the curiosity he guarded in the portfolio.

And yet the two are inseparable. The precise degree to which they are inseparable became clear to me only when it was already too late. But let me not get ahead of myself.

I sat. He breathed in deeply. He looked about the empty bar. He gave a disdainful laugh. Then the performance began. The loose foolscaps I'd glanced, when I'd spilled them in the wood, formed the opening scenes of a drama. He'd been working on this play for three years. What was he saying? More! He shook his head fondly. As fondly as a disappointed parent.

It had been rejected, it went without saying. And not just once! Oh by God not just once! By an entire raft of theatre companies! If he'd a mind to, he could wallpaper the toilet with the rejection slips… At each rejection he'd be despondent for months on end. But then, without warning, he'd spark into weeks of feverish revision.

I hadn't my reading glasses with me, but in any case he never allowed me to hold a sheet for more than a few seconds at a time. My eyes ran along the pencilled notes and red arrows, fired untidily between the regiments of type. Revision, rejection. Rejection, despondency. Dejection. Revision, resubmission. Then dejection, again, when the rejection slips returned like homing pigeons, more swift and peremptory at each revision.

He swiped the final page from my fingers and slid it into the satchel. 'Written anything yourself?' he asked, suddenly suspicious.

'Oh, nothing much.' A shoebox hovered briefly before my unfocussed eyes. 'Notes. Nothing so grand as a play.'

'You see, that's what they don't realise. That's what nobody realises.'

He stopped. He looked at his hand, inert on the portfolio. The fingers were short and pale, with scribbles of orange hair. At length the left hand raised his pint and, surprised to see it there, he took a draught. I waited. He replaced the glass onto its random pattern of wet circles. The hand returned to its squat. Evidently he thought he'd made his point.

'But what's your play about?'

'About? What is my play about? I subtitle it,' he declared, grandly, '*Opera without Music*.'

'But what's the subject of this opera without music?'

'Oh, that! It's…' he shook his head. 'It's a melodrama.' He began to tap the case with a blunt index finger, hesitant to continue. But at some length he went on, as though in an aside, 'written in verse.' At this final word he snorted in the direction of the barman.

'I'm sorry?' I wasn't sure I'd heard him right.

'I daresay that's why I've had no luck having it put on. The repertory companies, you say? Ha! All they want to do is to play it safe man.'

'And is it… the plot, I mean…?'

His eyes bulged. His face swelled. He could barely contain the hilarity. 'Of course it is! Christ!' He slapped his thighs and looked about the bar, triumphant. 'What else would it be about?'

Then he leaned in to me, all confidential. 'If you must know, I even go so far as to call it *The Cuckold*!'

'*The Cuckold*,' I repeated, in awe.

'*The Cuckold*,' he winked. '*The Cuckold* shows you all the… *crap* a cheated husband has to put up with. I don't pull my punches.'

'But did you say "in verse"?'

'By God,' he laughed, not having heard or, more likely, ignoring me, 'I'd dearly love to see Stephanie Dujardin's face if she ever went to see that play. By God, I'd dearly love to see that! The whole damned Frenchified family!' He slammed the table with his palm and looked at me triumphantly, even raffishly, as though I too were a victim of his despicable in-laws. 'Oh by God, that would be rich!'

Later, when I was alone and in the flat, when I'd had time and leisure to consider the night with all its bizarre shenanigans, my uncharitable soul began its whisper. *A body is found, hanging from a tree. Forensic tape seals off the scene. But the search of the copse uncovers nothing suspicious. Foul play is not suspected. Then a satchel is found. The press-hounds are mildly interested. Who is this man? What brought him to this pass? Perhaps if that satchel could speak…*

A news story is born. It develops momentum. Someone tells someone the battered old bag contains the manuscript of a play. A cheated husband! Someone else lets out a few lines of dialogue. The outlines of a plot. The news story takes on a life of its own, rising from the grave of the suicide, as you might say. A director spots an opening. Word goes around…

So then, the bungled suicide might well have been Chester Maher's final bid to have his magnum opus performed! If only he'd had the nous to pull it off. One thing was certain. He'd brought a second trousers-belt, to stop his pants from falling about his ankles. That argued forethought. This was no spur-of-the-moment act of desperation.

I lay back, hands behind my head. And this man knew Mother, in the old days? This melancholic bear? He growled.

He insulted. He exasperated. He was a dab hand at turning the deaf ear – had done each time I'd begun on Mother. But time enough. The angler, sensing the big fish, becomes tentative.

I determined to grapple him to my soul with hoops of steel.

Chester Maher. It's been the best part of a decade since I laid eyes upon the man, and yet he's as vivid to me as if I saw him a week ago.

One day, when we were in the Portobello flat – he'd just walloped me unmercifully at chess – his eye caught sight of one of my charcoal sketches. A standing nude, male. It was not one of my happier efforts.

'What's this all about?'

'Just something I do.'

'Something you do.'

'A hobby.'

'You haven't been at your *hobby* very long.'

It wasn't one of my happier efforts, but he could have shown a little diplomacy. There again, he'd snorted at every move I'd made at chess. 'A few months,' I lied. I made to take the sketch from his hands. It more than piqued me to see his thumb had smudged the charcoal. 'Not very long.'

'You go to a class, I suppose?'

'It's just a hobby, you know? To kill the time.'

'But you go to a class.'

'Once a week. Look, it's just something I thought I'd try my hand at.'

'To *kill* the time?' The way he drawled the verb made this an indictment.

'Well if you must know, I enjoy the whole business. It relaxes me.'

'So you said,' said the suicide. 'It kills the time!'

Why in the name of the merciful Christ did I allow him to see a sketch?

'It doesn't kill it. What it does is, it alters your perception of time. On a longer pose, on a half-hour pose, say, you become so absorbed in the whole business, you really couldn't tell if two minutes have passed or twenty.'

'You have more, I suppose.'

In those days I hoarded items. On top of the wardrobe there were a number of sketches, some of which were passably executed. There were even a few I'd dared set under the supercilious arch of Ms Zamorska's eyebrow. I now felt a strong urge to justify my pastime by calling as witness the best of these.

'I've a few. Give me a minute to sort through them.'

'Show me the lot.'

'The lot?'

'Every blasted one of them. I've a mind to see how this business works.'

Some minutes later the bed, chair and floor of the studio-flat were covered in contortions of the human form: males, females, old, young, three-minute sketches and twenty-minute poses. The sudden proliferation of so many leaves resembled nothing so much as a Last Judgement. I hadn't realised I'd done so many.

Chester Maher touched one of the nudes with a toe.

'That's one of your more recent efforts?'

I bent down over the page, edged it away from his shoe. It contained the torso of a woman in brown chalks.

'No. That one was last year. One of the first weeks, in point of fact. We were encouraged to try out different materials.'

He snorted. 'And that one?' His foot was hovering perilously over another sketch of the same female model, charcoal, but this one greatly foreshortened. She'd been laid out on a mattress as though dead, feet to the fore.

'That one too. Last year.'

'In that case,' he shook his head and sighed. 'In that case, I can't see how you can say you're making any progress. Them two is better than the rest of them, if you want my candid opinion.'

'You could be right,' said I, irritated. So far as I was concerned he could stuff his candid opinion up his melancholy arse. 'Like everything else, it's two steps forwards and one step back.'

'Or vice versa,' he trumped. Who does this... *fucker* think he is?

Of course the crux of the problem was thatI knew well he'd picked out the best two sketches. The two worthy among the damned. So I quieted myself by gathering the blackened pages in hasty sheaves from the floor. I'd never have shown them to Mother in the old days, that's for sure. Even supposing she could have seen them. Or maybe I would have. What weakness is it that makes us crave approval?

His comments had me in check. Me to play.

'You've no hobbies yourself?'

'Hobbies?'

'Hobbies, you know! I'm aware you write. You told me yourself you write,' I added, as though he might deny it.

'I wouldn't call that a hobby,' said he. 'Oh by Christ, I wouldn't call that a hobby.' I had by this juncture cleared the floor and the chair of its multitude. I pushed the untidy ream back on top of the wardrobe, my hands trembling with adrenalin and vanity. I could scarcely bear to look at my guest.

Silence extended throughout the confines of the room. When I glanced in his direction, I found he was staring out towards St Mary's dome, his hands in his pockets. I wondered what held me from asking him to leave. Finding nothing better with which to occupy my own hands, I began to straighten up the bedclothes, and then to tip the cold ash from the ashtray. It was full from the last night that Yelena Zamorska had stayed over. It was already a week old.

'Oh by God, I wouldn't call writing a pastime. Not at all. A pastime, you say? A *pastime*! But I'll give you a pastime if you like.' He turned from the window and looked at me, ingenuous, unaware of the brief tempest he'd stirred up inside me.

'Tell me, have you never looked at the heavens?'

I squinted at him. Was this a trap? I was still smarting from his peremptory dismissal of my struggles with the human form.

'I'm not sure I follow you.'

'The heavens. The stars, man. Have you never had any interest in the stars?'

'Astrology?'

'For Christ's sake!' he bellowed. 'Astronomy! Astronomy!'

'Oh, astronomy.'

If he noticed a tincture of sarcasm, he was masterful at hiding it.

'You talk to me of losing your sense of time? There's timelessness for you. There's the realm that doesn't change.' Now his eyes were round as a child's. 'I put together a little observatory out the back of the house. Nothing too fancy. A place to keep the telescope. A shed, an old chair, a couple of books of charts, that's all it amounts to.'

'You've a telescope?' He'd succeeded in interesting me.

'Seven-inch, reflecting. Nothing much. Nothing fancy. But my point is, what I'm trying to explain to you is, you don't need nothing too fancy. Sure the lights of the city have entire galaxies drowned out, man. Orange and brown and yellow, as if the whole cosmos was burning. You can hardly make out anything these days against the glow of the city.'

'So then why do you bother?'

'Ach, you understand nothing! I'm after telling you. It's timeless. It's *beyond* time. Can't you understand what I'm saying?' A stubby finger pointed to the ceiling. 'Year-in, year-out, the zodiac turns slow circles over our heads, like the great cog of a clock. Taurus, and then Orion, and the Twins. Then Leo, like a bloody great question mark. You see, at those times, at the times when Stephanie…' He shook his head and broke eye contact with me. I was left hovering awkwardly over the bin, the dust-coated ashtray limp in my hand.

'Think of what *you* do,' he said, nodding towards the floor that had been covered with charcoals. 'All them bodies you draw. They're all caught up in time. Caught like insects in a web. But the stars!' I sensed he was drawing towards an aphorism. He always gave the impression that he was rising towards an aphorism. But as usual, the aphorism failed to materialise. 'Did you know, she used to be so beautiful she could quite literally take your breath away? When first I met her.'

'Who? Your wife?'

'My wife? My *ex*-wife. Stephanie Du-*jardin*.' All of a sudden a huge, clumsy, childish smile broke over his face. It was the first time in the many weeks I'd known him that I'd seen anything like it. He reached his hand into the back pocket of his pants and took a couple of steps towards me, his body-space pushing mine back towards the bed, two kings in an endgame. As the smile grew blurred from the proximity of his bulk, a wallet was conjured.

I examined a small passport photo in the window of the left corner, a woman of about thirty with luxurious hair, feline eyes and an unblemished complexion. But there was something harsh in her comportment. Handsome, I would have said if I'd been pressed for an adjective. Instead I muttered limply, 'She looks French.'

'Of course she looks French!' he cried. 'How could she not look French? That's Stephanie Dujardin. *Dujardin*, for God's sake!' He reversed the wallet as if he needed to be reassured by the image. 'At the time that photo was taken, she told me she wanted us to be together. Forever. Can you imagine the effect of that? A woman like Stephanie Dujardin, telling the likes of me that she wanted us to be together? Forever? That was in Paris.'

I had slipped out quietly, obliquely, from between mattress and wallet. Black king to king's knight one. Still smiling fondly at the photograph, he'd scarcely registered the manoeuvre. I watched him from beside the door in anticipation of his next move. He shook his head, and the smile grew rueful. 'Paris! It was crazy of me to imagine that she'd ever survive the drudgery of this town.'

Then he fired a look at me that was ablaze with sudden anger. But he failed to articulate this anger. Instead, he pushed rudely past me, swung the door ajar and stepped out onto the landing. He was angry for having confided, I've little doubt.

He left the door open behind him, and my eyes remained fixed on the torn shoulder of his coat as he made for the stairs. These he at once began to descend, but at about the third step from the turning he hesitated and looked back towards the room. His head was by now at a level with my knees.

'You see everything changes, in time. Everything tarnishes. Even the most precious memories become tarnished. You think she doesn't love me? Just because of her infidelities, is it?' I was all ears. Maybe this time we'd reach the elusive aphorism! 'Ach, if it was only that easy! Anyone could have walked away from that.' He was waiting now, as if there were a question that I was supposed to ask. I rummaged through my brain, but found only gewgaws.

'And astrology?'

For a moment, he looked as though his face had been slapped. I tried again. 'The heavens?'

'The heavens? The *heavens*, is it? I'll tell you then. The ancients were right about the cosmos. It's the scientists have it wrong.'

'Chester…'

'The moon and the stars and the planets all belong to a celestial sphere. Down here, on the sublunar muckheap where we crawl about, everything goes to pot. In a blink of an eye we're old. But not the stars. The stars,' he wagged his finger up at me, 'are eternal. That's why I turn my eyes to them. It gets me away for a while from this mildewed world. This mildewed, Godforsaken city.'

Is it any wonder, I asked the banisters after his ferocious head had sunk entirely from view, that this man tried to hang himself? More fool you for having stopped him. More fool you for putting up with his figaries.

All the same, on the following day I made a small bonfire in the back yard and, one by one, I let the life-sketches fall into the flames.

VI

*T*here were three consequences arising out of the previous visit.

One was that I discretely dropped out of life-drawing class. Somehow, my enthusiasm for capturing the human form on paper had been irreparably blunted. Of course the whole debacle, and the secret *auto da fe* that ensued the following morning, were sources of wry amusement for Yelena when next I saw her. And nothing I said would alter her opinion a whit: it was wounded vanity that was making me drop the pursuit.

But had I dropped chess, when he'd so easily routed me?

Another result, though it took a long time for this to happen, was that I finally got to sketch herself. If nothing else, this fact must add weight to my contention that it wasn't entirely out of wounded vanity I'd packed away the charcoals. But then, a good many months had passed before that memorable night. We'll have time and leisure to revisit the occasion, when, as they say, the occasion arises.

The final upshot was, from that day on, myself and Chester met in town. Again, this wasn't so much pique on the part of yours sincerely. Or it wasn't exclusively pique, and the proof of that is that I continued to meet the man at all! Since neither one of us was any great shakes on the phone, we hit upon an arrangement to meet on every second Tuesday in one or another café in town. He never again graced Portobello, and as for me, it was already Hallowe'en before I finally got to visit the Maher estate on the Old Cabra Road, with its home-built observatory.

About a month or two after the charcoal fiasco, Fate found a new thread to twist into the braid. I was walking outside the railings of Trinity College when I saw a comical figure caught up between streams of snarling traffic. He must've been trying to follow Thomas Moore's finger to the portico of the old Protestant parliament when the lights caught him out. Bikes, cars and buses bore relentlessly down on Westmoreland Street. They revved, growled, screeched, blared their horns, and the figure turned, tilted, wobbled and pivoted. It was all he could do to retain a precarious balance. A flatulent bus blew raspberries, a truck farted black exhaust fumes, a hysterical motorbike was almost his undoing. Then the briefest of gaps appeared to his rear, and he tumbled back onto the traffic island. It was at that moment I recognised the man.

But just as I drew level the lights changed once more, and he scurried from me to the portico of the bank. 'Chester!' He scarcely acknowledged the shout, and I sprinted until I was level with the old, torn shoulder. 'Chester, where are you off to?'

'Quick! For Christ's sake we'll lose her!'

'Lose who?'

He turned, stared, all but had an apoplectic fit. 'Stephanie Maher!' he sputtered, hands raised like Jim Larkin. Then he drew instantly ahead of me, weaving between a couple of buggies and sidestepping a newspaper vendor. 'Hang on!' I called, knowing well he wouldn't. But I was a good deal younger, and I kept pace without too much difficulty. Stephanie Maher! Soul was hugely excited. We'd finally catch sight of the scarlet woman! In the flesh, as they say.

We ducked and weaved through the throngs that were crossing the great bridge. We passed O'Connell's gull-spattered plinth, and then Sir John Gray and Smith O'Brien, and Big Jim Larkin himself, though we fell short of the temperate embrace of Father Matthew. All were gazing wistfully to the south side. We bore left. We insinuated our way through the GPO's columns. We struggled through the shoppers of pedestrian Henry Street, past the hucksters and over the buskers, until we'd reached the entrance to a great glass mall. Here, at last, he paused.

'There she is. You see?'

I could not see. I peered over his shoulder and saw none among the shoppers to suggest the French woman I'd once glimpsed in his wallet. A number of years would have passed, it's true, but surely not so many that she'd become that stooped figure with the wheedling cart. Or your one, laden down double with the bags. Or old biddy, there, with the blue-rinse through thinning hair.

'Where?'

'There! There!' He was waving his arms about vigorously, exasperatedly, and was nodding his head in the direction of a shoe shop. But I saw nothing beyond a child with a satchel, staring in through the window. A severe woman in a red plastic raincoat stepped out and took her hand. But although this one was young enough, I could not square her with the photo I'd been shown.

'Stephanie! Stephie!' Both woman and child turned to face the hollering lunatic. So did half of the shopping mall. 'Steph!' He lurched forwards. The woman shook her head and paced rapidly away, pulling the child after her. I noticed that, beyond her, Chester Maher's antics had begun to attract the attentions of a security guard. Only the little girl, whose head was turned back towards us, seemed unperturbed by the scandal.

The woman had a brief and efficient word with the guard while pointing unflinchingly at Chester. She then pulled the child forcibly behind her and made for the nearest exit.

'Stephie!' called the accused, hopelessly. But the guard had by now intercepted him and baulked his further pursuit. Soon after, we were frog-marched out through a different exit, and found ourselves, once again, under the sky.

'I'd never have recognised her, you know. Not from the photo.'

'Who? What are you talking about?'

'Stephanie. Your wife.'

'My *wife*?' He could not have looked more perplexed if I'd just said 'your talking dog'.

'Well who was she then?' His eyes were still wide open, baffled, mismatched. Involuntarily I touched his shoulder. 'Who was that woman?'

'How the hell should I know!' He shrugged my hand off in exasperation. 'How should I know what she gets up to these days, or who she hangs around with!' Suddenly I had a vision of the face of the child, so pure, so serene, as she was being led away by the other. 'Then that,' I tried, 'was your daughter? Stephanie Maher is your daughter?'

'What?' he blurted, and slapped his forehead with violence. 'Of course she's my daughter! Whose daughter do you think she is?'

I watched, abashed, as the flames died slowly in his face and, slowly, gave way to ash. Each minute his visage aged another year. 'She's turning her against me.' He looked directly at me, or into me, much as he'd done on our very first night. Today, shoppers were milling about, and the voice scarcely moved above a whisper. I had to strain to hear his words. 'Bit by bit, month by month, she's turning her against me. She begrudges me every blasted minute I spend with Steph.' There was a catch in his throat as he breathed in. Discomfited by it, he began to thump his temple with the ball of his palm on every stressed syllable. 'She puts every conceivable hazard between us. Every conceivable excuse. Always at the last minute. You can't begin to imagine her tricks!' Women and children had gathered to watch the bizarre figure who was striking his own head so pitilessly. 'And her grandmother, that harpy! She wants to have the two of them move to France!' And he danced a desperate jig. 'To France!'

'France?' I shook my head and took his arm. But I was unable to move him out of the eye of the crowd.

'Even with her here, every fortnight it's more difficult. Stephanie Dujardin sees to that! Oh by Christ she does! Soon enough,' he shook his head, laughed horribly, 'soon enough that child won't even remember who her father is.'

I tried again to move him. Useless.

'But you must have rights. The courts must grant you access.'

He was no longer aware of my presence beside him, if he ever had been.

I never saw Chester Maher happier than when he was with his daughter. I write this with no irony. It was a ferocious love, and he an innocent in its flames. Most of the year he was a card-carrying curmudgeon; with her, he was more child than she.

But there were times I'd witnessed a very different side of him, neither child nor curmudgeon. This was the dark side of the moon. Already, over the first months, there'd been more than one occasion where it was as if someone had quite literally pulled the plug on him. And he could remain disconnected for weeks on end. Then he'd miss our appointments. Or he'd show up listless and late. He'd be unshaven, unkempt, his hair lifeless. And while he remained in eclipse his eyes would stare, vacant, dead. Or worse, would turn suspicious. What he was suspicious of at these times I've never fathomed. He'd go so far as to mutter incoherencies that put me in mind of Mother in her dementia. Except of course Mother mouthed the foulest obscenities.

He once actually said to me that in 'the Polish woman' I was looking for my mother. Good Christ! For Mother? Had he no memory of the woman?

For her part, Yelena frequently did call me a kid. And not always affectionately either. 'You're kid of thirty-five, do you know that?' Of course I argued the toss with her. 'How can I be, when I looked after my own mother from the age of twelve? D'you really think you learn more about life in one of your colleges?'

'No. But still, Willy. You are like adolescent.'

'You're saying that because you think I'm jealous of you.'

'Well! You are jealous of me.'

'Anyone in their right mind would want to know where… would have a right to know…' I was stymied. How to complete the sentence without saying that forbidden word, 'girlfriend'? I'd no wish to provoke a row. But I'd no wish to let it go either. 'You of all people know what it means to look after a disabled mother.'

'Well? What's your point?'

'I looked after mine from the age of twelve. Twelve, Yelena! I had to teach myself to clean and to cook, and to see the bills were paid. You think it was easy to squeeze a few bob out of Mother? And it was up to little Willy Regan to give her each day her daily insulin! And all this when most fellas my age were still doing their twelve times tables! Don't talk to me about being a kid.' She was unimpressed. 'And it's not as if I wasn't reading either. Hundreds of books, Yelena. Novels. You name it! Way beyond anything they were doing in school at the time.'

'Oh sure! Novels!'

'Well what's *your* point?'

'What do you learn from novels, Mister? Words. Stories. You can't grow up by reading novels.'

I thought for a moment of the long pageant of adulteresses that had filled the pages I'd read. Emma and Effie and Anna. Tess of the what-you-may-call-ems. 'I worked for a while, too. Don't forget that. I was a clerk for Doherty and Fitzgibbon.'

'But still, you are *pzcgthzzz*.'

'What does that word mean?'

'It means you are an innocent. A naïve.'

'So you keep repeating. Just because you keep on saying something doesn't make it true.'

'Okay. I give you example. So why you let this man stay in your place?'

'What man? Danger?'

'You say me you don't even like him! And still, you let him boss you around in your own flat.'

'Well…' I began. She had a fair point. I clapped my hands together and rubbed them. 'But I got rid of him!' She squinted at me. 'Well he's gone, isn't he? And besides, he was stuck for somewhere to stay.' I stood up straight. 'It *amused* me to let him stop over for a time.'

'It amused you.' She had a way of blowing smoke into the air that was the very genius of irony.

'I thought I might learn something from the man. He's a... well, he's been around the block.'

'I tell you what I think. I think,' she began, lighting a new cigarette off the old stub, gaining a few seconds to polish her Polish thoughts, 'that when this man reappear from straight out of your schoolyard, it shows you have never grown up. It proves you are still little Willy Regan in short pants and he is still the schoolyard bully, ready to boss you about.'

'But that's absurd!' I stared over her head. It seemed to me that I'd started out trying to have one argument, but had yet again been sidetracked. I suddenly heard in my head, for the second time in so many days, Chester Maher's words: 'If you ask me, it's your mother you're looking for.' Yelena had turned her back on me, and my eyes admired her impertinent bottom. It might have been a teenager's. If there was one thing I was not looking for, it was my mother.

She turned around, and the teenager vanished. But how had she led us down this byway? In twenty years, I'd never hit on the mechanism to have Mother talk about what I wanted to discuss. Pocket money, free time, that sort of thing. Maybe if I gave the dialogue a lurch. Out of the blue, as they say.

'Did I tell you? I finally met Chester Maher's little girl.'

'No! You don't tell me. When was this?'

'There last week.'

'Last week? And you haven't told me before now?'

'I haven't seen you! How could I tell you? You were with...'

Once again I was stymied. Who had she been with? The one from the university, with the foreign name? Or the other one, the one with a boat? Even after all her hints and intimations, even after the names casually dropped and the *this cannot be relationship*, I still had no actual proof.

Proof! Who was I kidding?

'You were otherwise occupied.'

'And so?' Again the ironic cigarette smoke.

'So?'

'So what is she like?' She stared at me. 'This girl?'

'Oh! The girl…'

With Stephie there, Chester's illuminated face would take on the exaggerated features of a cartoon character. To see him at such times was to see a kid of fifty. I had put his age at quite a number of years more than that, and the figure came as a surprise. There again, when Mother was his age she'd looked nigh on seventy. The ravages of insulin and Cork Dry Gin.

'I will finally see out the half century,' he said to me one day, apropos of nothing, 'this New Year's Eve.'

'New Year's Eve, really?'

'Half a century,' he went on, ignoring me, as was his manner. 'It makes you think. It makes you feel sometimes like you're as old as the Earth. You feel there was never a time when you weren't on it.'

'You were never born on New Year's Eve?'

'I've always hated that damned day. Everyone else seems to want to cheer and make a song and dance of it. And this millennium business will be a thousand times worse! But for me, along with the calendar year, I'm burying another year of my life. I've never cared for it. What business had my mother giving birth in the dead of winter?'

'Fifty,' I nodded, 'so that would make it, what, 1949? I've an idea it was a particularly cold winter.' Mentally, I was comparing his dates with Mother's. He'd have been too young, I knew bloody well! 1949 confirmed the fact. Besides, there was the small matter of a tiny note stuck into Mother's prayer book. 'W' was not 'C', no matter what way you turned it. But we'll get to that, in its place. 'I was born in…' I would have told him where, if he hadn't been following his own thread of thought, quite oblivious to my presence.

'In a ward of the Coombe Hospital, in the dead of winter,' he resumed. 'I suppose it's the cold weather that gives us goats our famous disposition.'

'I thought you'd no time for astrology…'

'The goat! Ha! There's some truth in that.' I examined his head for goatish features, but discovered nothing out of the ordinary. 'They say we're ruled over by Saturn. Now there's a gloomy God for you. Devourer of his own children! The Greeks had a better name. Cronos, they used to call him. The God, I mean. I don't know what they called the planet.' He was fiddling with the spoon of his coffee as he soliloquised. 'Of course they knew nothing at all of the outer planets, for all their philosophy. I'll tell you one thing for free. It's Pluto that rules over this gloomy kingdom. The city of the thousand tribunals, says you.'

'City of Dis,' says I. 'Isn't he Pluto?' God alone knows where I'd picked up that particular nugget. If he was impressed he didn't show it. 'But you can't believe the planets have any influence over us?'

At first I thought he hadn't heard that either. He continued to stare at the coffee spoon, turning little spirals in the yellowed cream that was festering halfway down his mug. But all at once he fixed his eyes on me and dropped the spoon.

'Look,' he commanded. 'Look!' He'd begun to shuffle about awkwardly on his seat, drawing attention to himself as he went through his several coat pockets. 'Look. Do you see that? And that. And that.' Each phrase was punctuated by a small brown bottle, which he slapped down on the table before me. By the time he was finished, a quintet of them formed a chess miniature. I gazed at him, awaiting an explanation.

'Look,' he said again, lifting the first bottle and unscrewing it. He tapped out a few oblong capsules onto his hand. 'Look,' he said again, and from the second bottle he tapped out three smaller pills. 'Look,' and from the third, a number of sky-blue tablets, and so on until his palm was quite full.

'Those are my planets,' he declared triumphantly, after suitable pause for effect. Unbeknownst to him, he had the waiter's divided attention. 'Those are the planets that influence Chester Maher. Uppers, do you see, and then these are stabilisers, to make sure I don't go too high. Those innocuous-looking devils are lithium. These, barbiturates. And these fellows, they're to help me sleep. So you see, this solar system,' he closed his fingers over the entire confectionary, 'is all the planets I need in my horoscope. It's their orbits pull my humours about.'

'But you don't take all of them?' His unflinching eye dared me to disbelieve it. 'Not every single day?' He snorted at this. The question was beneath contempt. Infra dig, as they say. The waiter turned back to a table he'd been clearing. A bluebottle slipped down the window onto its back, and vibrated intermittently. The clock advanced by slow degrees.

'There's been something I've been meaning to ask you,' I said at last, when I despaired of hearing another syllable from the man. I had no appetite for another coffee to justify our stay. But in any event, there was a question I'd been burning for some time to ask him. 'How exactly did you know Mother?'

'Your mother? Your mother was a very fine woman!'

'So you've told me. But anything more than that is more than I know.'

'I knew her,' he resumed the slow circle over the cream that was by this time nothing more than whey, 'when she lived in Gloucester Place.'

'Gloucester Place?'

'Now, that shook you! You didn't know your mother was a north-sider! She only moved to the Liberties once she had you.'

'Go on!' So that meant I was a north-sider? Good God! 'So you're from Gloucester Place? I mean originally?'

'I didn't say that. I said I knew Moll Regan when she was in Gloucester Place. That's all I said.'

The clock moved on. Another five minutes, I thought, and I'll leave. The bluebottle had begun to spin in frenzied circles. 'I first noticed her,' he resumed, with no further prompting, 'when I was a lad of about twelve. She would have been fourteen or fifteen at the time. She used to look after a little chap who was lame.'

'That must have been Maurice. He was born with polio.' A black and white image of a grinning urchin in orthopaedic shoes had stood vigil by Mother's bed, even through her dark years. The uncle I'd never met.

'He died not long after Moll Regan left with a babby in her arms. I wonder, now, who that was.' He winked at me. It was a cruel wink. 'I remember, at one time she used to push this urchin around in a pram. A huge bat-like contraption, the way they used to be in the old days. Colossal, overlapping wheels, like you might get on a bicycle. He used to love to ride in that, the little lame fellow. Even when he was six or seven years of age. He'd watch them playing hopscotch and cat's cradle like he was little Lord Muck in his carriage.'

'And how did you know them?'

'I used to go to school around there. Sometimes we'd get into fights with the locals. Oh they were rough tribes living in those parts right enough. She had freckles in summer. And a face like an elf. I can see it as clearly as if it was yesterday. Now, would you believe that?'

I thought for a minute of the child being dragged through the mall. Little Stephie Maher.

'But why did she leave Gloucester Place?'

'Why? Ha! Why do you think, now?' There was something faintly comic, faintly sinister in the way he leered. My gut turning to concrete, I shook my head. 'Because the dad bet the head off her! And there was an older brother too that gave her what for.'

'That'd be my Uncle Jimmy. An unsmiling bastard. He's dead too this long time. A house fire.'

'A house fire begob. Well maybe he deserved it, the way he used to bully her about. A humourless bloody bastard. So one night, Moll Regan flew the roost. Told nobody. Just wrapped up her babby in a bundle and flew the roost. It was years before they found out where she'd flown to.'

'Years? Are you sure about that?'

But Chester Maher's face had become a blank. I wouldn't bet he even heard the question.

Some twenty minutes on, just as the bus was approaching his stop, where it was my custom to wait with him, he laid a hand on my forearm. 'I'll tell you something else,' he winked. 'Moll Regan was the first person to give me a number of sleepless nights.'

Now this winded me. This took the wind quite out of my sails. 'Because… she was pregnant?' I'd no wish to betray the seasickness his unexpected words had brought on. What was his Cheshire grin driving at this time?

'Because she was pregnant! That's very good! You have it, but you don't have it.' By this point, maddeningly, the asthmatic door of the bus had concertinaed open. He was already counting out his change.

'So what happened? What did she do on you to give you sleepless nights?'

'I'll tell you,' he said over his shoulder. 'I found out that Moll Regan was planning to fly the roost.' What was it about that bloody phrase? 'And I found out, what's more, that it was to the Liberties she'd be flying.'

'How did you…?'

He tapped his nose 'Moll Regan was only a young slip of a thing. Scarce halfway through her teens. It crossed my mind I should do everything I could to prevent any foolishness. It crossed my mind I should tell the father. In fact, for years afterwards it crossed my mind I should've told the father.'

He'd paid his fare. I looked pleadingly at the bus driver.

'I'll leave you with this question. How different would your life have been, would both your lives have been, if I'd turned tattletale and told the father what I knew?'

The door wheezed asthmatically. I was left watching the back of the bus as it laboured up the road. Flabbergasted, I think, would be the word.

VII

*M*y writing is disturbed by the mewl of a tomcat. It's a parody of the human, the wail of a demonic infant. This has been going on for three nights now. On the first night the yowling intruded into the room, I laid down my pen and clambered across the bed, then peeped out past the blind. The moon must have been close to full; in its oblique light the cataract of the far window glared luminously. I felt too uneasy to remain in its gaze.

On the second night I endured the torment without leaving the desk or the bedside notes. It's true I couldn't concentrate while the cacophony continued; that I threw down the pen in disgust. But in any event, the serenade was soon cut short. There was a horrid screeching like metal being torn, a clatter of dustbin lids, and then nothing.

This time I'm already crawling over the rattle-jointed bed just as the perverse racket ceases. I wait. Nothing. In the pressure of silence I hear my heart pound its cage of ribs with miniscule fury. I push aside the blind and press my cheek to the pane. But the silvered yard is empty, what I can see of it. The laneway, empty. Then the yowling of the child-cat starts up again, somewhere to the left. This is intolerable. Ever since prison, the small hours are the only time I can write.

I let the blind drop, and turn back to face into the room. My eye is tricked by the shadow, the arachnid shadow that palpitates beneath the hook over the bed. Another yowl penetrates the room, and I make a vow on its absent crucifix: *sooner or later, by fair means or foul, you will disappear, my feline friend.*

I'm wandering. I shouldn't allow a cat's crying to disperse my thoughts as if they were a clutch of foolish brood-hens. But when I return to the desk, the white page accuses me. Across its top is a single sentence. The night's labour has produced a single line, which I stare at as if it were a column of ants: 'Yelena Zamorska had, at this time, two other steady liaisons that I'm aware of.'

I crumple it up. A lie! A damned lie! I was no more aware of 'steady liaisons' than I was aware of the cell where the present story would end. The trouble is, I've allowed the chronologies to get mixed up, again.

She zipped up her jacket, shook out her blonde hair, and tripped to the door. 'He! He! Is man!' She stuck out her tongue, laughed, and was gone. That's where I left off my story, so far as 'steady liaisons' are concerned.

To get the chronologies straight, it was over Easter that she returned to Krakow to renew her visa. Or to obtain the university stamp that would allow our crowd to renew it for her. And it was in early April, while she was still away, that I chanced upon the trial of Joseph Mary Danaher. The mistrial of Joseph Mary Danaher.

So far, so good.

Now as said, I'd already been dancing attendance on Ms Zamorska for three months when our butterfly's waltz set me blundering into Chester Maher. The famous bonfire of the vanities that his one and only Portobello visit had provoked took place before Danger began his squat in the flat. Of that I'm sure. There were no bucking bodies in bucking charcoal lying about to provoke his bucking mirth. So then, that fiasco took place between January and April. But when precisely was it that 'He! He! Is man!' first transmuted into Adam Rakoczi, that hated name?

There was another, an O'Byrne or O'Brien. Owned a boat down in Athlone, it seems. But I don't even know for certain if he was a rival. Of one thing only I'm certain: by our anniversary (our anniversary! ha!) the name Rakoczi was engraved into my gut with acid.

The months passed with little change to the routines that I'd established, or that had established themselves willy-nilly. Life-drawing classes were dropped from my social calendar. Danaher appeared and disappeared, Yelena returned, and in her turbulence my emotion was once again a straw. That summer I attended fewer sessions at the Four Courts. Or perhaps there were fewer to attend. 'That,' Chester scoffed, 'is what's meant by summery justice.' July, August, so desired by one and all, I've always found fallow months. Courses are put on hold. Life dawdles. Even the newspapers seem to idle in the long afternoons.

For his part, Chester Maher delighted and infuriated in equal measure. His big news was a powerful new scene he was composing for his play. Or more accurately, that he was about to compose. It would, he declared, clinch the final act of his *Cuckold*. But he refused to let me peruse the foolscaps he guarded in the moulting portfolio.

All at once it was October.

I sat with Yelena one afternoon, deep in our secluded theatre in Stephen's Green. We were alone. Alone except for the verdigris statue of our poet, Willy Yeats. Ever since she came back from Krakow, he'd become our poet. All that summer we were discovering together his lofty rhetoric out of a dog-eared paperback Yelena had picked up for a song in one of the second-hand bookshops she delighted in. There was a paper she had to prepare for Krakow University, a comparison with some national champion or other from Poland. This project had been the basis of her renewed visa. If the whole affair wasn't a fiction. But that's another story.

It was she who suggested I help her. I wondered how, precisely. I've little doubt my schoolmates had memorised the great man's lines on squalid Dublin. The shivering prayer; the greasy till. But I'd left the classroom too early. Or I'd forgotten. In fact, the only thing I was in a position to correct her on, that first day she'd asked me, was that the man's name wasn't pronounced yeast. 'You see, Willy,' she cried, 'that's exactly the local knowledge I need!'

Now, in the shadow of the stern bronze, we'd recite aloud to one another from her book. Or we'd quarrel over a verse or a line, even at times a single word. Or a detail of history. It had been a constant embarrassment to me that a foreigner was able to poke her fingers through the holes in my knowledge of Irish history. And as for geography, as I explained to her, my head was built after the manner of one of those postboxes whose world is divided between 'Dublin' and 'All Other Places'.

I'd read dozens of novels on the sly, of course. In the old days. But then, my adolescent mind would range down the sewers of a pasteboard Paris, or over the huge steppes of the falling dark. What little local history I knew I'd picked up from the stories I'd read aloud to Mother: James Plunkett, or Walter Macken. Mother was particularly fond of Plunkett. But Janey Mary, with her nail-marked feet, was hardly social science.

So, to begin, I was invariably embarrassed in our spats. I enjoyed them all the same. So did she. Maybe, if we'd been sparring partners instead of lovers, so to speak, the whole business might've lasted. But besides enjoying the barney, they gave a goal to the long hours I spent alone in the reading room of Rathmines Library. 'Give a man a goal,' Mother used to say, 'and he's happy.' So I began reading up on the thousand-year-old capital, so rent with contradictions. Cobbled out of them, as you might say. I began to collect from R. F. Foster and J. C. Beckett a copybook of brave new words: escheatment, suzerainty, desuetude. 'To fall into desuetude.' For a period, I fondled that particular phrase. At every turn I'd try out ways in which to ingratiate it into my conversation. But with the passage of months, it fell from favour.

There was another motive driving my studies. A rival. This was some foreigner she'd met out in UCD on the study-abroad programme who was meant to be some sort of an expert on Mr Yeats. She'd let slip that particular dog of war early on. And so, in our game of catch-up, I even went so far as to order at the library desk *This Filthy Modern Tide*. It was a book-length study of the statesman-poet himself, and I wanted badly to trump Yelena and her expert foreigner. A memorable title, too, though there was no filth in it that I could find, and precious little that was modern. But the language was so convoluted I'd have fared no worse if it'd been written in Polish. It was, I believe, what they term an academic treatise.

It did provide me with one rare victory all the same. 'This is perfect, Willy!' she'd cried, delighted.

'What is?'

'This title. I will call my treatise *This Filthy Modern Tide.*' And I daresay she would have if, as I say, the blessed thing had ever been written.

On this particular day I'd begun to talk about, Yelena had forgotten the book of poems. To pass the time, which, as they say, would have passed anyway, I'd been telling her about Mother. She loved to hear about Mother. So I started on how, in the days when we lived in the Liberties, Mother used to spend hours on end in front of a television set. This was a PYE, an outsized antique with a huge dial and mismatched rabbit-ears, whose picture continually slipped its frame. The flicker would transform the room into a huge aquarium in which Mother spent her evenings, still as a rockfish. But I suppose the sound wasn't altogether bad. All the same, once it gave up the ghost, she never demanded I replace the set.

'I'll tell you something that'll give you a laugh,' says I. 'Mother was absolutely cock-a-hoop about the free TV licence. In Ireland, if you're blind, you're entitled to a free licence. By God, she loved that! She never tired of telling the neighbours about it. But here's the gas thing. During all the years that she was able to see, when I was still at the Christian Brothers, it had never once crossed her mind to get a bloody licence. Now! How's that for logic?'

'But she sounds wonderful!'

'She was,' I shrugged, 'my mother.'

For my part, I went on, I was mightily pleased to see the back of that old PYE. I'd always despised television, the sedative household god. Even as a solitary adolescent, I could never see the point in its inanities. But Mother wouldn't brook attending its altar alone, and I'd have to sit on the sofa, she on her burnished throne, for hours on end. It was my charge to consult the *RTÉ Guide* and then to tune in the appropriate channel, at the appropriate hour. Of course, the lines skipped and jumped and the picture faded in and out of snowstorms, but after all it was the sound that counted. I taught myself to read and write unnoticed, even occasionally to draw, by that unsteady glow.

I'd become adept at ignoring the metallic voices that hissed from its circuits. But Mother was innately suspicious of me, sole fruit of her loins. Every so often, when the slippage became acute, she'd become suddenly irritable. To this day I wonder at this trick she'd acquired. Perhaps there was some hint in the soundtrack that I was too obtuse to notice. Or perhaps the strobe effect was apparent, even to eyes rheumy with cataracts. 'Fix the picture, Willy,' she'd rasp. 'You're hanging alive with laziness!' Or 'You're bone idle' – that was another of her expressions.

'My mother too,' interrupted Yelena.

'Your mother what?'

'She hates to watch TV alone.'

'But you're missing my point. The point I'm trying to make is, I'd have to settle the bloody picture for her, even though she couldn't see the damned thing!'

'But I think it is you that misses the point. The point is that she could not stand to watch TV alone. If the picture was not good, then it was obvious you were not watching it with her.'

'But that's absurd, Yelena. It must have been just as obvious I'd not the blindest interest in watching the damned thing in the first place.'

'Well, people are absurd. So Adam can't stand it when he is cooking dinner but I have something tiny while I wait because I'm starving.'

I snorted. It seemed to me that ever since she'd returned from Krakow to UCD, the name of Adam had begun to crop up with provocative frequency in her conversation. Adam Rakoczi. As usual, it led to an awkward silence. But Yelena refused to censor other men's names from our talks. To have done so would have been to admit that there was something untoward in the set-up.

'And so now you are sulking.'

'I am not sulking.' I'd turned away from her and was staring out over the artificial pond. 'Far from it, in fact.' A pair of drakes drifted into view, two mandarins that had escaped from a Chinese print. I stood up and approached, letting on that they commanded all of my attention. 'In fact, if you want to know, I was going to ask you something. Something that'll probably surprise you.'

'Oh? Okay, Mister. You can ask me.'

I turned to look at her. She had placed a cigarette in her lips and her eyes shut to slits as she cupped a match. Behind her back, a flock of starlings wheeled and shoaled with a single will, turning the sky into an ocean. The air had begun to turn cold of late, and Yelena was wearing the same coat and muff as a year previously. Another year, yellowed and discarded in the rush to the new millennium.

'I was going to ask you… if you believe in an afterlife.'

'An *after* life?' she questioned, blowing up into the sky a stream of smoke and then laughing. 'After what?' It was growing dusky, and her features were becoming less distinct. 'I expect you mean do I believe in God?'

'What I mean is,' I answered quickly, as if I knew what the hell I'd meant, as if I hadn't simply been erasing the hated name of Adam from the air, 'do you think this is all that there is?' I made a sweeping gesture with my arm to include the pond, the trees, the loose-bowelled starlings. The flock reeled indecisively above the reflective surface, bracing for a departure they'd perpetually postpone. Months later, I found they were still stabbing the frozen grass.

'You're a funny man, Willy Regan. What on earth makes you ask me this?'

'I don't know,' I said. But I could hardly leave it at that. 'Maybe it's all the history I've been reading. The rebels, hurling defiance from the rooftops in the name of the dead generations. Never seeing what came of it. "The dead generations"! What d'you think about that for a phrase?' I began to warm to the subject. 'Or else it's all the faces looking sternly out of black and white photos. Dressed up in fancy costumes, back in the days of the Castle and the Crown.' A park constable threw us a glance as he made his rounds. I nodded after him. 'The DMP, you know? There's a marvellous photo of one of them directing trams by the Rotunda, like something out of the Keystone Cops. And then, the tenements. The hoards of the poor. Doorways gaping like foul-smelling mouths. The whole inner city,' I declaimed, 'nothing but a lurid grin of gaps and cavities.' Yeats had gone to my head. And I knew that she knew I was doing my damnedest to impress her with my rhetoric. To strike out Adam Rakoczi's name. 'They must have thought their world would last forever.'

'Nothing lasts forever. If it did, we would all go mad.'

'But this present mania for tearing down, this constant clatter of pneumatic hammers, how can that be any improvement? Have you tried to count the number of cranes, or the wrecking balls? I swear to God, Yelena, the whole city is one God Almighty building site. You want to hear Danaher on the subject! It's as if we've become afraid to say anything is ever finished in this town.'

'Well?' I watched the tip of her cigarette trace a slow arc before her, a firefly attracting a mate. 'You can't live in a museum.'

I was getting nowhere. But not ready as yet to give in to silence, I began to wheel like the starlings. 'Constantly ripping everything up, in the name of progress? Every day laying new foundations, new pipes, new cables, all across the same patch of ground?' I seized on an image I'd put into my journal some nights before. 'All you ever get that way is scar tissue.'

I imagined from her dim features she was serious. Impressed, even. But a breach in the clouds bathed her in flames of the dying sun, and I saw she was still laughing at me. A thin spoor of blue smoke trailed over her shoulder, the faintest of scarves. 'And what does any of this great speech have to do with the afterlife, mister man?'

'Well, what I mean is,' I looked back over the water to the trees, trembling in short-lived ochres and yellows. There was a waterfall of leaves each time the wind moved. I shivered. 'What I mean is, is this really all that any of us gets? One passage through the restless city? And then it's all over and done with?'

'But Willy, there's more to the world than this city of yours.'

'No there's not! There's not, Yelena!' My own passion came as a surprise. I moderated the tone. 'Or in any case, it all comes to the same thing. A hundred years from now we'll all be dead and forgotten.'

'What do you prefer? You want that there is judgement? Irish Catholic!' She stood up and made the sign of the cross with the ruby butt of the cigarette, laughed a third time, then flicked it from her in a cascade of sparks. 'I think that talking about your mother has made you so gloomy today.'

I shook my head. 'Doesn't any of this interest you?'

It is no use. I can't concentrate with the infernal mewling outside. I'll have to leave off this... this *confession*, for another night. And tomorrow. Tomorrow, first thing, I'll pay a visit to the hardware store at the corner of Talbot Street.

We'll soon see what a quart of rat poison won't do, my friend.

PART TWO

VIII

*T*here's a dream I have. A recurring dream. A dark aeroplane, massive as a sea-monster, is plunging through night clouds. The windows are a rosary of golden beads. In that double-logic that governs dreams, I'm able to watch the plane's fall, even though I'm a passenger inside the plummeting fuselage. The clouds part upwards in grey shreds of mist, and the great body of the aircraft is rocked with turbulence as it crashes through them. And I'm a terrified face, a wet petal, pressed to the rounded window just to the fore of the wing.

Dark air rushes upwards. In our hurtling descent I sense disaster rushing towards us. Vaporous rags are ripping so fast from the base of cloud that already the lights of a town poke through. It's a field of inverted stars. And then the cloud is breached and we float above a great city, ambers and reds like tiny dancing flames. Just for a moment its vast constellation is set out beneath us. But then the plane rocks, violently. The window disintegrates. I'm thrust out into the black air. I fall, catastrophically. I plunge towards the city's asphalt streets until, just before impact, I'm bolted awake. Every sense is alert and pounding. I'm sitting up in bed in a state of horrible panic.

This is a dream I've had, ever since I can remember.

It visited me again on the night before Danaher re-emerged into my circle, surfacing from whatever netherworld he inhabited, breaking through the surface of mine like a bottom feeder. Or maybe the dream came on the night previous to that. It's difficult to be precise after so many things have happened.

But I do know for a fact I'd spent the morning in the company of Maher and child. At first Stephie refused to speak to me, or even to extend her hand when I dangled my great paw before her. She stepped behind his bulk, as if he were a huge planet that could shield her, and she looked at the ground with a finger in the gap between her teeth. But once the three of us were hunched over ice-creams in some fast-food outlet, her shyness melted. Mine also, to a degree. Never having had much intercourse with mothers, I'm unused to children. My own darling progenitor could scarcely abide the breed. But this youngster mistook my clumsiness for playfulness, and even giggled at me. She was at that age when children lose their milk teeth and grin like miniature vampires.

Chester was a changed man with Stephie about. He became even less observant than was his wont, as if there were no more world than his diminutive daughter. His face floated, semi-submerged in unfocused flaccidity. It floated, as you might say, in the amnion of a vague smile. His features were blissfully stupid, except on those occasions when he became aware of the relentless march of hours. Then they'd surface and grow hard.

At all other times he played the clown. In one game he'd squeeze his thumb between two fingers, as though pulling away the girl's nose. Or he'd let her pull at his ears. I was taken aback at this easy interplay between such disproportionate beings as Chester Maher and a five-year-old. Unkindly, I compared the great red gargoyle head to the elf-like face of the girl, luminously pale, but freckled over the nose like an April meadow. *It's a wise child indeed,* whispered Soul.

If Chester Maher shared my suspicion, it altered not one iota his affection for the girl. She called him 'Dada', and that was proof enough for him.

That same evening, I'd met Yelena in a bar that was popular with her university pals. There was a gathering of mature students, so-called. Around her table, foreign accents prattled. At this time I had the curious idea that, whatever her motives may have been, she was doing her damnedest to engineer a meeting between myself and her Yeats expert, Rakoczi, with the result of course that I was on edge all the time we were in that blasted bar.

Later, to make up for it, as we strolled along the canal in the direction of the bedsit, I began to recount the events of the morning. It was by no means the first time I'd resorted to Chester, since she invariably laughed at my descriptions of the man. But today, I couldn't find the comic note. 'So Stephie was finally collected at three o'clock by the self same woman I'd seen her with previously – she of the red plastic raincoat. After that he became stiff, subdued, quite impossible. I might as well not have been there.'

'So that he loves his daughter more than he loves you. You cannot tell me you're jealous!'

'If she is his daughter, Yelena. I have to tell you I have my doubts.'

'But you men are so stupid! What difference can it make?'

'You don't think it makes a difference?'

'Listen, mister man. Do you not say me she calls him "Dada"?' It was a curious thing with Yelena, the stronger she felt about an argument, the less perfect her grammar. This disparity would inflame both her passion and her imprecision still further. 'Do you not say me he call her her daughter?'

'*His* daughter. Course he does. But all the same…'

'But all the same…! But all the same…!'

'All the same, Yelena, I expect that a man likes to leave a trace. Some evidence he's passed through the world. Maybe that's why he chooses to write. Or to make statues or paintings or bridges. Or even a fortune! Anything at all that might outlive him and say to the world "I did this, I passed through here."' I stopped and looked at her. 'A woman too, I expect.'

Above her glasses, her plucked eyebrows were hoisted into a child's drawing of a gull. 'Still you don't answer my question.

What difference it make, that he is the real father or that it is some other man, so long as the girl call him "Dada"?'

'What's "Dada" got to do with it? "Dada", Yelena? "Dada" is just a word!'

'No, Mister. "Dada" is everything to do with it. Is not just word!'

'And what's that supposed to mean for God's sake? How exactly is it more than a word? And a child's word at that!'

'This is why you will never be a poet, Willy.' Her mouth twitched. She knew she'd scored a goal.

'Who says I want to be a poet?'

True, I had mentioned my journal on a couple of occasions. I hadn't ventured to show it to her, though. As things turned out, I never would. We began to walk again, but one of us hesitated on Charlemont Bridge. A bat was zigzagging low over the canal, irresolute as a suspicion. Like a crack running through the porcelain of dusk, as some poet had put it, wanting to leave his mark. That was in my journal.

'I'm no poet like you. I'm Willy Regan. I'm not Willy Bloody Yeats.'

'So then, Mister, where's your trace?' Two direct hits! I was beginning to founder under the assault. Yelena was watching me with wide eyes and a pursed mouth, a great cat toying with its quarry. The bat fluttered erratically over our heads and I recoiled from it. I had the idea that in its blind haste it might falter against one of us. 'But all the same, you saying that the girl's real father doesn't matter, that's nonsense. That's like telling me you'd be happy to pass off a book of someone else's poems as your own, just so long as it was your name appeared on the flyleaf.'

'So your friend Chester is plagiarist?' She was enjoying herself now. I knew, because she held her lips taut so they wouldn't betray the smirk.

'I never said it wasn't his child. I said I thought it mightn't be his child.' It was vital to figure out where the invisible boundaries of this game lay. If I crossed one, she wouldn't come home with me.

'It?' She cuffed my ear with her muff as she pronounced the pronoun. 'This child is *thing*?' The bat was back in my sight line, tracing its imperfect polygon about our heads. I pointed it out to her. 'If it crashes into your hair it'll have to be cut out.' I'm not sure where I'd come across this particular piece of lore. From a mother blind as a bat, I've little doubt.

'Aha!' she cried, 'and so the bat is "it", too. So maybe this child is a bat?' She was playing with me. But I gave her lighter tone no credence. I knew bloody well there was a purpose behind her ruse. She cuffed me again. 'You will never have a child, I think.'

'No, I daresay I won't.'

We had paused on Charlemont Bridge because she was engineering a pretext not to come back to the flat. This was my own suspicious bat. I had to be bloody careful. 'Truth is, I've never really given it any thought. While Mother was alive, there was no reason to. Mother would never have countenanced another brat in the household.' I laughed. 'To tell you nothing but the God's truth, she was never cut out for motherhood! She never tired of telling me I was an accident, and a bloody great one, too. I can still hear her… *if I hadn't've had you, Will Regan…*'

Uninvited, I'd gatecrashed Moll Regan's late childhood. Sometimes, when the ugly humour was on her, she'd date her diabetes to this calamity. The implication, of course, was that she'd later paid for *if I hadn't've had you* with her eyesight. This snippet I didn't share with Yelena.

'I wish I'd met this mother. She sounds great!'

'Ah!' I said. 'She wouldn't have wanted to have met you, though.'

'Oh? Why do you say this?'

'Mother would never have accepted the idea of my having a girlfr…' There! I'd blundered across the invisible line. And boy did I know it! Yelena could never abide the word. Girlfriend was an insult. Girlfriend was a notice of ownership nailed to the wall. She turned from me and buried her cheeks in her muff. 'It's cold. I go home now.' I knew of old there was no reasoning with her once she'd reached such a pronouncement. Hadn't she been angling for it all along?

'Suit yourself.'

I watched her furs recede into the evening. I waited as long as dignity could stand it, then ambled in ashen fury along the canal bank. I imagine my face was glowering. *If Yelena intends to engineer a breach,* whispered Soul, *it's because she's arranged to meet one of her mature students.* So-called.

'Who's the doxy?'

A short figure had stepped out from behind the wicker curtain of a great willow, and was blocking the path. The spoor of deodorant annihilated six months in an instant. It took a few moments more to make out the cockerel's baseball cap. 'Danger! What has you in this neck of the woods?'

'You haven't been reading the papers, bro?'

I shook my head. Behind him loomed the very arch under which, six months before, he'd been set upon. Where I'd performed my unlikely heroics. They do say destiny delights in symmetry.

'Nor looking at the news?' His disbelief broke the back of the final word so that it fell into two syllables: new-ess.

'You know I don't bother with a telly.' After the debacle at Charlemont Bridge I was in no mood to engage in conversation, much less with Joseph Mary Danaher. But he stood stubbornly in my way.

'Why' I sighed. 'What's happened?'

'She's only bucking gone and died, that's all!'

I shook my head again, 'I'm not with you.' I was still preoccupied with libidinal frustrations. To put it plainly, my balls throbbed. I wished only that this odoriferous apparition would disperse into the night air.

'The old bat as was in the coma.' Danaher took a step forward, pushing before him a huge holdall and the aura of cheap scent. 'She's only gone and died on us.'

Now, I was not at all happy with his inclusive 'us'. Instinctively, I took a half-step backwards. 'The old woman is dead?'

'They pulled the plug on her yesterday morning.'

'The one you hit with the…?' What was it he'd hit her with again?

'Amn't I after telling you? Yesterday morning! It's all over the papers, man.'

I shook my head again. I've an idea I may have tut-tutted. I wouldn't put it past me.

'So are we going to stand here all bucking night? I'm frozen stiff waiting for you so I am.' He was clutching an enormous holdall and it buffeted against me. Even in the darkness, his forearms were comic-strips, their tattoos drained of colour. Then I saw him wink. Or this may have been another trick of the darkness. 'She's not going to come back to you, if that's what you're waiting for. Not tonight, bro.'

'Who?' For a second, a bony, white-haired phantom rose out of the canal.

He turned his head away from me and spoke out of the side of his mouth. 'Your lady-friend.' The low derision of these four syllables was as close as he came to humour.

'She's hardly that, Danger.'

'So who is she then?'

'Nobody. A friend.'

'A *friend*.' Beneath the hat, a chuckle: *kyak kyak kyak*. 'Right!'

We walked in silence. I was unable to hit upon a single pretext to deter the man from coming back to the bedsit. On the other hand, I'll say this. His eruption into the night drove all jealous thoughts out of my head. That's what company will do.

We'd no sooner got into the flat than he strutted about as if he owned the place. It appeared he wanted to be sure there was no one waiting in ambush, hiding under a bed, lurking behind a door. He even checked the wardrobe and the kitchen presses for God's sake! All the time, as his head darted hither and thither, stabbing, pecking, he kept the enormous holdall gathered protectively to his chest feathers.

When he was happy there was no jack-in-the-box about to surprise him, he sat on the bed, set the holdall beside him under one wing, reached into an inside pocket with the other, and pulled out a brown paper bag. He looked at me, sizing me up, weighing whether or not to pass it to me. I don't know what I was expecting at that moment. A brick of money? A firearm?

He prodded the package towards me. 'Go on!'

'What?'

'Jemmy.'

Ha! It was nothing more lethal than a naggin of Irish whiskey. 'No, I…'

'Have a Jaysus drink, Regan! Go on!'

I guffawed.

'What's so funny?'

'Nothing,' said I, wrinkling the brown paper down the neck of the bottle and unscrewing its cap. Breaking the seal. 'Nothing at all!' I took a huge swig and gagged on the high-octane fumes. I had to hand it back to him, coughing, laughing, sputtering, unable to see him for the tears.

He stared at me, looked at the bottle, tried a mouthful, rolled it over his teeth, winced, swallowed, stared hard into my eyes. He was calculating how much it was in his interests to befriend me. 'Here,' he pushed the Jameson once more into my hand. 'Drink up. A bird never flew, as the fella said.'

I took another swig. 'Mine did!' And then the giggles took me again.

Kyak kyak kyak! Careful, whispered Soul, *he's after something.* But I was too giddy to pay much heed.

'Who is she, this bird? What's her name?'

'Her name's…' My torso was still laughing. But I was growing mortified by the laughter. I felt like a schoolboy who, caught out on a prank, fights down the spasms. 'Her name's… Yelena.'

'She's a foddener?' Suddenly his eyes became slits. 'Here, she's not a Roosky is she?'

'A Roosky?' I was still prone to aftershocks of giggles, and bit down into the lining of my cheek. 'No she's not Russian. She's…' The tooth hit a nerve. 'Yelena's Polish.'

'Polish, bedad!' He sniffed, rubbed beneath his nostrils with a finger, and if I hadn't laughed all night, the ludicrous figure that his Ireland top and army surplus camouflage bottoms cut beneath the bobbing red cap would have done for me entirely. 'Well, that's all right then.' Was he trying to provoke me?

'I'm not with you, Danger. How do you mean "that's all right then"?'

'I mean,' he said, sucking on the neck of the bottle and looking about the walls as if the answer were written there, 'what I mean to say is, the Poles, you know what I'm saying? The Poles, man! The Poles do hate the Rooskies. Hate them! To them, it's the same as the Brits is to us.' He nodded, satisfied. 'So that's all right then.'

'I see.' I didn't see at all. The laughter had died a death inside me. Be on your guard!

'Does she stay over much, this Ye-*lay*-na?'

'Oh no,' I chirped. 'Scarcely at all, in point of fact.' Silence began to weigh into the room. I cast about for a topic. 'I was just thinking, Danger,' I tried, 'if it was the doctors pulled the plug on the woman in the coma…' He jolted. 'Well, what I mean to say is, how can it be first-degree murder?'

'Who said anything about first-degree murder?'

'I thought…'

'I never said anything about first-degree murder. You must be imagining things.' Was he annoyed? He sucked again on the bottleneck. His eye was sizing me up, for the umpteenth time. He held the naggin out, more tenuously.

'What I said was, the old bitch died on us. That's all I said.'

'But if the guards…'

'If the guards come after me, I have my back well covered. Don't you worry about me, bro. It's not the guards I've to worry about.'

'So then…?'

Our faces traded question marks.

'Look it, I'm never going to do time for some old biddy who was at death's door anyhow, I can tell you that for free. There's others will go to the can before I ever do.'

It was time to change the subject. I had the sudden, bizarre image that the holdall he clutched contained the old woman's body parts. 'So, uhm, what's in the bag?'

'What? Never mind what's in the bag!' He seized it convulsively. 'The bag has nothing got to do with you!' He was on his feet. 'It's none of your fucking business what's in the bag, right?'

'Take it easy! Jesus!'

'This bag has nothing got to do with you, Regan. You never go near this fucking bag.'

Bucking had become fucking. It was a gauge of how serious he was. 'You go near this bag, Regan, I swear to you…'

'Take it easy! I was making conversation!'

He began to pace around the room furiously. 'Conversation is right!' He was concentrating on the presses and cupboard. 'I swear to you…' He was now pawing around at the top shelf, the selfsame alcove in which once, a lifetime ago, I'd buried my life sketches. He turned and stared at me. 'Don't so much as sniff at this bag when I'm not here, do you hear me?' He then rammed the holdall halfway to the top of the wardrobe. A padlock dangled dangerously from its zipper.

I made a gesture to show that nothing could have been further from my mind. But it was hard not to laugh. Manoeuvring the holdall onto the shelf was causing him an inordinate amount of difficulty. Danaher was not a tall man, and the bag was not a cooperative bag. Once more a canine dug mercilessly into the lining of my cheek. 'Here, let me help.'

He fired a basilisk look. The sports bag was evidently a holy of holies. So I sat back on the bed to enjoy the comic labours. I was imagining how I'd describe them to herself when next I saw her. A mocking tale or a gibe, to please a companion.

'I need to lie low for a couple of weeks.'

The growl came out of the side of his mouth as the bag teetered on the brink and the padlock swung dangerously. But the words had punctured the comedy. I felt I might suffocate under them. The possibility of 'my lady-friend' staying over any time in the near future would be entirely stifled by his presence. 'I swear to you,' he darted another warning glance, then returned to his tiptoe struggle with the bag's recalcitrance, 'I'll be back up in a couple of weeks, Regan. If you've so much as sniffed at this, I'll know about it.'

The oppressive air lifted as suddenly as it had fallen. 'You're not staying, Danger?'

'Too risky, bro.'

'Looking after your old man are you?' I had the vague memory of a father. Demented. Alzheimer's, or something.

'Me da?' He stared. Was I accusing him? 'I have to get the hell out of this city.' The bag was by now as far inside the cache as was possible for Danaher to stuff it. Still on tiptoe, he pushed at the top door of the wardrobe, but it failed to close beyond the halfway point. The bag nosed out, a huge grub bent on emerging from its comb.

For my part I was ready to be entertained once more. Yelena could stay over. If she ever had a mind to.

'So… where will you go?'

'Limerick.' He tensed and spun around, his face scarlet. 'Never mind where I'll go! Where I'll go is none of your bucking business!'

'Course not! I didn't mean anything by it. Conversation!'

'You didn't see me. You didn't hear from me. You don't bucking know me, right?'

'That goes without saying, Danger.'

He grabbed up the bottle from where it sat beside me. 'In fact,' his eyes grew to two ping-pong balls, 'for your information, I'm having you watched so I am. Even as we speak. I swear to you. Twenty-four hours a day, bro. You say one word about any of this to anyone and I'll know about it. And then…'

He touched his nostril, narrowed his eyes, and nodded, once.

The next day he was gone. But if there was one thing I was learning about Danger's departures, it was that they inevitably bore a sting in the tail. 'Come down with me as far as Harcourt

Street,' says he. At the place the road forks, he ducked into a repair shop, shoes mended while you wait. I was mildly surprised. I'd never seen the man in anything other than designer runners.

'Key,' he growled.

'I'm sorry?'

'Give us your Jaysus key, Regan.'

Can I begin to describe the cold dismay that congealed in my belly as I handed my door-key over to the shopkeeper in the brown coat who bore a bizarre resemblance to Geppetto, and listened to the flippant whine of his copying lathe?

This turn of events upset my peace of mind immensely. The cell's sanctuary was no longer inviolable. It's curious: over the many months I'd been with Yelena, the matter of a spare key had never come up. Presumably, she hadn't wanted a key, with all that its possession might imply. Now Danger had a copy. In fact, he'd taken the original and left me with the copy! It was an intolerable situation, and after a couple of nights' insomnia, I visited a hardware store and screwed a chain to the inside of the door. Only then did I sleep.

At odd times, my eye would be drawn to the half-open press, bulging with its pupa. But I was not inclined to invade the bag's sanctity. It may have contained the woman's disarticulated corpse for all that I knew, or cared.

But secrets were another matter. He'd sworn me to absolute secrecy before he left. 'Swear on your mother's grave, Regan'. On Mother's *grave*? On that forlorn six foot of earth out in Glasnevin? Needless to say, I felt under no great constraint as regards his precious secrets.

'I think what our friend Danaher is most concerned about,' said I to Yelena one day not long after this, 'is that they'll reopen the case.' I was improvising, as they say. Making conversation. 'The grounds have shifted with the old woman's death.'

'So now it can be murder case?'

'Precisely. The legal basis has changed, you see. You can't apply double jeopardy. Because he was never tried for murder.

Breaking and entering. Aggravated assault. But not murder. Murder's a different ball game entirely.' This was unadulterated bluff on my part. I was conjecturing. Or extrapolating. I imagine there were vestiges of hearsay in what I said. After all, the tabloids were full of the story. But I had Yelena's keen attention, and that was a coveted prize at the time. In fact, it was herself who had started me on the subject. 'But worse again, where our friend is concerned, is all the new publicity. Seems he ratted on some dangerous characters, and now they're after him. I'll lay odds that's why he's gone back into hiding. Course the papers are having a field day. The radio, too.' A sudden thought hit me. 'Come here, can I ask you something? What do you think of the Russians?'

'Don't change the subject, Willy!'

'I'm not!'

She ignored this.

'You like this man?'

'*Like* him? No, I wouldn't say "like" is the verb, exactly.'

'Then why you let him back in the flat?'

Now, I hadn't told her Danger had been inside the flat. Not only that, I remained at all times hovering in the vicinity of the window for fear she'd catch sight of the precious holdall peeping out behind her.

'Who says I let him back in the flat?'

'There is smell. Is not your smell.'

'Ha ha! I'm glad to hear it!'

'Don't make joke. I don't trust this man.'

'Well, neither do I. Jesus, Yelena. He killed a woman. Or even if he didn't, he's a double-dyed bloody criminal no matter what way you look at it.'

This set her train of thought off in a different direction. Or at least, that was the impression that maybe she was trying to give. One way or another, it was some time before she spoke. 'Tell me then. So you would never do something that is criminal?'

'Criminal?' I echoed. She'd straightened her back. Her tone had been casual, the question far less so. 'In what way criminal?'

She shrugged. She didn't want to reveal her hand. Not as yet.

'If you look at it one way, you could argue I already am a criminal. Danaher did in that old woman, even if he didn't pull the plug. You could argue, if he's been in the flat, then I'm aiding and abetting a fugitive. Charges or no charges, he told me he battered the woman in.' I had a sudden whim to dye myself in the blackest of hues. To lend myself an air of mystery, as you might say. 'In the eyes of the law, that makes me an accessory after the fact. And an accessory to first-degree murder, if you can believe the press-hounds. At the very least,' I said to her, lowly, 'I could be charged with obstructing the course of justice.'

'But you say me you don't know if they've even reopened the case.'

'But they're bound to! We don't get so many murders in this country. Not random attacks on old-age pensioners. The tabloids are baying for blood. They'll reopen the case all right, you wait and see. And then what am I to do? Snitch on the man?'

'Snitch? What means snitch?'

'To snitch is the basest of all crimes. The lowest of the low. It's a mortal sin in the underworld. To snitch is when you betray someone's trust.'

'In what way betray?'

'When you tell tales on them behind their back.'

'Like when one schoolboy tells the teacher what another has done.'

'Precisely! Exactly! It doesn't matter a rambling damn that the other is the worst blackguard in the classroom. You don't go to the teacher, that's all there is to it.'

She thought about this for a moment. She took off her glasses and wiped them, and for a few moments fixed me in her myopic gaze.

'But still you don't answer my question, Willy. Do you do a crime?'

'I'm not with you. What crime?'

'Well. Suppose that you found a way to make money that is not quite legal.'

I laughed. 'Like the bloody MacMurrough Tribunal?'

'I'm being serious. Why you always make joke? Is not quite legal, but is not like robbing someone's house. Maybe is hard to see who loses. So do you do it?'

'But give us a concrete example, Yelena. What have you in mind, insurance fraud? Not declaring my *taxes*? I'll give you a queer one,' I went on, unsure what game she might be playing, 'there was a case over in London of a woman was working in the Bank of England. She was in the section where they burn the old notes. Consign them to the flames. Now this woman's scam was, she used to stuff her knickers with handfuls of old notes. Twenties, fifties. All due to be destroyed. Later she'd place them by dribs and drabs into a deposit account. It ran to thousands before they caught on to what she was at. All the same, it's hard to see who exactly she was defrauding by her little pastime.'

'But she was arrested, this woman?'

'Oh God yes. Arrested, tried and convicted. The press-hounds loved it! It was the detail of the knickers that caught the public imagination.'

After this, Yelena let the subject drop. She climbed into bed, and we made love. All over by seven o'clock. But as she fidgeted for a match to light her cigarette, I looked at her in a different light.

I knew well it'd be only a matter of time before she again sounded me on the theme.

IX

*S*o the bag is stashed in the flat. We're getting on. Soon we'll be in Glasnevin. I know for a fact that Glasnevin happened after the fever, and the fever happened after Hallowe'en. And you could argue that Hallowe'en was the first time I could've got an inkling of the disaster towards which we were all hurtling.

In between Hallowe'en and Glasnevin, Danger resurfaced and took half of his stash away with him. I know that for a fact because that was on the day of the fog, and I told the story of the fog to Yelena on the way out to the cemetery.

One more character has to be introduced: Ciarán Crowe out of St Audoen's. But that was after the cemetery, because that was the day I didn't get to ask 'who is W?' Everything in its place.

Hallowe'en, fever, fog, Glasnevin. Then all hell breaks loose.

There was one Greek myth I always admired above all others. It's the story of a fella who tried to outfox his fate. He'd been banished as a baby to a distant city after his parents heard a black prophesy about him. But then, when he grew up, he came across the same prophesy and, getting the wrong end of the stick, he'd fled that distant city. Where should he wind up but back in his native land? Killed his own mother. Or he married her, I forget. But the point is, by the very act of running from his fate, he

96

ended up fulfilling it. The gods had foreseen that too. His fate had closed in on him like the two jaws of a trap.

Now that is symmetry.

I'd had Chester out to my place only the once, and on one occasion only was I invited to visit the Maher abode. Invited officially, as the saying goes. Later visits happened in a more or less casual manner. Chester was at this stage living alone, in that legal limbo they call separation. Limbo was a terraced house somewhere off the Old Cabra Road.

It must've been the eve of Hallowe'en. All through the city, enormous stacks of crates and boxes had been piled high on the public greens, awaiting only the riotous match. I've a memory, too, of hoards of child-ghosts and child-demons flitting between the houses and parked cars. Every so often, one of them would detonate a firecracker, and then they'd run squealing from its cascade of sparks.

Chester had invited me to view an astronomical event through his seven-inch reflector. It was the transit of one of the heavenly bodies. Or it was a lunar eclipse. I don't remember. I have a memory of watching the huge yellow knuckle rising as I left the bedsit, wondering if the clouds could be trusted to keep their distance.

I don't know what delayed me that day. I wasn't feeling the best, that much I can vouch for. My temperature had topped a hundred and one, and there was a metal taste on my tongue. So it was already well into the rush hour when I was setting out. On a whim, I hailed a taxi. Now for thirty years, Mother had drummed into my skull that luxuries the like of taxis were the height of profligacy. Luxuries led straight to the poorhouse. She'd any number of old sayings to back her up. *Look after the pence, and the pounds will look after themselves. Penny-wise and pound-foolish. A penny saved is a penny earned.* But the hour was late, my knowledge of the Cabra estates was scant, and I was unaware of any bus route that crossed the river.

'You haven't been following the MacMurrough Tribunal, boss?' I'd been staring at the taxi-meter, mesmerised by the ticking of luminous numbers, wondering how they tallied with Mother's grave prediction. This bark broke her spell. Rising out of an open denim shirt, the driver's bull-neck broke into heavy, frowning folds. These in turn tapered into a seal's head. The furrows deepened greatly as he angled to stare at me in the rear-view mirror. Candid eyes looked out from a hairless complexion.

'No I haven't.' This was a lie. A white lie, as they say.

'I'll tell you, they should lock up the whole bloody lot of them and throw away the key, so they should. Make an example out of them.' The eyes were still framed in the coffin of the mirror. I nodded at them, vigorously. It might beggar belief, but at thirty-something years of age, I was entirely unused to cars. The box of the taxi, it seemed to me, was hurtling recklessly through the city gridlock. I was horrified at the scant attention this great seal in his cowboy shirt was paying the impatient horns to the right of us. Soul took flight, and for the rest of the journey was nowhere to be seen.

'That's what they should do,' the feckless voice barked on. 'But of course they won't. It's one law for the rich in this country. D'you know what I'm saying, boss? It'd be a different matter entirely if it was the likes of you and me. Then you can be bloody sure they'd lock you up as soon as look at you.'

The baby-blues were back in the mirror. Oh God, I thought, please make him watch the road.

'I've a brother-in-law is in the 'Joy,' he threw at me after a pause, just as the car rounded a dog-leg. A colossal juggernaut, bearing down on us, blasted its horn at the manoeuvre. I swallowed a knotted rope of anxiety. For Christ's sake! Looking down, I noticed a crucifix, swinging like a pendulum beneath the dashboard. On the licence number pinned beside it was a photo of what appeared an older man, one with a full head of hair. Who was this lunatic behind the wheel?

'D'you know what he done?' I shook my head. Please, please make him watch the road. 'He attacked a pusher was always hanging around the daughter's school. Lorraine, my niece. Put him in hospital for himself, with two-dozen stitches to the head and a fractured collarbone. Eighteen months they gave him for that! Eighteen months, and the dealer gets off scot-free?! How's that for justice for you! Anyone pushing drugs on school kids, I'd have them walled up alive inside their cell so I would with nothing but their drugs.' We were now stuck fast at traffic lights just before one of the bridges. In the absence of immediate danger, my eyes returned to the meter. It continued to clock its tally, with no regard for our actual progress through the city. 'I swear to you, anyone went next or near one of my kids with drugs, it wouldn't be in hospital they'd have to look for them. It'd be out in Glasnevin.'

A huge hand moved to the side of his neck. 'I see you're looking at this.' I hadn't been. But now my eyes were drawn to a crimson half-moon that arced like needlepoint through his skin as far as a missing earlobe. 'D'you know what that was?' My head shook in the diminutive mirror. 'That was a junky so it was. Tried to hold me up with a hypodermic needle. So when I grabbed it out of the bony fucker's hand, what does he do? He only throws himself onto my neck and bites into me. A good job I didn't get an infection out of it. HIV-positive, you know what I'm saying? I'll tell you, you meet all types driving a taxi around this town. No use telling the guards either. Not where it's a junky is involved. They don't want to know. But you lay so much as a finger on one of them in self-defence, that's another story entirely.'

'Terrible,' I said. My eyes had become fixed on the hoof-print of teeth, set into his skin like a tattoo. A rite of passage. Suddenly, as he changed lanes, his voice jumped an octave. 'And then there's these fat cats has been creaming millions out of us for years, selling the city to the highest bidder! And nobody to touch them! That MacMurrough Tribunal they have, sure Jesus that's only a mockery. Do you think any of them fellows will ever do time?' The indignant scar flushed indigo. I imagined his Adam's apple, pumping away like Danaher's as he drew breath. 'They will in your eye! Making fun of us from their mansions up in Dalkey and Howth, that's all any of them buckos is good for.' All they're *buckin'* good for, I thought. Would he have a go at the Russians next? His eyes still on me, he missed the change of lights until an angry blaring behind us alerted him to the fault.

Rush hour. Has ever a phrase been coined with more sarcasm? It took us fully three changes of traffic light to shunt over the bridge. The clock's estimate swelled flippantly from £11.90 to £13.00, and Mother's ghost poked my ribs in dour satisfaction.

'What do you do yourself, boss?' he asked, once we'd gained the far bank. For a second I was tempted to say I was a land speculator. 'I'm between jobs.' This was my stock answer. It had been honed by years of deflecting barbers from their polite meaningless words. He nodded gravely. He seemed to be considering how to respond. In the interim my hand, deep into my pocket, was calculating blindly whether I'd have to return to the south side by foot. As said, I was not feeling at all well.

Another twenty minutes went by. Or perhaps it was the tedious passage through the traffic that was dilating time. 'Tell us,' he asked, as we swung up past St Peter's, 'do you ever pray at all?' This time I was sure I'd misheard the gravel-voiced question. 'I beg your pardon?'

'For a job. Do you ever pray for help to find a job?'

'Pray?' I repeated.

The creases in the bull-neck once more deepened as he gazed into the mirror. 'I was three year unemployed. What d'you think of that? Three year!' Once more, the crucifix danced wildly as we lurched about a corner. A child dressed in a sheet and another in a witch's hat ghosted past the window. The big sister's face was a mask of vocalised abuse. I thought of little Stephie Maher with her vampire smile. She should have been spending Hallowe'en with Chester, not me. But the Dujardin woman had reneged on the arrangement.

'Nearly cost me my marriage so it did,' gasped the voice, hoarse as sandpaper. 'At that time I was hitting the bottle pretty hard. And d'you know who it was that saved me?'

Jesus, I thought. He's going to say Jesus. If Soul hadn't been frightened from the car, we'd have made a wager on it.

'It was the brother-in-law.'

'The same one that's up in Mountjoy Gaol?' To this day I'm unsure where this detail was pulled from. I'd been so ill at ease throughout the journey, I hadn't thought his words had registered. But in school, and even more so with Mother, I'd always been able to pull off the same feat. His eyes now clamped upon me with so much intensity I was sure we'd collide with the back of a bus pulling flatulently onto the road in front of us. My fever must've been up over a hundred and three. 'They've no right to put a father away for trying to defend his childer. And the other bugger gets off scot-free! Where did you say you were going to, boss?'

'Old Cabra Road.'

'Old Cabra Road. But it was the same brother-in-law that made me see the light, all the same. Set me on the straight and narrow so he did.' We rounded a drunken corner. To my immense relief, I saw the words 'Old Cabra Road' nailed to the wall. Somewhere in the distance a derisory firework whined and popped.

About halfway along the street he pulled the cab over and, making no move to indicate we'd arrived, he continued the husky monologue. 'He lived for a good number of years over in the States. Boston, Massachusetts. You've never been yourself?'

'No,' I said. I might have added that in point of fact I'd never been outside the confines of the city. But then I might never have got out of the taxi.

'They've a different way entirely of looking at the world over there.' A great, meaty arm had stretched as far as the passenger's headrest. 'Work hard, play hard. That's the motto. No room for messing around.' He pivoted about, and the taxi began to reverse waywardly up the street. 'That's their attitude when it comes to crime, too. It's three strikes and you're out. There's a lot to be said for it. And do you know what, the same goes when it comes to Jesus Christ. I'm serious. No room at all for messing about there. What number did you say you were looking for, boss?'

I pulled from my pocket the slip of paper Chester Maher had given me and passed it to him. Halting the car's retreat, he squinted at this by the light over the mirror. He then scrutinised the nearest of the houses. 'Must be the other side of the road. Tell us this, did you ever hear tell of John 3:7?'

'No,' I said. My arms had pressed into the seat as the car swung a U-turn.

'No,' he repeated. I had the briefest idea he was about to give out to me. 'No, me neither. It was the brother-in-law had to explain it. "Unless he is born again, a man cannot see the Kingdom of God." Are you with me?' He stopped the car, definitively, by ratcheting the handbrake. For the first time he looked directly at me, without the medium of the mirror. 'That's the Gospel that is. John, chapter three, verse seven. And it was the brother-in-law told me, too, "Don't be ashamed to pray". That's great advice, boss. Don't be ashamed to pray. Because the answer mightn't always be yes, but you can be sure of one thing, your prayers is always listened to.'

I wasn't sure if he was expecting a reply to this. The silence grew inside the taxi until it was squatting beside me like an unwelcome passenger. 'So how much do I owe?'

The arm, thick as a club, moved from the seat back and executed a deft fiddle with the meter that tipped the fare into a second decade. 'Twenty will do you, boss.' Mother, that malicious spectre, poked another bony digit into my ribcage. The driver folded my reluctant banknotes into the top pocket of his cowboy shirt and winked at me, deadly serious. 'You see, you can never tell how exactly your prayers is going to be answered. But they will be.' He slapped the steering wheel with both palms. 'The ways of the Lord is strange, did you ever hear that saying? Here's yours truly that was long-term unemployed, and now I'm driving the brother-in-law's cab for him while he's doing time up in the 'Joy. Making a few bob, too. Now, that shook you!' He leaned forward and spoke out of the side of his mouth, as though he were imparting a great confidence. 'You were looking at the picture earlier. I seen you doing it in the mirror.' He tapped the photo beside the crucifix, which at last hung still. 'Sure I don't even have a driver's licence, never mind a taxi licence! And how would the likes of you or me ever afford a plate?'

I smiled queasily and shook my head, wondering how to take my leave.

'Here,' he said, 'I want you to take this.' He reached into the other breast pocket and pulled out what looked like a business card. The candid eyes never left me. 'You're ever in trouble, boss. You ever just in need of sound advice, you go there. Have a good long talk to one of the pastors for yourself. Will you do that? Do you promise me now?' I waved the card at him and slipped it unread into the arse pocket of my pants.

He squinted an eye at me, pretending to shoot me with a finger. 'And remember what I said to you. Don't be ashamed to pray.'

The car squealed out from the footpath. The horn sounded twice as it disappeared into All Hallows night. Looking about, I had a sudden vision of the front dashboard, on which lay the slip of paper with Chester Maher's address. What house number? My hand slapped my forehead, hard. John 3:7 laughed back at me. *The ways of the Lord aren't half as strange as you are, you bloody lunatic!* called Soul, after the car. Together again, we vowed never again to ignore Mother's warnings.

I'd have returned home there and then if I'd found myself in the vicinity of a bus stop. I was really not feeling well. I'd slept poorly for several nights, and all at once the accumulated fatigue overtook me. My forehead was smouldering, my saliva was iron. I looked about the unfamiliar streets. A huge moon was largely obscured, and along with sulphur and smoke there was the smell of drizzle in the air. To put the cherry on my bad humour, I was sure to have missed whatever astronomical event Maher had invited me here to witness. That's how painful our progress had been across the city. But here I was, miles from home. So in the end, I rang the bell of the house that was closest to me, and asked if anyone knew where Chester Maher lived.

'Ma!' The door was answered by a heavily pregnant teenager. 'Ma! Young fellow wants to know where... what did you say his name was?'

'Chester Maher.'

'Young fellow wants to know where Jester Mare lives!'

'Who love?'

'Jester Mare!'

I waited as a shadow distorted and dilated in the frosted glass of the hall door. From behind the pregnant daughter's shoulder a woman's head, wrinkled as a windfall, peered out. Diminutive, not five foot.

'Mare? No, I don't think there's anybody be that name on this road.'

'Maher,' I adjusted the vowel. 'Chester Maher.'

She shook her head. 'No. Jacinta, you never heard of anyone be that name?'

'There's Josie O' Meara the seamstress lives down above the takeaway. Maybe that's who he's looking for.'

'But Josie's in the Mater since Tuesday last week with her hip. No, Mister, I don't think so. You must have the wrong road. You don't know what number your friend lives at?'

If I knew that, I thought. 'Middle-aged man, not very tall,' I tried. 'Roundy face.' I riffled my memory. 'Married to a French woman?'

They looked at each other, mother and daughter. Or grandmother and granddaughter. They have children young in the estates. 'No, I don't think so. Not unless it was Josie O' Meara you wanted, but she's in the Mater Hospital waiting on an operation to replace the hip.'

'No, Chester's definitely a man.' I threw my final dice, on the cusp of cutting a retreat: 'Wears an old mackintosh with a tear here?'

The pregnant girl threw back her ponytail and cried out 'He must mean Loopy Loony!', and the old crone cackled as she repeated the nickname.

Chester, who lived three doors nearer to the turn, pulled me straight in through the hallway and kitchen and out to a cluttered rear yard. There was by now far more than a mere suggestion of drizzle on the wind.

'Hurry for God's sake!' he cried. 'It's already started! The clouds have it nearly blotted out!' He'd stopped behind my shoulder and I was left at a loss as to how to proceed. There was no sign of a telescope. Or at least, nothing you might find on the bridge of a man-o'-war. All I could see, low down amidst the clutter and debris, was a miniature circus cannon. Any minute, it might fire a daredevil midget over the neighbouring wall.

'Here! You'll miss it! It'll be over any minute!' Chester bundled me to one side and threw himself down on all fours to worship the dwarf's cannon. Once his fingers were within an inch of its body, they became infinitely solicitous.

After half a minute he was satisfied he had the tube correctly trained, and he motioned me to squat down beside him. I looked from his sycophant's pose to the pale disc of the moon, cowering behind veils of mist and smoke. But what was I to do? Shivering, I knelt beside him. One of his hands rose to prevent my further approach. 'Hold on! No! Damn it, it's gone.' I looked back up and saw, to my surprise, that over the rooftops the moon was now stripped of her rags of cloud and stood in splendid nudity. 'She looks pretty clear to me.'

'Ach no! The shadow! You've missed the shadow. It's gone.' And so disgusted was he that he would've had us both return indoors at once if I hadn't pleaded and begged to be allowed to put pupil to eyepiece. He grunted, and turned his back on me.

What revelations! Once my eye adjusted to the bone-coloured glare, the view astounded. It was more beautiful and deathly than I could possibly have imagined, a great realm of dust and silence. As my gaze moved towards the perimeter darkness, shadows carved out a bas-relief of mountain, crater and valley. I had about a minute to admire the alien landscape before the lens became blind with mists.

'But what a fantastic place!'

'Anyone would think you'd never seen the moon before,' grumbled Chester. He seemed to doubt my enthusiasm.

'But I haven't! Never like that. Good God, man, it's an entire world unto itself!'

'What were you expecting, green cheese?'

We moved out of the drizzle into the kitchen. In the doorway behind him, a melancholy apple hung on a string. I was only out here on sufferance after young Stephie Maher had been whisked away by a harpy mother. The apple must have reminded him, too, of this fact. His body and his conversation lurched away from it. 'The whole universe is littered with landscapes the like of that.'

'Is it?' I cried, to help distract him. I'd had no idea. Or I'd had a vague idea. But I'd certainly never imagined you'd be able to see such places from a back yard off the Old Cabra Road!

'There's more worlds up there than there are people on this… *planet.*' He spat the word 'planet'. 'There was a time,' he went on, dryly, 'when they'd've burned you at the stake for saying so.'

'Go on!' I said.

'You don't believe me? There was a great man once by the name of Bruno. Giordano Bruno. A Dominican priest he was. Four hundred years ago, they burned him alive. You know what heresy he was burned for?' I smiled wanly and shook my head. 'His sin was accurately describing the extent of the universe.'

The apple hovered in the corner of my eye, a solitary moon in the empty cosmos of the Maher household. 'But can there really be so many worlds?'

'As many as there is grains of sand in a desert. More.'

'Go on! But not with air, and seas, and weather?' The drizzle was whispering across the dark window. He nodded at me. Oh yes.

'And life?'

He opened his mouth, let out a low, mirthless laugh, and walked me into the hall. It was only after the front door shut behind me that I thought to check the number. 37. A shock of static raced through me. John, 3:7. Wasn't that what the cowboy had said? Truly the ways of the Lord are strange!

It took me the best part of two hours to get back to the bed-sit. There was a persistent drizzle, and I was without a raincoat. I was increasingly feverish. But I was determined to walk. My mind was too quick with the pale contours I'd seen. The revelation! The fantastic geography had driven all fatigue from my bones. *More worlds up there than there are people on this planet!* The moon's perfect circle was suspended behind the cloud like the big bloody aspirin out of the story I used to read Mother. It helped direct my steps southwards.

The sensations of the evening, and of the previous few weeks, converged and blurred as I blundered through the estates. I passed several bonfires, their branches hissing and protesting the damp. These disgruntled pyres made me think of the heretic they'd burned. How unrepentant and supreme he must have felt, having witnessed the lunar face! Heresy. Hearsay.

Then I was on familiar ground. I crossed the river at Wood Quay. I was thinking to pass under the arch of Christ Church, but the grim concrete of the Civic Offices held my attention. I could see again the indignant creases on the taxi driver's bull-neck, hear again the hoarse bark: *They should lock up the whole bloody lot of them and throw away the key.* And I imagined fantastic punishments for the land speculators, eternal punishments that might take place in the barrenness of the lunar landscape. Buried up to the neck in their own dusty foundations. And tormented by indolent devils in hard hats and check shirts. Ha! Ha!

It was turning cold, but I was burning. I mounted the hill under Christ Church arch. I turned right at the Lord Edward Fitzgerald and past behind St Pat's, in the general direction of Stephen's Green. When we lived in the Liberties, Mother had grown weary explaining to me why there are two cathedrals so close together. One within the city walls and one without. She'd drummed that into my skull, though I couldn't for the life of me remember which was which, nor see where this wall was supposed to have stood. But anyway they were both Protestant, so what did it matter?

I'd got lost one day trying to explain the cathedrals to Yelena. We'd been in to explore one or another of the vaults. A cat and a mouse had got mummified, caught forever in the tomb of an organ-pipe. That had tickled her. Now, as the fever smouldered, I could actually hear the Polish intonation: *But still you don't answer my question, Willy. Do you do a crime?*

On a whim I took a detour to the left. Marsh's Library. Kevin Street. A delicious shiver ran down my spine as I ran my fingers along the railings of Stephen's Green. Which one of us doesn't fantasize about a crime? I called inside. Which of us wouldn't murder an old pawnbroker? It goes without saying I hadn't the slightest inkling of how near the edge of the precipice all four of us actually stood.

But my fever could hit on no magnificent deed, no heist that would take my soul beyond the pale of good and evil. When the jealous agitation was on me, could I strangle my beloved? The prospect was laughable. I could no more imagine myself in that role than I could Chester Maher.

Chester Maher. Chester Maher. It came as a shock every time I remembered the straights in which I'd first found the man, dangling from a tree like a bloody great bell. Or like a birdcage. He'd once told me the human body is the perfect prison. 'The Earth is a prison,' he'd said. 'And a clever one. There's no walls or wardens, because your sphere has no need of walls or wardens. Walk as far as you can in any direction, and you're right back where you started. *That* is a perfect prison.' I wonder had I told him about my Norwegian sailor. 'But even better than the Earth is the body. The human body's a prison that can hardly be improved upon. The human body's a cage you push along with you wherever you may go. It's visceral, you see. You can't get out of a cage the like of that.' Then he asked me something curious. Had I ever heard of what they call sleep paralysis? I hadn't. No? You wake up, and nothing will move. Not so much as your mouth, or your eyelid. You lie awake, perfectly conscious. You're in a panic. If some one were to hold your nose shut, you'd suffocate. But it's as if you're buried alive in your own body. Can you imagine anything more fearful than that? I couldn't. 'The body is a bitch,' he declared, rising towards an aphorism, 'and the world is visceral!' (I must've told him about my Norwegian sailor!) Had he an answer? Maybe the tree was his only answer, his final bid to fly that cage. *Make suicide a capital offence*, as some wag had scribbled on the side of the Four Courts.

Crime and punishment. Punishment to fit the crime. I saw briefly the junky, hurling himself in a frenzy on my taxi-man's neck. *Anyone pushing drugs on school kids, I'd have them walled up alive inside their cell.* So that he must gnaw his own flesh. Feeding off his habit. So that the punishment fits the crime. It all comes out, if you look at it one way.

The railings imprisoned the green. I thought of the statues, locked up inside. Yeats and Emmet and Wolfe Tone. They were imprisoned in bronze, just as we were imprisoned in our bodies. But the old woman wasn't. Not any longer. The doctors had pulled the plug on her.

I wondered if I could kill an old woman for her possessions. Danaher's rooster's strut briefly appeared under the lion couchant of Newman House. *The next thing she's standing there behind me, with her white hair down around her shoulders and her white nightdress, looking just as bony as death itself.* 'You died unrepentant,' I called to his ghost. And then I imagined in what grim purgatory his sin should be eternally expurgated. He'd be zipped into a holdall which reeked of tracksuits and eau de cologne! Ha ha! Bundled into a hollow by a troop of demons whose hides were covered in foul tattoos. I knew I was laughing, hilariously. But the city was deserted, and the only sound was the echo of my laughter along Leeson Street. If I'd been more perceptive, I'd have heard Fate laughing back at me.

When finally I made the bedsit, I was soaked to the skin. I was, moreover, exhausted. Once I'd shut the door on the city, the temperature burned through the skin of my forehead. Now, all the weight of fatigue returned. I towelled my hair with the first jumper to hand, and then fell onto the bed without switching off the light or removing my damp clothes.

These were the beginnings of a fever that kept me confined to the flat for the next number of days. How long precisely I can't say. It was an unreal time in which I was visited by no one mortal, but lay listlessly upon the unmade pallet, watching the light in the window grow and fade, grow and fade, and listening to the vicissitudes of the traffic. I rose only when thirst raged, or when my bladder pressed. For the rest, I drifted in and out of uneasy dreams of uncertain duration. I was too limb-heavy and listless to do more than crawl under the covers or kick them away from me. All the while, when my arm fell from over my eyes, the light bulb burned like the eye of an inquisitor.

And then, one afternoon, the light bulb was extinguished. The memory of hearing a scratching or scraping, an ill-fitting key troubling the lock, made me prop myself up on unsteady elbows.

Two figures, it seemed to me, were standing at the foot of the bed.

X

I felt the back of a hand cool on my forehead, and a glass of tepid water was pressed against my lips. I coughed and spluttered, pushing it away. I then lay back into the pillows and squinted up at the ashen blonde head of Yelena Zamorska.

'How long?'

I could feel, by the soft pressure of linen on my skin, that I'd been fully undressed. The window had been thrown open unto the evening traffic. The air in the room was largely purged of its staleness, though I could make out the trace of a cigarette.

'Do you mean how long it is since I find you?'

I nodded, mouth too dry and membranous to form a sentence.

'It is maybe two hours since I find you lying here.'

'Before that, how long?'

'I don't know. You were supposed to meet me for lunch two days ago. But you have much stubble, Willy. I think must be a week.'

'Water,' I croaked. She put her arm around my neck and leaned my head forwards until my mouth met the rim of the glass. The water was warm and sweet. I swallowed it slowly, allowing it to soak my chapped and tingling lips. I lay back, extraordinarily weak, and closed my eyes. 'Weren't there two of you? When I woke I thought I saw two of you.'

'Yeah,' she said, or I thought she said. I looked about. She was now standing over at the window and had lit up another cigarette.

Time had evidently skipped ahead. She drew in slowly, exhaled into the darkening air outside. 'And so you didn't show up, and then you didn't call me. But I was not worried. I thought, probably Willy is mad at me. You know the way sometimes you get mad at me. And then you act so like a child trying to punish his mother.' She looked over at me, I think smiling, and then turned again to the window. The cigarette glowed cherry red as she drew deeply on it, then dulled again. 'So two nights ago from the bus I see that your light is on and that the curtains are not shut. I think, okay, he's in. But still he doesn't want to call me. So let him, I say. But then last night it is the same thing. Still the curtains have not been shut and still the light is on. And I remember what you say me about this Danaher person. So maybe he's come back. Then I think, is this why Willy doesn't call me? Now it's been nearly five days. Of course there could be something wrong. Tomorrow I'm not working, and I must go and see.'

'But I don't understand. How did you get in?'

She turned, drawing on the cigarette, and the glow it cast over her complexion made her appear triumphant. 'The lock is not so hard to pick.'

'You never picked the lock!'

'No,' she said. 'I call Adam. It's Adam who knows how to do this.'

'Then there were two people! I thought as much.' I lay back, winded by the hated name. A Yeats expert, and now a handyman. I determined on the spot that another trip down to Geppetto was on the cards to have a spare key whinnied out for her ladyship, to make damn sure it'd never happen again. 'And so where is he, this man who can pick locks?'

'He has gone to buy some food. You know that you've no food at all in your presses?'

I must've drifted into unconsciousness soon after this. When I awoke, the room was humid, fragrant with herbs and spices. There was a clatter of utensils coming from the kitchenette area, and snatches of a conversation which I strained to make out. My stomach growled, a starving animal. I propped myself up against the headrest and coughed, deliberately. The sky above Mary's dome was quite dark.

'So the patient is awake?'

This was Yelena. Her form was silhouetted in the alcove that marked off the kitchen area. She turned in profile and said something or other I didn't catch, and a male voice responded in a handful of monosyllables. Z's. J's. Tak, tak. Their language was not English. Polish, or Russian. I found out much later, when he'd briefly made the newspapers, that Rakoczi's stock was from all over the East.

Presently this second figure, in an apron and bearing a large saucepan, appeared behind Yelena, and said something low into her earlobe. Suppressing a giggle, Yelena advanced two steps. The figure behind set down the saucepan and began to stir it luxuriously with a ladle. He then tipped the contents of the ladle three times into a cereal bowl, which he passed forwards as carefully as if it were a sacramental vessel. This offertory released an even more marvellous choir of herbs into the room.

Yelena walked carefully to the side of the bed and allowed the steam to waft beneath my nostrils as she set the bowl down. 'You must be little hungry,' she stated. It was in a flat, functional tone that made me think of the psychiatric nurse who'd attended Mother at the end. 'This soup will do you much good.'

The truth is that by now my guts were yapping and writhing about like a sackful of puppies, so diabolically aromatic was the atmosphere inside the bedsit. If it weren't for this bodily betrayal, I'd have told the chef where he could stick his precious ladle. But if cavorting hunger was in no mood to be cheated of its prize, neither was pride ready to throw in the towel without some sort of a show. 'What's in it?' croaked Pride, pulling a disapproving mien.

'I don't know. Adam, what's in the soup?'

Still wearing the apron, Adam Rakoczi took a couple of steps into the room. The ladle was a thurible an altar boy might carry. I made out a large, almost hairless forehead over thick-framed glasses that reflected like two television screens. It was a middle-aged head, not at all what I'd expected. Just as surprising, Yelena was taller than him by several inches.

He blew out his thick lips and tallied a deprecating roll call of roots, tubers and herbs. His pitch had a trick of falling through every syllable, as though he were trying to excuse each item's inclusion. His English was correct in the main, but lacked any modicum of enthusiasm.

But entrails and imagination made up for any deficit. Every carrot and swede was at once an ideal that set the puppies fawning and whimpering inside me. Struggling with their outrageous hunger, I closed my eyes and instead conjured again the tableau of the crazed addict, clamping teeth into the elephantine skull of my taxi-man.

'It will be getting a skin if you let it grow cold.' This was Yelena, her voice still that of a matron. I wondered at whom the performance was aimed.

'I'm not at all sure I'd be able to keep it down,' rasped pride, triumphant before the fall. Even Hunger was temporarily impressed.

'Come now, Willy, do I have to spoon-feed you like little child?'

With this, the citadel crumbled. 'Very well,' I sighed, scalding my thumb in my haste to pick up the bowl. I had no wish to play the invalid to whatever role she'd dreamt up. For her culinary lover's amusement, I have little doubt.

After I'd had second helpings and risen from the bed, a bottle of claret wine was uncorked, and then another. A great feeling of well-being was slowly infusing my body, this in spite of the fact that I was at last in the presence of my great rival. My hated rival. But oddly, his presence was helping to defuse the tension brought on by 'Adam Rakoczi'. Those exotic syllables had always brought to my imagination the figure of a much younger man, tall, undoubtedly blond, looking at the world through the arrogant blue eye of the Baltic. This clown with the lopsided grin who sat opposite me at the table could scarcely have been more different. He was wallowing myopically in his forties. His dark hair was unkempt and receding, and from a blue unshaven jowl the thick lips protruded like a thing obscene. His forehead was expansive, his eyes a deep-set, lugubrious brown diffracted through huge rectangles of glass.

Rakoczi had been expounding for some time in his self-deprecating manner something concerning funds and exchange rates. The words fell listlessly from his protruding lips, and I'd struggled to follow the convolutions of his exposition. But now he sat back, the tips of his fingers touching. The gesture demanded a response.

'I'm not sure I get you. How's your scam supposed to make money? It seems to me all you'd be doing is robbing Peter to pay Paul.'

'Robbing Pyotr…?'

'Just an expression,' I explained. The wine had set a dull fire in my belly, and I was animated by its glow. I began to toy with the corks, palming one as would a cheap conjurer, pretending to transform it into its companion. To my mild surprise, there were by now three corks on the table. 'Robbing Peter to pay Paul. It means you borrow from one creditor to pay off another. Abracadabra! Then you do it again, the other way around.'

'Robbing Peter to pay Paul,' he nodded, satisfied. But the fingers, squat inquisitors, continued to tip each other lightly.

'But then, you're not even fobbing off creditors.'

'Fobbing…?'

'Postponing. Not paying. Jesus, man, are you not following the MacMurrough Tribunal?' I stared at the twin television screens.

'No.'

'If, as you say, your friends in Odessa have the cash up front, then there's no creditors that need to be fobbed off that I can see.' No reply. 'But what I don't get is, where do I come in? I open what? Three accounts?'

He looked at Yelena when the number was mentioned. I took her silence as assent. But where was the scam? 'It seems to me that all I'd be doing is moving funds endlessly about. I really don't see the point of it.'

'But this is precisely the point.' The glasses, two great aquaria, flashed from Yelena to me. 'This is precisely the point.'

I nodded and sucked in, trying to look wise. 'I still don't get it. It's real money we're talking about? Nothing counterfeit or phoney about it?'

'Of course.'

'So where exactly do I come in?'

'I explain you already.'

'But why don't you do it yourself? Or Yelena, for that matter?'

'Because in your country,' he said, filling the wine glasses slowly and exchanging glances with his girlfriend, with my girlfriend, with nobody's girlfriend, 'it is as if we do not exist. We are shadows. We are people who are without reality. Is very difficult for us to open account.'

'Whereas I…' I prompted.

'You are like living person, with body.' He held his hand over the table, and a shadow moved to the corks. 'My shadow can't move cork. But when you move your hand, then the cork move. And besides this,' he shook the final tilly of wine into my glass, 'these days no one is suspicious of Irishman who have money.'

'I don't know about that,' I smiled, raising my glass to them both. 'It's not as if I ever had the chance to put that proposition to the test.'

Yelena smiled back, and taking the hint, Adam Rakoczi counterfeited her smile.

The following morning was lost to a hangover. But by early afternoon I was feeling altogether better than for a number of weeks previously. Quite in tip-top form, in point of fact. There was a high, cloudless sky such as one often gets in November, and through the window the great bulk of the verdigris dome was lit like a planet.

I imagine that's what put Chester Maher into my head. Chester, whose bitch of a wife had yet again robbed young Stephie from him at the very last minute. All about his kitchen I'd seen the debris of the Hallowe'en games he'd prepared for her. There were masks and a witch's hat on the table, there were nuts and sweets and a barmbrack, still uncut. Saddest of all was the solitary apple suspended from the doorway with coins stuck into its flesh.

Now, yesterday had been a Monday – so Yelena had informed me when I'd come out of my fever. My standing arrangement with Chester was three o'clock on every other Tuesday. We hadn't met the previous Tuesday. I glanced at the kitchen clock. If I hurried, I could still catch him. I'd have plenty of time to worry about Rakoczi as I walked. When I finally left, a raw wind was blustering in from the direction of the docks, driving truant leaves west along the canal.

The flat had been quite empty when I'd risen. There'd been no evidence of the previous night's conversation, nothing beyond a trace of cigarette smoke and three bottles of Bordeaux that stood sentinel beside the bin. On the table, three corks were lined up like terms in an arithmetic equation. The three shells of the conman's game, if I'd had wit enough to see it.

With a mind blank as the ozone high over the city, I struggled to recall any details of the financial scheme that Rakoczi had outlined. In which Mr William Regan of Portobello was to be the central player, if you don't mind! The only bit I could recall with any certainty was that, as his gastropod lips had put it, I was the one figure here whose hand could move the corks about. With everyone else's it was shadow play. Was it out of Yeats he'd culled that gem? One way or another, the accounts would have to be in the name of yours sincerely.

Shadow play. In the beginning, when I'd first begun to escort Mother on her interminable rounds, I'd toyed with the idea that the streets were phantoms in the midst of which I alone was real. It's a common schoolboy fantasy. The entire city of dust and voices was conjured into being only as we made our way along its shabby streets. I got a great kick out of that. The shop fronts came into existence only as I turned my eyes upon them. As soon as I turned my back, they vanished into thin air. I could trick them, if only I span about fast enough.

Mother pertained to the real world, that much was obvious. Her bloodless hand gripped my shoulder, constant as a yoke. The marks are still there, somewhere, under the skin. One pace behind, she was nevertheless my guide through the phantasmal stage-set. But here was a conundrum. How could the visible world, the world of three dimensions, be conjured into being for her, whose eyes were dead? What disappeared when she turned around?

Oh I was a precocious child all right, in spite of my lack of schooling.

I looked about me at the expensive brick façades that line the canal. The centre I'd walked with Mother wasn't quite so grand. Thomas Street and Francis Street and Guinness's brewery; Moore Street, and Parnell Street as far as the North Circular. It was here, on that memorable excursion with Danaher, that I'd been allowed to glimpse his entire ecosystem of bottom-feeders, with their lingo of nods and winks and nudges. Now here was a new stratum. This was another domain of shadows, only here the whispers were in Polish, or Russian. Here the woods reverberated with their 'tak, tak'. There were z's and j's and v's in the air, and a plentiful lack of vowels. Which goblins ruled here? I wondered. Which laws prevailed?

As my feet wandered, my mind wandered. I found I was avoiding the tiny gaps between the paving stones. Now, back in the days when Yelena's infidelities were still in doubt, I used to play a game: *if I land between the cracks then she's not 'seeing' another man; if the third car to pass isn't green then she's not 'seeing' another man.* That sort of lark. One afternoon, during this period of pavement hopping, Yelena had come back to the flat with the bones of a poem in her bag. In Poland, though once again she alluded to the country only by referring to an obscure village whose name cried out for a vowel, she'd been commissioned to write a poem. It was the anniversary of some liberation or other.

She told me they'd already published it over there, in Polish. What she now required was to render the bones of the poem into English. 'The bones of the poem' was her own phrase. The title eludes me. 'The Grove of Birches', or maybe 'Glen of the Birches', I'm no longer sure. Birches, in any case. What I do remember is the poem's remarkable accumulation of crows. Crows of every kind stalked its branches: black crows and hooded crows and rooks and ravens and great carrion crows.

I'd hit upon the happy cacophony 'raucous chorus' for some similar pairing in the original. And she'd been delighted, much as she was delighted with my 'Filthy Modern Tide'. 'You see, Willy, this is what I need!' The rest of the poem escapes me, all but the final words: 'Under a grey exfoliating sky.' I remember the sky with absolute certainty because she was annoyed I didn't 'get it'.

She'd brought with her a huge Polish-English dictionary. I saw at once she'd fecked it from the local library. She of course denied this. She looked offended, cried no, she'd borrowed it. So I of course pointed out that you can no more borrow from the reference section! The next thing, she fell onto the bed in a wild fit of the giggles, her boots kicking into the bedclothes. Now, I'm not sure how she was in her other liaisons. I never asked. With me, spontaneity was the very genius of her sexuality. If anything had the aura of planning or expectation, she recoiled like a nun from it. But that day, with late sunlight streaming through the open window, the unexpected laughter released the most unbounded desires in her. She clasped me to her as if she hungered to make us one flesh. She stared at me in frantic disbelief, and she bit my mouth until it too began to grow savage. I was so astounded at the strength of the wave that swelled up in her, I scarcely noticed my own pleasure.

Afterwards she was calm and affectionate. We lay in the bed and she smoked and talked about her childhood. Later again, we ate sardines and bread and drank from a bottle of sin-coloured wine that I'd been saving up for Mother's anniversary. 'I'll stay here with you tonight,' she said.

In fact she stayed two nights. On the second day we worked again through the bones of the poem, improving on the crib that she'd penned in the margins, flirting, discussing, thumbing through the dictionary, and I marvelled at the words that appeared to me like strands of barbed wire, so relentless were the clusters of consonants. Poland, I thought, must be a dark place.

There was no sign of Chester at our usual haunt. I waited for the best part of an hour, and then gave up on the man. It was not the first time he'd failed to show. But I'll be damned if, on this occasion,

I didn't have a presentiment that things were not quite right. On that I'd swear. But there was no point in waiting indefinitely either. I set out on my wanders once more while it was still light.

Is there a pattern that governs our steps? Or do we continually stub our toes against coincidence, and shrug off the indignity by invoking divinity? My mind still mulling over Rakoczi, and my feet still avoiding the cracks in the pavement, I arrived, quite by chance, at the quay opposite the Customs House. Not long before, I'd read how the great building had been sacked during the latter stages of the War of Independence. The last throw of the dice of an exhausted shadow army. What had held my attention was how, in their assault, an entire archive of deeds and registers had been reduced to ashes. Then, a bare year later, what irony! In that fratricidal madness that followed the Treaty, the squabbling factions had put the Four Courts to the match. And so the only duplicate of that archive, complete since medieval times, was destroyed.

Meditations in a time of Civil War. I imagined the sky filling up with flocks of charred pages, crows rising from a field of stubble. And it seemed to my imagination, still troubling over the paradox of Mother's sightlessness, that in the twin conflagrations, far more than the memory of dead generations had been lost. And then those lines came floating down to me out of Yelena's poem: 'Under a low, exfoliating sky'. Was that what she had in mind?

The day was by now quite cold. To my right I saw a sea mist, as coarse as a brown habit, beginning to drift in over the East Link. To the left, a low, feeble sun had disappeared behind Liberty Hall. It wouldn't be long before it set entirely. Not long to rush hour, then, with its lava flow of cars to the western suburbs. In those days, the lower quays were derelict. No high-rise developments challenged the easterlies as they blustered in from the open sea, driving the demented gulls before them. 'I'll go home,' says I with a shiver. I walked with shoulders hunched, and the street lights began to flicker on over my head, prematurely as it seemed.

The mist was by now moving like breath along the river, chill and wet to the cheek. Everything beyond the railway bridge had already dissolved into amnesia; into a river of ghosts. The fog is the ghost of the sea, I'd read, once. The freezing humidity must've had a deadening effect on the transmission of sound, too. I was surprised to find there was already a diminishing series of red circles idling westward along Aston and Wellington Quay. If I were to try my hand at poetry, I'd say the penumbrae, thrown out into the vapour by throbbing tail lights, resembled nothing so much as a procession of votive lamps. I shivered involuntarily.

By the time I was pushing around the perimeter of Trinity College, the fog was so dense it was no longer possible to make out the milky circle of the old Parliament. Maher once told me how, around the time of the Act of Union, its windows were apparently bricked in to avoid paying the window tax. Daylight robbery, he'd quipped. Today it would hardly have mattered. The entire south-west corner of College Green was dissolving. Figures, stooped and scarved, or clutching upturned collars about livid faces, loomed abruptly out of the freezing nimbus and dissipated just as abruptly once they'd passed me. It seemed I was alone in making my way counterclockwise about the railings.

A few yards, that was the extent of what you could see by this time. Where, now, the circle of ten miles' radius my sailor said we drag with us? I'd plotted, mentally, an itinerary home: Grafton Street and Harcourt Street, curved like spinal columns on either end of the green. Then on to the black canal. These locations would only come into being in proportion as I made my way along them. Mother's vision was as curtailed as this, I mused, my sight soaked up in the damp blotting paper that had invaded the city.

But this was no solution to the general problem of blindness.

And then a curious thing happened. An unpalatable coincidence, of the kind you don't just stub your toe against; you trip over it. The kind that sends the jitters running through you. I'd registered the sound. It was a tapping or scraping, as if bamboo were being dragged over the pedestrian paving. What the hell was it, now? I stopped at the base of a lamp post, its crown an ochre aura in which tiny droplets were suspended like faults in glass. Suddenly, a figure loomed out of the whiteness and banged into me. We entangled at the very moment the tap-tapping registered. I'd time to observe the fluttering, sunken eyelids beyond the dark glasses before we managed to disengage from one another.

'Sorry,' said I as I pressed his cane, which had fallen, into groping fingers. 'An evil night,' said the blind man. Then 'I wonder are the buses still running?' I was unable to enlighten him, though I told him I doubted it. Meanwhile, Soul was whispering, *how does he know there's a pea-souper?* He sank forever into the mist as I was again apologising for my clumsiness. Then out of the fog a thought arrived, so vivid it held me. Fate is blind, they say. If a divinity did govern this infernal city, had I just collided with it? 'Bah!' I shivered. 'Nonsense!' I let his memory dissolve into the wispy forgetfulness that had settled on the world.

When I'd continued a good many steps up the spine of Grafton Street, a whim made me take a road that had opened to the right. All my life I've been the dupe of such caprices. I continued until the next left opened, and groped along until another left, and then a right. Or vice versa. I read once how it takes talent to lose one's way in a city. It's there in my journal. Until now, I thought what it meant was that it was hard to get lost in a city. But with the streets opaque, it would've been no mean feat to keep one's way. Quite soon I was lost.

I'd grown up in the Liberties. From an early age I'd guided Mother daily about her huckster shops. It seemed astonishing that Will Regan could go astray in his own back yard! But the fog had altered the landscape after the manner of a bad dream. What should have been familiar had been made strange. Twice I thought to have reached Patrick Street, only to find my idea mistaken.

After a while I found I was labouring up a slope. In this part of town? There was no such hill! And yet the gradient was horrible steep. It made me wonder whether I hadn't descended to the river without realising it. I could imagine no other explanation. I paused to listen. I ran my left hand over a silent granite brick. What thread had Mother used to negotiate her lightless labyrinth? Crossing the street with hands outstretched, I all but stumbled through a railing that ran upwards. Some sort of floodlighting beyond was glamorising the fog. Winetavern Street? Not at all! Fishamble? I followed the railing's ascent towards the summit. Could that hallucination be the hull of Christ Church?

'Don't say a fucking word!'

The voice materialised behind my ear a split second before I heard it. Instantaneously, a rough arm was about my throat, clamping my Adam's apple. 'Don't say a fucking word and I won't touch you, right?' I tried to move my head to signal my assent. A minute slipped by, or what seemed like it. Amplified by the fog, our breathing was bestial. But I was aware of another noise. Another presence, somewhere in the fog. This was a rhythmic, mechanical hum that was menacing the road somewhere above us.

A pin scratched my throat. 'D'you know what that is? That's a fucking syringe that is.' I rotated my eye sufficiently to see locks of hair like seaweed about a livid complexion. 'So give us your cash, and no fucking nonsense.' He sniffed. All the time he'd been shivering violently. And now he sniffed. The droplet glinted at the end of his nose. 'You don't, and I'll shoot this dose into your fucking throat so I will.'

What happened next I didn't understand. Not for a minute. Suddenly he took fright. The low, rotary growl, which had been deepening, burst upon us with a great hiss and clatter. An orange eye glared across us. Or glared across me, since my assailant had already melted into the fog. I fell backwards against the railings, pushed back by the roar of sound. And then the dragon receded as abruptly as it had arrived. I clutched the cold iron staves until its rattle had rounded a corner somewhere beneath me.

A shudder seized me. It was deathly cold. All at once I threw myself from the rails and began to run. I ran until my lungs were bursting and a stitch had opened in my side. I ran as though the phantom mugger were hard on my heels. I clambered along parked cars, I careened about lamp posts, I scrambled over a humpback bridge. Faces loomed, and I fumbled past them. A dog's head wrenched at a chain in an avalanche of barking. When at last I could run no more, I found that I was in the courtyard outside St Mary's, Rathmines. I wasn't two hundred yards from my door! What blind instinct had taken over, guiding my flight? Was this what Mother had used to navigate when I wasn't there to take her arm? And the blind man who'd stumbled into me earlier, did he have such instincts?

Now I was so close to home, I began to feel easy again. I even began to think of how I'd frame the story for the amusement of young Yelena.

I was to see her again in three days' time. This date I'd wrung from her the previous night while Rakoczi was out of the room. The place was her idea. A grand trip to Glasnevin cemetery, to track down the graves out of the poetry of Mr Yeats. It was a project she'd talked about for some time now. She cuffed me. 'You can show me where is buried your mother.' So now, as the roar over the canal lock sounded to one side and I tasted its fetid breath, I began to cobble together a narrative for her entertainment. How in my own back yard I'd managed to lose myself in the fog. How a junky, with seaweed for hair, had risen from the river to seize me by the throat. How his pestilent needle would certainly have done for me, if I hadn't been rescued by an enchanted street-sweeper.

But my narrative was cut short when I reached the foot of my building. There was a light blazing in the bedroom window.

XI

'*D*anger! You're back!'
    'I'm back.'

My heart hit the floorboards without a bounce. Hoody and cap were hovering beside the window, where the corner of the net curtain was deflected by two nicotine-stained fingers. The hood in the hoody.

'There wasn't no one asking after me this last few weeks?'

'No.'

'You're certain?'

'No one saw fit to ask *me* about you anyway.'

The eyes fixed me like two rivets. I noticed he'd grown a pencil moustache while he was away. 'And come here to me, Regan. What about just now? You didn't see no one standing across the way just now?'

In this fog? Was he joking?

'I didn't see a soul.'

He turned back to the window. 'Only I thought I seen one of the cunts waiting for me in Heuston Station the minute I got off of the train.' I stared at the back of his cap with intense distaste. I couldn't have felt more repulsed if I'd encountered a giant vermin in the flat, twitching at the curtains. 'Who was waiting for you, Danger? The guards?'

He stared back at my ignorance with subdued rage. 'Not the bucking guards!' he hammered all five syllables equally. 'Not the bucking guards. Jaysus Christ!' And then he added, with something like a grim snigger, 'The DPP has nothing new on me, bro. And they never will what's more. I took good care of that.'

'Who then?'

Was I trying to rile him? 'The bucking Rooskies! Jaysus, Regan!' With this outburst, his chameleon face altered hue. Frustration blanched to suspicion. The eyes narrowed accordingly. 'Whose is the bottles?'

'What bottles?'

'There's three empty bottles of vino sitting inside so there is. And there's three dirty glasses with them what's more.'

'Oh,' I said.

'So don't tell me there was nobody in here. Who was it? Regan, if I find out…'

'No one,. Jesus! It was friends.'

'*Friends!*' You would have thought he'd swallowed a gnat, the way he spat out the word. Then his head jerked back and forwards mechanically, with its bantam cock's aggression. 'Here! Where's me bag?' Now, twice since I'd come in I'd seen his eyes flit to the press in which the oversized bag was pupating. From its snout the padlock still dangled out into the room.

'It's where you put it, Danger. Where else would it be?'

'If I find out, Regan…I swear to God…' He strutted past me and made straight for it. But the strap must have been snagged on a catch, for he tugged several times, to little effect. I'd forgotten how short he was. Stepping up beside him, displacing him, I ran my finger blindly along the strap and slipped it over the catch. He jerked the bag past my ear and allowed it to topple onto the bed. Then, with much ostentation, his fingers tried the padlock that secured the zip, while his eyes drilled straight into me. When he was satisfied it hadn't been tampered with, he pulled a fistful of coppers out of his pocket and flicked his head towards the stairwell.

'Here,' he said, 'run down to the pub and get me twenty Caddles.'

I shook my head, not to refuse, but at the condescension of the man.

'What're you grinning at?'

'Twenty Caddles. It's exactly what the mother used to call them. Only she only ever got tens at a time.' He stared at me as if I were soft in the head. 'Here,' he cried, thrusting his fist into my hand and laying there a few sweaty coins. 'Go on.' I shook my head, but I went. His voice followed me as far as the banister. 'And Regan, don't be in too much of a hurry to get back.'

I counted about twenty minutes before I returned.

'Where the hell have you been?'

'I went as far as the canal. You told me not to…'

'Never mind about that. Here, give us the bleedin' fags.' From his wide-eyed expression as he held out his arm, it was obvious he was testing whether or not I'd been to the pub at all. No doubt he suspected I'd been sneaking about in the fog, consorting with a host of imaginary pursuers. The new pencil moustache twitched, as though he were sniffing the air.

I waved the box in the air like a flag of truce.

He took his twenty Carroll's in one hand and pushed forwards the other, which until then had been concealed inside the hoody.

'What?'

'Take it!' he cried.

'Oh.' I found I'd accepted a small, sleek phone. 'What?'

'Now listen to me carefully. I'm going to be lying low for a few days in a safe house. Then I'm getting the hell out of this country.'

My eyes took in a couple of plastic bags, very full with what appeared to be bricks, squatting by the door. But there was no sign of the holdall. It must've been obvious I was scanning the room for it, since he nodded violently towards the press. The door was now securely shut.

'In a few days' time I'll be giving you a shout. I ring you. You don't ring me. Do you get it?'

I shrugged. Was there any point in telling him I hadn't the faintest idea how to use a mobile phone? I'd scarcely mastered the ATM, for God's sake! Or, for that matter, that I hadn't the foggiest what his number might be. 'I ring you. You don't ring me. Right?'

'I get it, Danger.'

'When you hear from me, Regan, then and only then will I explain to you exactly what you've to do.' He nodded at the press. 'Where you've to bring the rest of the gear. Understood?'

'You won't be coming back for it?' I tried to hide my relief behind the question mark.

'Too dangerous. Were you not listening to me? I can't show so much as my nose anywhere in this town any more.'

'I can see why you're heading abroad.'

'Who the *fuck* said I was heading abroad?'

'Jesus, Danger! You did. You just said it now.'

'I swear to you, Regan. If I find out you've grassed on me…'

But I never was to find out what would have happened to me if I'd dared to grass on Joseph Mary Danaher.

I've reread the last number of pages. It seems we're getting somewhere. To the heart of the matter, as the saying goes. Keep an eye on that holdall!

There hasn't been hide nor hair of that bloody tom in a week. Looks like the poison I laid out has done for his caterwauling. Tonight, only the creak of the wardrobe and the tick-tick of the radiator punctuate the silence.

I thought it through. Cats are supposed to like liver, right? So I went to the family butchers and bought a calf's liver, half the size of a bloody cat! The butcher's assistant took my extravagance in his stride. That night, I laced it with the rat poison I'd picked up earlier. I dusted it with enough of the stuff to put paid to nine cats. Then I laid it on the very bin-lid I'd watched him clatter across the previous night but one. The following morning, there was no trace of the liver.

Bye bye, moggie!

'ABANDON ALL HOPE, YE WHO ENTER HERE!' The wreath-sellers to either side of the gate gave me a queer look. 'Crazy man!' smirked Yelena.

'Know what they call it? The dead centre of Dublin.'

Hallowe'en; Fever; Fog; Glasnevin. From this point on, we can begin to talk of dates with a degree of certainty. They can always be checked against police files.

We're getting on.

I'd entertained Yelena with the story of the fog all the way out to the cemetery. No sooner had the chess-piece towers on the wall swung into view than my heart soared high. Now it was up with the rooks. 'So is time for your "casual comedy", Willy?' she teased. A while since, we'd been teasing out a Yeats poem, fighting street by street over its details. She'd sustained the fiction of her academic paper for so long now that, visa or no, we were both coming to believe in her *Filthy Modern Tide*. If things had turned out differently, she might've even published the bloody thing.

'I still say you're wrong, and I don't care what Mr Rakoczi has to say on the subject. By "casual comedy" he means the rest of the time. The daily grind.'

'No, Mister. It's you who are wrong. I say you on Friday, the comedy is turned to tragedy only when they are shot.'

'If you say me, Yelena, it must be true.'

'Don't make fun of me, bastard.' She was frowning a little too deliberately, a child playing at being cross.

'You know of course what they wrote on the grave of your man was killed there last year in Connolly Station, and he trying to jump onto a moving train?'

'What?' she pouted.

'"Sadly Missed".'

'Oh, ha ha, funny man!'

We pushed in through the main gate. My spirits danced the instant I saw the first tomb. The graveyard had always been a favourite haunt of Mother's. She liked it so much, she'd taken a more permanent residency.

'The round tower,' I pointed, 'is for O'Connell. He's the only comedian here. And the granite boulder is for the tragedian, Parnell.'

'Where is Parnell? I don't see him.'

'Over beyond the mortuary chapel. A cholera pit, near the plots where the religious are buried. I'm sure,' said I, 'there was no irony intended in that.'

'The religious what?'

'The religious. Here, we just call them the religious. Like the righteous, or the damned. They bury the regular clergy by their orders in great, communal enclosures. Creatures of habit, says you.' She ignored the quip. 'I dare say that's how they'll file out on the Day of Judgement. It'll help the angels to sort them.'

'I think it is the devils who will sort your religious.'

I guffawed. 'The Irish Catholic and Apostolic Church is starting to stink like a corpse. Ever since the days your compatriot Karol what's-his-name paid us a visit! Have there been as many scandals in Poland?'

But she'd no wish to talk about her country. 'I'll tell you one thing that's buried out here,' says I. 'Romantic Ireland. It's with O'Leary in the grave.'

'Who is this O'Leary?'

'Famous football player scored against Romania.'

'Crazy man!' That was the fourth time she'd called me that. With Yelena, it was a sure-fire sign she was feeling frisky. It was fifty-fifty we'd wind up in the sack. If I didn't balls it up that is. 'Actually, he was an old Fenian was much admired by Mr Yeats.'

'So where do we find this grave of O'Leary?'

'Dunno. If it's anywhere, it's sure to be with the rest of the rebels. What you'd call a republican plot!' Another pun lost to the damp air.

'Where are buried MacDonagh and MacBride?'

'And Connolly and Pearse? No, ma'am. There's a monumental garden in Arbour Hill, watered by their patriots' blood.' Now, when she was of a mind to, Yelena had the handy knack of slipping a pinch of levity into my unleavened humours. So I tried for the umpteenth time. I winked at her. 'In the name of God and the degenerations.' But the quip fell flat as a slab. I saw her peeking at her watch. 'It's okay,' I said, 'they'll wait till we get there.'

'Everyone else,' I went on as we walked, 'everyone who was anyone in the struggle, is buried out here though. Both sides of the bloody punch-up that followed the Treaty, one laid right on top of the other! That'll be fun and games to sort out on Judgement Day.'

'The Struggle! The Troubles! I love how you call things in Ireland. But the Emergency, this one is my favourite.'

'We like to play things down I guess. History's been bloody enough around these parts without talking it up.'

'You should come some time to my country, Mister.'

'I'll wait for you to join the Community first.'

We poked around the republican plot for some time without unearthing O'Leary. Over the city, the sky had begun to take on an ominous tincture. I saw Yelena again glance at her watch. She was keen to see Mother's final resting place before the rain came. We moved down a yew-lined avenue with little time to dawdle over the more ludicrous names and vanities: the last of the three publicans, whose plot was a whisker wider than his two companions; the child's dolmen over Skin the Goat's grave. All around, leprous Christs and crumbling angels tallied the mottled quarry. Stone too has its diseases.

'Ever been to a Church of Ireland boneyard?' I asked. 'Their headstones are decorated like the frontispiece out of an antique book. "Here lies Nathaniel Smith, Faithful Departed. Volume III. Printed by George Faulkner of Essex Street in the Year of Our Lord MDCXVI."'

'Maybe that's what a graveyard is to your God. Is a huge library, where he can pick out any of the lives he wants to read.'

'*My* God?'

We rounded the corner to that row of crooked slabs where lay Mother's mortal remains. It was gap-toothed as the gawp of a tramp. To the left, three generations of stockbrokers, all named Edmund Godwin. In dignified oblivion. The last had died fifty years ago. To the right, in the next plot but one, flowers in plastic domes yellowed for a lost twin. She'd drowned at the age of thirteen. And in between, seven members of a family named Burke, all with the old names: Sonny, and Sis, and Babs. Dubliner than thou.

I shuffled at the foot of Mother's kerb where Yelena was standing, head bowed. I was unsure what posture to adopt. 'So what do you think *my* God would read from this one?' my voice broke the rook-scratched silence.

'"Margaret (Molly) Regan, 1947-1997, RIP."' She touched the letters with her finger. 'It doesn't give very much away.'

'No.'

'You visit her?'

'Every anniversary and birthday. Religiously, as they say. I do sprinkle the holy ground with a sup of the Cork Dry.'

'Cork Dry?'

'Gin. She was fond of the gargle, Mother. Had a good tipple every night of her life.'

'She did not!'

'I'm telling you! Neat, or with just a dash of Cantrell & Cochrane. Slimline on account of the diabetes.'

'What means neat? Not tidy?'

'Neat means straight out of the bottle. Don't think for a minute that being blind made it any harder for her to locate that merchandise either. She'd a nose like a highland terrier.'

'You're a bad son, Willy.'

'I'm only speaking the truth.'

She considered this for a minute, eyes on the headstone. 'You don't know where is buried your father?'

'How in God's name would I know that? Sure he's probably still alive, the bugger.' A shiver ran through me at the old thought that I might one day bump shoulders with a man bearing my aged features. 'I'll tell you something funny about Mother though. She had this little prayer book, a hangover from her confirmation days. Actually, I think it was only a penny catechism.'

'What is catechism?'

'Ach. Who made you? God made me. Why did God make you? That sort of malarkey.'

'So why *did* God made you?'

'Will you let me finish my bloody story? So anyway, she clung onto this prayer book, even after the eyesight went. I mean, it wasn't like she could read it, and of course she'd never the patience to learn Braille. But any day she went to church, that little penny catechism had to go with her. You'd swear she was afraid the priest might ask her a question out of it! So this one evening we're on our way down to St Audoen's for the Friday novena when she stops on the very threshold. "I haven't me *buke* with me, Willy. Would you ever run back and get, it son? I'll wait here for you go on, it'll take you two minutes is all" So to cut a long story short, there was never a point in arguing with her. So I trot back to the flat and get hold of her *buke* for her. And that's when I discover what she's been using all along for a buke-mark.'

I nodded at Yelena, inviting her. Begging the question. 'Well?'

'I say a bookmark, though of course she could no more read than she could dance a jig. It was a keepsake. A sacred relic. An old envelope, with a note inside. The ink was faded. Five words, that's all it was, Yelena. Or four words and an initial. "It can never work, W." Very curious. So of course I check the envelope. The postmark dates it about five months before yours truly was born. So what do you think of that? "It can never work, W."'

'But who is W?'

'Exactly. Who is W? I told you I'd always a hunch I was named after my da.'

'But you don't even know is man. W might be Wilhelmina.'

'Wilhel-*meen*-a? Please!'

She frowned. 'So where is this note? Do you still have it?'

'Ah! It lived inside that prayer book, you see. And when finally they laid her out in the madhouse, they placed that book in her dead fingers. I hadn't the heart to root it out of their grip.' I nodded at the headstone. 'So you could say, chances are, it's my father is buried in that grave with her.'

She fingered an earring. 'And have you ask your friend who is W?'

I stared at her, dumbstruck. 'You fool. You bloody fool!' If I'd a hat, I would've thrown it down and danced a hornpipe on it. On the rare occasions I'd caught a glimpse of Mother's early years through the chinks in Chester's monologues, it was like found money. 'You bloody fool, Will Regan!' I gripped her shoulders. 'How was it I never thought to ask?'

'Because you are bloody fool?'

Mentally, I ran through the days before I'd have the chance to ask the man. Nine days, if the bugger showed! It was interminable. I shook my head wildly. Just then, the first fat drops burst on the grey slab. 'Come on, we'd better go.' I caught her again glancing at her watch as we set off.

We were returning along the main avenue when I saw a figure in a hood bearing down on us through the oblique rain. Yelena seemed not in the least surprised at this apparition. The man was already on top of us before I made out the face of Adam Rakoczi, livid in the rainwater. The wet lips were two slugs, mating.

'I bring the papers to sign,' he said, looking at Yelena but addressing me.

'What papers? What're you doing out here?'

'I bring the papers.' Now his eyes turned into his anorak, under which bulged a secret cargo. 'The papers, like we talk about.' He looked back to Yelena, and the two of them began to

bicker in their patois: *zh; vh; ch*. 'Tak, tak,' the echoing axe. After
a while Yelena turned to me. 'You need to sign these papers to
make possible transfer into your account.'

'What?' I laughed, pulling a strand of her bedraggled hair.
'Here, in the rain? It'll run like cheap mascara.'

'So where we can go?'

It happened that the door of the mortuary chapel was
unlocked, and we sat into a pew, water dribbling onto the flags.
A hand touched my knee. Hers. I looked at the dog-eared pages
that Rakoczi passed over to me, understanding next to nothing.
One bore the logo of my own bank, the several that were under
it had been typed in a foreign alphabet. Backward letters, like
Alice might've seen through the looking glass. I laughed and
shrugged my incomprehension. Rakoczi looked to Yelena, his
face a blank cipher.

'You must sign here,' she supplied, her nail varnish tapping a
line, 'and here, and here, and then here.'

'But I don't understand a word it says.'

'Willy, we explain you…'

They began again, pianissimo, their symphony of hovering
insects. Then Rakoczi rose from the pew. As he stepped into
the aisle he made a class of apologetic curtsey towards the altar,
a down-payment on a genuflection, as you might say. He then
retreated to the rear of the church on ludicrously groaning
soles. I smirked. I tried hard not to smirk. But I smirked. Yelena
snuggled up beside me. 'What you want to know, crazy man?'
she purred. 'I explain you anything you like.' A palm leaned on
my thigh.

I glanced over my shoulder. Rakoczi was lolling in the last
pew, his eyes beatifically on the ceiling. I tapped a page which
was in Cyrillic. 'Be fair, chuck. For all I know it might be an
organ transplant you have me signing up to!'

'I tell you already. Is bank!' Out of the looking-glass alphabet
her nail varnish traced out the scaffolding of the word.

'How do I know it's not a blood bank?' I quipped. She
cuffed me. 'You shouldn't make joke. Is church.' My smirk

returned, more fixed than ever. Yelena was about as religious as a tabby cat. 'What else you need I explain you, stupid man?' she whispered, tickling my ear.

I shrugged, fingered through the papers, and feigned the sign of the cross. Then, like the scholar in the morality play, I signed the infernal things.

XII

*A*round this time, the skeletons in the cupboards at the MacMurrough Tribunal were beginning to reek to high heaven. The headlines, those blowflies of public indignation, were revelling in the stench. Broadsheets frowned, radios jabbered, and tabloids howled in execration. Unimaginable fortunes had been made. Great swathes of land had been rezoned, field after green field covered over with brick and dust and asphalt. The whole city chattered of backhanders and envelopes and offshore accounts, and every mother's son was at once jury and financial regulator.

One day, idle with curiosity, I made my way to Dublin Castle. To fill my lungs with the atmosphere, as you might say. They call it a castle, this Georgian doll's house. Yet for all its childish geometry, for seven centuries the city was terrorised from inside its shadowy offices. Spies and informers. Lackeys. Castle hacks, drummed up by the British from Dublin's nether-world. I looked at the gathering of press-hounds. 'Now they're our own hacks,' I smirked, feeling the lack of a companion. I'd have even settled for a Danaher, *kyak kyak*. Anyone at all at whom to direct my witticisms.

Or Mother! Mother would have revelled in the high tide of sleaze. She had ever the lowest opinion of the political classes. By God, I'd swear that woman could sniff out corruption at a hundred paces. Every evening, as a mixer for her digestive Cork Dry, she'd have me read aloud such columns of The *Irish Press* as dealt with scandals and recriminations. This could take some time, as she'd the habit of interrupting every second line with a scornful ejaculation. Gin and bitters, we called these sessions. Is it time for my gin and bitters, son? And the more local the exposé, the more she enjoyed it. She had no use at all for international news.

I marvel to think how little I knew of history in those days. Or of any current affair that gave off no whiff of scandal. The North might as well not have happened. But now, Yelena had used Rakoczi as such a goad to my vanity that I was an expert on everything from Poyning's Law to Wood's halfpence, from the statutes of Kilkenny to Surrender and Regrant. I surveyed the great doll's house, and I could almost smell the reams of historical papers that gathered dust in every corner.

A makeshift sign for the tribunal pointed into the interior courtyard. Here, Justice lorded it over the cobbles from atop her gateway. No blindfold. So much for the impartiality of the law, I thought, again feeling the lack of an ear. *And then*, echoed Soul, *they say whenever it rains, the scales tip to the left.*

I passed the flock of paparazzi idling with their cameras. Perhaps they were the very crows that had been bickering outside the Four Courts on the day I fell in with Danaher. Beyond them loured a red-faced Garda. His farmer's bulk blocked the way into the great chamber where the tribunal was in interminable session. I nodded too familiarly, and he ordered me with a deepening glower to 'Present your press pass for inspection if you please.' I made a show of going through my pockets, all the while trying vainly to peer around his frame. I came across nothing except some class of business card in my back pocket, so, for devilment, I asked him if a brown envelope wouldn't get me inside.

'You'd be well advised to keep your jibes to yourself.' He discharged his thick-tongued counsel at the lintel over my head.

Nothing to be done. With no appointments with which to fill out the day, I slunk outside the courtyard and I hovered. At any time before I'd become so sociable, the lack would scarcely have registered. Now, the days seemed shapeless without some intercourse to stiffen them. Any thought of being the city's chronicler had long since been abandoned, and from the time of the back yard bonfire of the vanities, I'd taken up neither charcoal nor chalk. These days, when I was alone for any length of time, I found that my nerves grew progressively fidgety. In fact, the craving for company had taken such a hold, I even looked forward to signing on at the welfare office, the last Thursday of every month. There I'd examine the anaemic faces I'd begun to recognise. I'd listen with joy to the banter and argument in the glacial queues that smelled of the charity shop. In short, I'd become a people fancier. It was a weakness that the rude intimacies of the prison cell would cure me of for good.

With damn all to do and all day long to do it, I hummed and hawed at the gates behind Justice's back. Then, as so often in these pages, Fate or chance or Mother took a hand in the proceedings. What the hell business had I with a business card in my arse pocket? I pulled it out, turned it over. It was a calling card, with a blue fish that a child might draw. 'Chapter of Christ the Fisherman, 14–16 Lower Abbey Street, Dublin 1 "… therefore be wise as serpents and guileless as doves… (Matt. 10:16)".' I gawped at it. What the hell hand had slipped this into my arse pocket? And then it came to me. The taxi-man! 'Don't be afraid to pray, boss.'

Damn it, I thought, I'll find the place. Soul sniggered. *And you wouldn't be the first Irishman, Will Regan, to have turned in despair from politics to religion!* I set off down Parliament Street at a good pace, happy that at last the day had a shape to it.

I'd already crossed the Liffey and was about level with the Winding Stair when I was arrested by a yell. It was stark, inarticulate, scarcely human. I couldn't for the life of me see what desperado had given vent to it. But instinct told me it had been directed at my progress. I scoured both sides of the quays minutely until at last I hit upon a figure scurrying through Merchant's Arch. The yell was repeated, its back breaking hoarsely over an octave, just as the gesticulating form stumbled onto the Ha'penny Bridge. It could only be Chester Maher.

Instantly my question soared like a gull over the Liffey. Who is W? Nine interminable days had been cut in two by providence. 'You're the last man I was expecting to see around these parts! I thought it was supposed to be your day with young Steph?'

He was out of puff. But there was a desperate cast to his eyes.

'Weren't you to bring her out to the zoo or something?'

'That's just it!' he panted. He shook his head. 'That's just it!' he cried. I allowed him a minute to catch his breath. 'Her mother…'

'Oh, not again! Surely to God…'

He really did look in a desperate state. He was floundering about for words, eyes flittering urgently from one bridge to another. 'Come upstairs,' I motioned to the café behind us. 'You can tell me all about it when you've sat down.' *And once we've that out of the way,* says Soul, *you can ask your famous 'who is W?', like you should've done months ago.*

'I went out to your flat,' he panted. He was looking up and down along the quay wall, for all the world as though he'd lost something there. 'But you weren't in.'

'No.' I waited another minute to see if he'd calm down, or at the least get his breath back. He didn't. 'Come on upstairs, Chester. We'll have a coffee, and then you can tell me what's happened.'

But the coffee had the opposite effect to what I'd hoped. Far from sedating the man, it set his nerves a-jitter. At this rate, we'd never get on to W. One phrase snatched another away before the first had time to alight. It was all I could do to keep pace with his flurries. 'She didn't have… I thought she mightn't… give me custody today because… but I don't see how she could have found out so… I certainly didn't tell her… you see, the bank… but I still have to see about another… it's not as if the repayments, before now… but now she's talking of France again… I swear to you, if she… if they… and Stephie has never even been to… my

God, what am I to do?… if this time…'

'Chester!' A sound not unlike a whimper met my command. 'Chester, slow down. Tell it to me one bit at a time. Stephanie Maher wouldn't hand over Stephie today, is that it?'

'She must have found out! For God's sake!' He slapped his forehead several times, and I felt the eyes of the place upon us. 'The bank! The *fucking* bank! What right had they? The bank *must've* told her!'

Calmness, my soul. W was beginning to tease it like a will-o'-the-wisp. 'You said something about repayments…?'

'But that's not the point!' He was hollering, his head an effigy of anguish or outrage, probably both. I smiled weakly at the waiting staff, begging indulgence. 'For Christ's sake! She says she's going to move back to France! For Christ's sake!'

'And she'll take Stephie with her to France?'

'Take Stephie with her?' He was on the point of tears, but tears which hadn't decided between fury or despair. 'Of course she'll take Stephie with her! God damn her! God damn her to hell!'

I could see that the manager, who'd come down from the second floor to investigate the commotion, was on the point of asking us to leave. So I pre-empted him. Chester's hand was fidgeting about his face as though a wasp was bothering it. Touching his forearm determinedly, I nodded out towards the Ha'penny Bridge. 'What you need isn't a coffee, my friend. What you need is a good stiff whiskey.' I left a reluctant fiver on the table, and then steered him, a blindfolded hostage, down the stairs and into the first bar to hand.

Months before, when we were comparing jealousies, I'd asked him if he'd ever fantasised about doing the old one in. Putting an end to her endless infidelities, like the black fella in the story. He'd smirked and shook his sardonic head. 'You don't see the tether that ties the goat to the post.' 'I don't see the…?' In place of answering directly, he'd recited a few lines from a poem. For someone writing a drama in verse, it was the only poetry I ever remember hearing from him. 'Each man kills the thing he loves,' he'd intoned, one hand raised, the other on his heart. 'The coward does it with a kiss, the brave man with a sword.' Or a trouser-belt, I thought.

The lines came back to me as we sat into the snug. There was no telling what a desperate man might do. By this time, W was little more than the grin of the Cheshire cat fading into the air. Double you.

'Start with the bank. What is it exactly the bank has told you?'

He sighed. The first whiskey had gone before the glass had ever reached the counter. The second had fared just marginally better. 'The repayments.' He lifted the empty glass and pressed it to his lip as though he were kissing a sacred receptacle.

'You're behind in the repayments is it?'

He stared deep into the mahogany, and after a long search trawled up the figure. 'Nine months behind.' 'And they're threatening…?' My prompt hovered about in the air, a hornet that had been smoked from its nest. His Adam's apple bobbed like the float on a fishing line when a perch is attacking the lure. 'They're threatening,' he mumbled at last, 'to repossess. To throw me out of my house and onto the street.'

'I see.' There was nothing for it but to stand another round.

'Listen, Chester. I'm no expert on financial matters, but a bank…'

'If she takes Stephie away,' he vowed quietly to the holy whiskey, 'I'll kill myself. I'll kill her,' he spoke to his reflection, 'and then I'll kill myself.'

Now, many months had passed since I'd made the man's acquaintance. In all that time, I'd scarcely given a second thought to the circumstance which had thrown us together. But all at once I was back in the winter copse beyond the Magazine Fort, and he dangling from a bough like an outsized Christmas decoration.

'Surely to God you can't be serious! Would you leave little Stephie an orphan? Sure how would that solve anything!'

'But what am I to do?'

'What are you to do? Fight her! Stand up to her! You must have rights…'

'A father has no rights,' he spat, 'in this country.'

I glanced into the mirror for inspiration. 'You pay alimony, don't you? You pay to support Stephie?' He nodded, unconvinced. 'Well there you are! That gives you a say-so, too.' Looking at his downcast frame, I'd worked myself into something of a passion. It goes without saying I hadn't the least grounds to support what I was saying. But what I told him carried all the authority of indignation. 'You're the biological father,' I went on, though nothing was less certain. 'And you've provided for her ever since she was a child. No one has the right to take her away from you just like that! Are you mad?'

'Stephanie Dujardin is her mother. Her *mother!*'

'Stephanie Dujardin can like it or lump it. You have your rights, too. And so has the girl. I've seen the pair of you together…'

'But what about the house?' He was determined to dredge up all the mud.

'The house! What has the house got to do with it? The house doesn't pay alimony. The house doesn't provide for the child. The house hasn't raised the girl as if she was…' I'd been about to say as if she was its own daughter. 'You have to separate the two issues.'

'I've to see the manager next week,' he conceded, 'to renegotiate the loan.'

'There you are! You see?' He was staring deep into the amber of his drink, mollified, as I imagined. 'I want no more talk of you doing anything stupid. Do you hear me now?'

Some time later, when I was just beginning to think that the clouds had finally lifted from his character and that W might hover into view from behind them, he muttered: 'There's another thing.'

'Go on.'

His speech was slow, considered and understated. 'I'm slipping.'

'Slipping?'

'I can feel it. I'm slipping.' My heart sank. I'd about had my fill of the dark side coping with Mother's dementia, and the cries and jabberings of the madhouse where she died still had the power to disturb my sleep. If Chester Maher was going into eclipse, I could throw my proverbial hat at 'who is W?'

'Into depression is it?'

'It's like you're walking on ice. You know it's only a matter of time before it gives way.' He stared for a long time into the cylinder of his glass, empty as a shotgun case. I reckoned the dregs of my cash and nodded to the barman to refill it one last time. 'You know damn well it's only a matter of time. You can feel the ice thinning. You can hear the groans. Then you go under. You go under, and there's no telling when you'll surface again.'

'But you have your pills. Your medication.'

'All the signs are there,' he went on, oblivious. 'Tightness. Anxiety. Panic attacks.'

One last try, I thought. 'But of course you're anxious! How would you not be anxious? Didn't you say yourself, the letter from the bank…'

'Ach, it's not that!' A hand slapped the table so hard the barman looked over. 'It's not that I tell you! It's not… specific. You understand nothing! It's inside. Inside! You're as nervous as a bag of cats. It's all the time. Never stops. It's giddiness, tickling the heart of you.' He took a deep breath. I nodded to the barman. He shook his head. No more booze. Just as well, I was all but broke.

Chester took a long last sip from his libation. 'This time, if I once slip under, there'll be no way back.' He drained the glass. 'Not this time.'

I saw again the constellation of tablets he carried about in his pockets. 'Can you not just increase the dose? More lithium?'

'I have increased the dose.' He banged the glass down on the table and glared. 'What the hell do you know about it?'

I'd lost all thought of the card, and of finding the *Chapter of Christ the Fisherman,* after that particular interview. But as Mother would drum into my skull, it's when you cease looking that you're most likely to find. I'd no sooner taken my leave of an acrimonious Maher than I quite literally stumbled over a sign on a back alley off Lower Abbey Street. A lecture was to take place. The eminent Dr Aaron Brockmann of Boston, Massachusetts. What caught my eye was the small logo to the bottom of the board: a blue fish, such as a child might draw.

I'll go in for the laugh, says I. But I can tell you, laughter was about the furthest thing from my mind. Was it the silent laughter of Fate, that fog-bound divinity, or perhaps of Mother, that I was attempting to laugh off as I climbed the rickety stairs? Abruptly, I found myself at the back of a large auditorium. There was a hum of conversation, or of anticipation. A considerable crowd, considering the place and the hour. I was just making my mind up not to bother when I was approached by a small man with round, flashing glasses and an interrogative drone that accorded well with them. 'Were you invited?'

'Not… as such. But I was asked to drop along at some point…'

'Who was it asked you? Who do you know here?'

'Is it not open to the public? Your sign…'

'Never mind the sign. I'd like, Mister, for you to tell me who, here, invited you?' At this juncture a large, bald hulk of a man in the back row pivoted about. Farther over, a bearded individual with covered head shifted about uneasily, one eye as it were on our proceedings.

'It's all right, Tom. I know that individual. He's okay.'

The minute I heard the rough bark, the hulk resolved itself into the taxi-driver. My eyes honed in on the bite mark, on the missing earlobe. *Never be afraid to pray, boss.* I shot a glance at the suspicious figure in the corner, who was wearing the hood of his anorak up. His eyes flitted instantly to the front.

The seat beside my taxi-man being vacant, I sat in beside him. 'Why the inquisition?'

'You know how it is, boss. You can't be too careful these days.'

'Careful of what?'

'The Chapter had some pretty bad write-ups in the press there last month. Totally biased it was. I needn't tell you. Very unprofessional what's more, seeing as there's a court case pending.'

'A court case?' I was out of touch with the law.

'Some young one says she was brainwashed out of thousands. A fool and her money, says you. I'll tell you about it after.'

'Then they took me for a press-hound?'

'It's like I say, boss, you can't be too careful.'

'That's funny, all the same! Because earlier on, when I tried to get into the MacMurrough Tribunal, they wouldn't let me in. D'you want to know why? Over in that place, you *had* to be a journalist to get in!' And I would've told him all about the Garda with his droll advice, but at this point, a glass chimed several times to the front of the room.

'Good afternoon, everyone.'

A plump-faced man with a great mane of white hair that fell over the glitzy suit of a car-salesman had taken the podium. 'Let me apologise for the delay in getting started. I'm afraid I've had some rather bad news.' A murmur of dismay rippled through the audience. 'It seems that Dr Brockmann's plane has been delayed. Fog in Boston.' The man's upraised hand quelled the disturbance. 'Man proposes, my friends, but it is God who disposes. At very short notice, it gives me intense pleasure to say that a young man has been inspired to talk to us. A very brave young man. We'll call him Michael.'

The man bowed, knowledgeably. He went through the motions of taking a sip of water from a glass. Pure affectation. 'For many years, Michael attended an Industrial School, here in our capital. The Christian Brothers. And it grieves me to tell you, my friends, that during all this time, when he was most in need of trust, Michael was sorely let down.' The man's face had flushed to the colour of raw beefsteak. Now, mutters of opprobrium swept over the congregation. I glanced at the beard in the corner. The man's posture had assumed such an uncomfortable aspect, you would've thought the hostility had been directed entirely at him. His eyes were shut, and he was shaking his hood slowly from side to side.

A youth still marked by gills of acne had been introduced into the auditorium and now began to fidget behind the white-haired man. We'll call him Michael. Our host put a generous arm about Michael's young shoulder, and nodded encouragement at him severally from point-blank range. But his opening syllable was a squawk. The white head nodded again, and the boy coughed twice into his agitated fingers. 'For eleven years…' he began, his voice trembling.

I soon lost interest in we'll call him Michael. What attracted my attention far more than his increasingly confident litany of abuse was the discomfort it was causing the character in the corner. I had the uncanny feeling I knew the man. At each new injustice, at every new outrage, he winced, or cowered, or his shoulders slouched lower, while always his head dropped farther and farther into an anatomy of dejection. What penance, what atonement, had compelled him to attend?

The room was abruptly seized with an aching silence. A lone person clapped. Its loneliness brought down a general applause that relieved any awkwardness. We'll call him Michael shifted from foot to foot, a parrot on a perch, until the man with the plum-coloured face stood forwards, again raised a hand, and the applause subsided. 'We thank you, Holy Spirit,' he assured the room, 'for inspiring Michael to speak to us today. He has borne witness, just as every one of us, my friends, is asked to bear witness.' Michael, an adolescent once more, nodded, blushed, nodded a second time, hovered, squirmed, blanched, nodded a third time, and was at last ushered to a free seat by an officious-looking woman.

'You came here, friends, to hear the eminent Dr Aaron Brockmann talk of the abuse systemic to the Catholic Church. The *systemic* abuse. Now, Michael gave us his personal testimony of what was, if you will, a personal abuse. Sadly, as we are

increasingly coming to learn, it was not an isolated abuse. Far
from it! But nevertheless, it depended on the depravations of
an individual. An individual who abused his position of trust…'

The shifty character had disappeared entirely into his hood.
We know that man, Soul insisted. Why is he here? What has he
done, to be here? Through his cowl he sensed that my gaze was
upon him, and he half-turned to the wall. 'I'd far rather you all
hear about the abuse of trust, not of an individual, no, but of an
institution. An abuse that Dr Brockmann has written about; an
abuse, my friends, that runs all the way from top to toe…' and so
on and so forth until an elbow nudged my ribcage. Out of the
side of his mouth, my companion muttered: 'The MacMurrough
Tribunal has nothing on this!'

A corner of my retina picked up a movement. I turned
in time to see our friend in the anorak slip furtively from the
auditorium. 'Listen,' I whispered, 'I'll catch you again,' and before
the taxi-man had the chance to draw down his astonished
eyebrows, I too had slipped out.

The anorak had made its way down towards the river.
But its owner, head now clear of the cowl, was hovering
at a street corner like someone who's received bad news. I
approached and then called out: 'I know you.' I watched his
domed head flinch, and hit upon a direction to get away
from me. 'I know you,' I repeated, and as I spoke, a name
at last attached itself to the features. 'You're Father Ciarán,
from Audoen's off of Thomas Street!' He flinched again, but
decided to turn about and face me, a brow domed like a light
bulb above a beard that greatly protracted the length of his
head. This beard was new, and gave the head the proportions
of a keyhole. It reminded me of someone famous. Who in the
hell did it remind me of?

I noticed with surprise that he'd lost considerable weight.
The cheekbones were prominent.

'You're Father Ciarán Crowe! Deny that!'

'Who are you? What do you want?'

'My mother used to know you, Father.'

This was certainly true. Mother had an intractable religious streak, even towards the end. If anything, it grew more entrenched as her delirium came on. At first Mass every Sunday morning of her life, at each Wednesday vigil or Friday novena, and at confession on the last Saturday of every month, Mother made a point of being the first to arrive at St Audoen's. And always of course with the penny catechism. We even had our own pew, to the left, three rows from the front. And when the service was ended and the altar bare, before I could leave the gloomy interior she'd drop a few bob in a slot and have me light a candle before one or other of the plaster saints. I'd watch the tiny flame cast nets of shadows over her wrinkles. I often toyed with the idea of just letting on to light it. But somehow, I knew this sacrament of hers had the power to register the candle flame through blind eyeballs.

'Your mother?' he said. My lack of guile had disarmed him.

'Moll Regan.'

He looked blankly.

'Moll Regan of the Liberties! Would be first at confession every last Saturday.'

'I'm sorry...' he shook his head.

'The blind woman.'

I watched his memory jog, and all residual suspicion fall away. 'You're her son? Willy? Ah, go on!' What, I wondered, had she said about me, in the shadowy intimacy of the confessional? And what grievous fault did she routinely accuse herself of? There was scarcely anything for her to tell that I could think of, unless tippling was a sin. And if that were the case, how many priests would stand condemned!

All at once, I was gripped by a ferocious sensation of déjà vu.

'Where are you heading now, Father?'

'Where? Back to the sacristy, I suppose.'

'Do you mind if I walk with you?'

XIII

I wonder what it was put it into my head to accompany Father Ciarán Crowe back to Audoen's that day. The Catholic Audoen's, not the medieval place down the road. Scratch at one name in this town, you're sure to unearth another beneath the paintwork. Dig, and who knows what bones will be unearthed. We live atop a charnel house.

I hadn't been next or near the place in a number of years. I'd inherited none of Mother's religious scruples. If I thought of the clergy at all, it was as a relic of a different age.

'I wonder,' said he, wearily, 'what your mother would have made of all these dreadful revelations.' The thought caught me off balance. With her nose for scandal, you might have considered she'd have revelled in them. But hers was a childish faith. It was a hangover from the simple routines of girlhood; its bedside prayers and offerings of flowers. And penny catechisms. Even in her dementia, she would never use an obscene word once she'd crossed the threshold of a church. Who was I to judge what it was all worth? 'I can tell you,' he went on, leaning on the parapet of Capel Street Bridge, 'it's tested my faith to the very quick.'

'It must be hard on all of you...' I didn't know with what word to round off the observation. Clergy? Priests? Religious? 'It is,' he said. He turned to face me, and looked at me with absolute candour. 'Do you know, I've spent two out of the last three years in John of God's?'

'Is that right!' Madness was fast becoming the theme of the day. 'I suppose I should be able to say it's Christ's way of testing me. If the physician was ever able to cure himself!' He smiled, desperately. 'Nothing is that straightforward any more, if it ever was. Do you know, when the revelations first began to seep out of Ferns, it was like a blow to the solar plexus. I was physically sickened. It was quite literally as if I was unable to breathe, for weeks on end.' The world, I mused, is visceral. Chester Maher had said so. Looking into his troubled face, I kept the thought to myself. A different thought was beginning to take shape at the back of my head.

'Almost every day,' he picked up the thread that led into the dark recesses, 'I have to ask myself is it the right thing to continue in the priesthood? Is it simply cowardice that keeps me in? I was one of the class of '64, Willy. Clonliffe College. I still have the year picture on my wall! All those fresh faces… So you could say, the priesthood is all I've ever known.' *We're all creatures of habit.* Shut up, Soul! 'Every day, the last thing at night and the first thing in the morning, I beg God for an answer. Is this what You want of me? Is this Your plan for me?' Capital 'Y'.

'Does he ever answer?' Small 'h'.

He looked deep into me. Or through me. 'I think,' he declared, despondently, 'what we're witnessing is the death of the Apostolic Church. To begin with, I was dismayed by the idea. How could God allow his Church on earth to have become so rotten, so corrupt? So corrupt that the bishops, and the archbishops above them, can put the welfare of the hierarchy before that of the very children that God entrusted to them?' He shook his head. He'd talked himself into a dark corner.

'You don't seriously believe this'll be the death of the Catholic Church? They've lived through some pretty rough patches before now.'

'Long had she dwelt in Rome when popes were bad,' he smiled. It appeared to be a quote. 'I don't know. I don't know, Willy. These days I'm not certain of anything. But one thing I can tell you. Now, the death of the Church is something that I earnestly pray for.'

'Go on!' I looked hard at the man. There was not the least intimation he was having a laugh. 'But do you mean that?'

'With all my heart. And with all my soul.' A demented gull swept past us. It might have been a soul astray. 'You're surprised to hear me say it. An ordained priest? It sounds like blasphemy to you! I grant you it does. But it seems to me, if the Gospel has one message, it's that there can be no everlasting life unless first we die. Like the grain that dies in the earth. It seems to me that the same law must hold true of the church. It must die, too, if it's to live. It's time to return to a more simple ministry. A ministry like that of the very first Christians.' He fell silent. For a while we watched the gull, tugging on its kite-strings over the Liffey's rebellious surface.

'So is that why you stay in the Church?'

'What do you mean?'

'To oversee her death?'

'I stay,' he said, after a long reflection, 'simply because I don't know where else to go. And I stay, too, because I continue to believe that there are those who need a priest. Simple people. With a simple faith. What are they to do?'

The thought that had been slowly fermenting began to assume the flavour of a proposal. Two birds with the one stone, as you might say. 'Father, can I ask you something?'

'Please do.'

'There's a friend of mine…' I began, in the way the guilty are said to. I then told the man everything I could think of about Chester Maher's predicament. I spared him neither the bizarre circumstances in which I'd found the dangling man, nor his periodic slides into depression. I even hinted he'd threatened violence, not only against himself this time, but against the estranged wife.

'And what would you have me do?'

'You might talk to him,' I said. 'I don't just mean because you're a priest. I mean… that other business. John of God's and all that. It sounds as if you'd have a better chance than yours sincerely of understanding where he's coming from.'

'It will probably be a case, then,' he smiled naively for the first time, like the peep of a sun in winter, 'of the blind leading the blind.'

'It might be just that,' I assented, laughing. 'Leave the nuts and bolts to me, Father. I can get in touch with you at the sacristy?'

'You can. Good luck to you, Willy. I remember your mother with fondness.'

'I'm not seeing any fucking priest.'

A week had gone by since the Winding Stair.

'Don't think of him as a priest. To tell you nothing but the truth, he doesn't seem to think of himself as much of a priest.' I should've remembered that as a child, if he'd ever been a child, Chester Maher had gone to a religious school. The Jesuits. He'd told me so, one sardonic day. Every spring, they used to go for a week's retreat to a religious house, somewhere in the Wicklow hills. 'Know what we used to call it?' he'd growled. 'Consecration Camp.'

He had a droll side to him, old Chester.

'So what am I meant to be seeing him for, this *priest*?'

'He'd understand better than me what you were saying to me about going through the ice.'

'What *ice*?'

'He's been in and out John of God's himself. He knows the score.'

'Suffering Jaysus! A depressive!'

I'd been peering closely at Chester Maher to see if there were any signs of his condition having worsened. I wasn't at all sure what signs I should be looking for. But in any case, I noticed little change. He was the same cantankerous bugger, eyes of flint, glower pollinated with eczema.

'What's the latest from the bank?'

'The bank, is it?' He shook his head. 'Ach, he gave me another two months, the young pup. Sure what else could he do?'

'Well that's good news.'

He held out. .

'Isn't it?'

'Oh, terrific! Don't you see me skipping about the place? And what am I to do the month after that?'

'Well Jesus, Chester! It gives you some breathing space, if nothing else.'

Some time later, as a concession: 'So tell us about your famous *priest*.'

'I wouldn't have called him that. Actually,' I went on, with a glimmer of guile, 'he was Moll Regan's priest.'

'Was he, faith?'

'He was. She'd never take confession, unless it was off of Father Ciarán.'

'I would never have taken your mother,' he sat back, 'for a spiritual woman.'

'I wouldn't have called her that either.' And I began to outline to him the discussion on Capel Street Bridge. Or more accurately, the soliloquy. He was silent, allowing my words to wash over his lobster's head, until I reached the detail of his prayer for the death of the Church. 'Did he say that?' He toppled forward and gripped the table. 'Did he say that? He never said that!'

'I'm telling you.'

'But that's unbelievable!' He was, to my eye, far more animated than a priest's apostasy should have warranted. 'But that's incredible! I… ha! Ha! Did he say that? There's a priest in *The Cuckold*…'

'The what?'

'*The Cuckold*! For Christ's sake, the play! The play! There's a priest in it. A Father Quinlan, from Ardee. He says exactly that.'

'About the death of the Church?'

'It's in the third act!' he cried, as though I doubted him.

The upshot of the disclosure was that he told me to go ahead and arrange the meeting with Father Ciarán for as soon as was convenient. He also told me to drop out to his house the following week to pick up a copy of the manuscript. An earlier draft. The most up-to-date was with an amateur dramatics company somewhere in Longford. I wondered how long it would be before it was returned, reviled, rejected.

'I'll tell you, when you drop over,' he winked, just as he was getting on his bus, 'how I got on with your famous priest.'

It's been a while since I've said anything of Yelena Zamorska. It's been a while since I've had anything to say. I'd begun to wonder, now she and her paramour had my various signatures, if I hadn't become surplus to requirements. But that was to do her an injustice.

On the following Saturday, at about eleven in the morning, I was woken by a knocking at the door. Christ God, I begged, let it be anyone but Danaher! Through the edge of the net curtain, under a sullen sky, the caller looked more like a door-to-door salesman than a small-time hood. I eased open the window hinges over Adam Rakoczi's bulbous head. We looked at, or past, or near, one another for some time without a word. My eyes wandered from receding hairline to protruding lips and back again. I shut the window with a grunt, pulled a coat roughly about my underpants, tramped down the stairs, and finally swung open the outside door. Once more, we stared closely past one another. 'You'd better come in,' I shrugged, when neither hairline nor lips deigned to move.

He sat inertly at the table while I toyed with the kettle and rummaged through the presses to conceal my annoyance. Or else it was my awkwardness I was hiding. The silence sizzled, or festered, whatever it is that silence does between two deadly rivals. What could this clown be doing here?

'Yelena's not with you, then?'

'She is down country.'

'Down the country?'

For a while I thought I'd exhausted his conversation. 'Do you know,' he asked, stirring a spoon around and around in the mug of tea I served up, without once tasting it, 'who is O'Brien?'

'O'Brien?' I pondered the heroes of the rebellion. 'Nope. I don't believe I do.'

'She is with man called O'Brien. Donnel O'Brien.'

'O'Byrne, is it?' The name snagged like a fish-hook. There was an O'Byrne, or perhaps it was an O'Brien. Suave. Expensive coat. We'd rowed about him once, when I'd seen them step out of a taxi. He was supposed to be her tutor or something.

'He's supposed to be her tutor or something?'

'No. Is not her tutor.' He stirred and stirred the tea. 'I think is barrister.'

'Well, well.'

'Yelena has gone with this man for weekend to Athlone.'

A flashy man with a flash coat and flashy russet hair.

'Athlone?'

'I think he have riverboat in Athlone.'

He would have! 'So they're gone beyond the Pale for a dirty weekend!' I snorted, sitting heavily opposite his glasses.

'What means Pale?'

'The Pale? The Pale was a ditch they dug around Dublin in the old days. It was to keep out the vermin who lived on in places like Athlone.' He was still caressing the milky tea with his spoon, urging it into slow eddies, absorbed as a schoolboy. It was harder now to think of him as a rival. 'Do you know what signifies my country?' he questioned the tiny whirlpools. 'It means, at the edge.'

'Russia means at the edge?'

'Not Russia. Ukraine.'

'At the edge of what?'

'At the edge of world. In the old days it was western edge, but now it is eastern edge.'

'That'll all change,' I idled, 'once you've joined the EU.' So she was with O'Byrne was she? 'No,' he said, as though he'd heard. He withdrew the spoon and tapped it nine or ten times on the rim of the mug. 'No. We do not join. Poland, where is from Yelena, she will join. But not Ukraine.'

'Why not Ukraine?'

'Is too big. Is too foreign.' He laid the teaspoon carefully on the saucer. 'Always, there must be edge to the world. You will see.' Was he a melancholic by humour or was it the topic that was causing his melancholia? The lugubrious lips scarcely opened as he spoke.

'So how exactly do you know Yelena? UCD?'

He looked at me with a new frankness. His brow was a ploughed field of furrows. But they were not frowns. 'I meet her in Krakovia at seminar. Then I translate her poetry for journal.'

'Into Russian?'

'Into Ukrainian. Is different. It even have different letter. Everyone think we are the same as Russian! Always Russian! When I tell them in customs I am born in Sebastapol, on Black Sea, they say me, then you are Russian.'

The Black Sea! It meant nothing to my postbox geography of 'Dublin' and 'All Other Places'. At a pinch I could have told him where he'd find the Galtee Mountains, or the three sisters, or in which four towns they'd raised their strategic sugar mills. But when he mentioned the Black Sea, he might as well have been talking of the geography of the moon. I shrugged my shoulders. 'But there are many Irish buried there!' he exclaimed, as if the detail would throw light on the subject. 'They die in Crimean War. It was after Famine, and many Irish join army to escape hunger.'

The Crimean War! He'd hit on another lacuna. Well, let it remain so. 'So then you're a poet as well as a Yeats expert?'

'No. I'm not poet. Yelena, she is poet.' He picked up the spoon and began again to circulate the tea. 'You say poetess, yes?'

'And so our poetess has run down to Athlone to write couplets with her *barrister*,' I guffawed. He grimaced, and his mouth listed into a leer. I hadn't realised what queer fellowship there is in misery. 'Tell me, is it O'Byrne or O'Brien?'

'I think his name is Donnel O'Beirn.'

'Dónal. And tell me this, have you ever met the man? Has she... Yelena, has she introduced you to this Dónal O'Byrne?' This question was not prompted by a suspicion that the pair of them might also be chasing O'Byrne's signature. If he was a barrister he'd have no shortage of money. That happy thought only came to me after Rakoczi had left. The question hadn't been prompted by anything so noble as suspicion. It was driven by a perverse impulse to see if my companion in misery would flinch. But the crooked grin held fast. 'No. I have not meet him. I saw him once getting into taxi.'

'Did you! And I saw him once getting *out of* a taxi! Maybe the same damn taxi! Ha ha!' The canoe grin tilted, the prow tipped into an eye, and then started a slow capsize. 'Maybe same damn taxi!' he laughed, mechanically. For a while he sat still, and it was only when he began to fidget with the spoon, and I feared he'd start to rotate the damned tea again, that I broached the obvious. In pace with the sky outside, my mood darkened. 'What's brought you out here, Rakoczi? It was hardly to chat to me about the Crimean War.'

He looked up from the spoon and his furrows deepened. This time they presaged intelligent comment. 'No. Is not about this.' He drew an envelope very slowly from his breast. 'There is,' he said, and he pointed to a figure, 'so much now in your account.'

I can't for the life of me remember the tally exactly. But it ran to five figures. I raised my eyebrows and shook my head. He might as well have shown me the national debt.

'I come here because we need more signature.'

I stood up. 'Would you ever stop that nonsense!' I walked over to the net curtain, and peered at the dome outside. Whatever I'd signed away in the mortuary chapel, I'd signed it away on the spur of the moment. I'd signed because Yelena had been there, goading me. Teasing my manhood with a smirk.

Today I balked. It's not that I was particularly worried about the implications of another bloody signature. There wasn't a penny of my own in any of the accounts for anyone to steal. But I was damned if I was going to give this character a signature in her imperial absence. 'Go on with you! I've signed enough papers already.'

'But is just formality. We must move this money out very fast.' He pulled out a second form. 'And this one. It need signature to say them you are resident here.'

'I don't read your Russian.' I had a desire to be shot of the man. He'd reawakened in me the sour suspicion that, all along, her majesty had been using me.

'No. Is in English. Is declaration of…'

'Listen, I'm not signing anything more, d'you hear me? I've signed enough of your damned papers already.'

'But is formality. It mean you don't must pay tax.'

'For your information, I don't must pay tax as it is. I'm living off the dole, or hadn't you noticed? Hadn't your Polish friend explained *that* to you?'

He did not appear to be in the least surprised at my vehemence. He sat at the table, not one whit put out by the turn of events. I glared at the back of his head. I don't know how it is that we come to form opinions of ourselves. Through the eyes of close friends, I expect. But I'd never had intimates. And none so blind as a mother's loving eyes. As I stared at the back of Adam Rakoczi's balding pate, a deep feeling of revulsion surged up in me. It was not aimed at him, precisely.

In fact, when I think back, what I felt in his regard was closer to indignation. I was angry at the indignities he endured through Yelena's carry on. That was it! I was angry that he was so spineless in the face of it all. You see a cowering dog, and you are impelled to lash out at it. All at once, I saw my own entanglement for the sordid mess that it always had been: I was one more fool with a lopsided grin capering about the Polish court.

And I made up my mind to be shot of her! In one second it was decided. Will Regan had made up his mind to be shot of her.

'Come on, Rakoczi, you're leaving. I've things to do.' I'd already picked up his coat and found I was holding it open for him. He might as well have not heard me for all the movement he made towards it. 'Come on, you're going.'

'But the papers? Yelena rang me yesterday to say…'

'Leave your precious papers on the table.'

'And then you will sign it?'

'Never mind whether I'll sign it! I'll take my own sweet time about it if I do sign it. When did you say Yelena was coming back?'

'She doesn't say. I think Monday.'

'Well you can tell Yelena, when you see her on Monday or on Tuesday or whatever damn day you do see her, that she can bloody well get in touch with me herself if she wants me to sign any more papers. I don't talk to footmen.'

He bandied a look at me as he left which I will never forget. It's hard to capture in words the craft of it. The lips had turned through a part rotation clockwise, and the forehead tilted forwards several fractions. He lingered thus in the doorframe. I know you, these inclinations declared. And I know this act and bluster. And most of all, I know we both know that when push comes to shove, you're not one jot better than I am.

There'd been no difficulty in arranging a meeting between Chester Maher and Fr Ciarán Crowe. In fact, the interview was taking place even as I was entertaining Rakoczi. When Tuesday came around I was keen to hear how they'd got on. I was doubly keen not to be in the flat that morning, on the off chance Yelena Zamorska called. *And I made up my mind to be shot of her.* I was living off the fumes of that giddy idea.

With an abundance of time on my hands, I caught a bus as far as Declan's on the Navan Road, and then struck out on foot for the terrace off the Old Cabra Road. It was a walk filled with joyous declarations. I'll split up with that scarlet hussy so I will, I shouted in strident silence to my soul. I'll tell her I've had it up to here with her whims and liaisons and her *this cannot be relationship*. She can go and take a hike for all I care. *And as for that lap dog, Rakoczi!* Soul laughed back to me. *We'll soon see what difference there is between man and mouse.* Soul was having trouble fixing on a precise animal.

I rapped at the door several times, allowed a minute to pass, rapped again, waited again, and was on the point of withdrawing. The house had a moribund look about it. But the barest flicker at the edge of the living room curtain betrayed a presence inside. I gestured and grinned. 'Chester!' I mouthed. The curtain abruptly twitched back into place.

Another minute dragged by. Once again I weighed the disadvantages of leaving. This time it was a rattle and scratch that detained me, and at long last the door eased open several inches, until it snagged on a chain. The eyeball that appeared behind it was dirty and unwelcoming. 'Chester! You remember I was to come out today?' The eyeball sustained a sullen vigil, the dull orb unrelieved by recognition. 'It's me, for God's sake! Will Regan! You said to come out to you on Tuesday…' The door snapped shut, but before I'd quite made up my mind whether to beat a retreat or beat at its panels with open palm, it groaned ajar. Chester Maher, in ungirdled dressing gown, shuffled down the hallway and into the dim cave of the living room.

'You do remember I was to come out, Chester?'

My host flopped into a tetchy armchair. He was neither observing nor ignoring me, and I was unsure whether to advance beyond the door. The smell of stale air was overwhelming; the furniture as listless and dishevelled as its owner. The face that I'd seen so often aflame with indignation had collapsed into fags and ashes.

'You weren't expecting me, I take it.' He snorted, or I had the impression he did. A spring in the armchair misfired. My eyes ran over his dressing gown and up to his stubble. 'Have you had breakfast?' Nothing. 'Will I wet a pot of tea?'

I took his inertia for assent, and made my way into the kitchenette.

Already, from the hallway, I could see all the symptoms of apathy scattered about the place: open cupboards; unwashed dishes; packets on their side. So this is what happens when the ice finally gives way. As I pushed through the doorway, I felt something light bob against my hip. It was the Hallowe'en apple, shrivelled to lurid sweetness. Tiny brown mouths were agape where the coins had been driven in.

The bin hadn't been emptied in the weeks since that broken appointment. In its throat were lodged a mask, a witch's hat, a dried barmbrack. Would all this drama be happening if it weren't for Stephanie Maher's antics? Should I try to track her down? But maybe that'd be the worst thing I could do. Judging from the mess of the place, Chester Maher was in no state to receive his daughter.

I looked at the table, at the evidence of unwashed dishes. Three days, at the least. I calculated that he'd slipped under on Saturday night or Sunday morning. I change to 'It'd'll do no harm at all to have a word with Father Ciarán to see if he kept faith with that appointment. *And while you're about it,* whispered Soul *ask his advice about the little girl.*

I returned to the twilight living room with two over-brimming mugs and a much better idea of what to expect. I was surprised to find he'd vacated the armchair. Instead, he was hovering by some random bookshelves, doing his best to hum a tune. He looked at the mugs that I set on the coffee table, and then he looked at me. Something in his aspect declared he was fomenting a thought.

'It's the concentration,' he said at last. 'I've no… there's no… *ability* to concentrate.' He shook his head. 'The axle spins,' and after an unfeasible gap, 'but there's no teeth left on the gear wheel.'

I'm not sure how long I spent there. The mugs were both cold before I left, that much I do know. But it wasn't an entirely wasted trip. For one thing, I came upon the typescript of his play. His opera without music. I held it up, and received his tacit assent to carry it away with me.

But dearer still, when I got back to the flat there was a little note folded up like a butterfly stuck into the jamb of the door. It declared that Yelena had dropped by. She'd forgotten her new key. She was most disappointed to find me not in.

XIV

*M*iniature victories of a subject people! Their insurrections leave no more trace than a folk song's refrain. *And I made up my mind to be shot of her.*

I determined not to be in on the next day either. But I could think of no pretext with which to fill out the hours. After a lot of restlessness I hit upon a trip to the sacristy of St Audoen's to see if Father Ciarán was in.

He wasn't.

Perhaps her weekend beyond the Pale had served to rejuvenate her. Perhaps it was that, in my mind's eye, my darling's hair and complexion had been painted as shabby as her comportment. In any event, the scarlet woman that called out from the window of a taxi was a damn sight more elegant than my new resolution would have wished.

'I've been looking all over for you, Mister!'

'Really.'

'It's true! Will you be at home this evening if I call?'

'What time?'

'I don't know what time, stupid. This evening!' The lights changed, and the taxi whisked her away.

Would I be at home this evening if she called? It was a difficult one. *Where would you go, to pass the time?* scoffed Soul. Soul, for want of a better word. *I told you, you should never have dropped out of life drawing*, it jeered. Don't be so smug, I answered, it was your dented vanity that kept me from re-enrolling in the first place.

But you can be in this evening, I reasoned later on, in the queue at the local SPAR. And when she calls round, you can let her know you've no intention of letting her in. Leave the door chained in case she remembers her key! *Better again, let her in*, trumped Soul. *But treat her with absolute coldness. She has to know you're not afraid to meet her.* Very good, and maybe I'll even pour her a glass of vino? Pour everyone a glass, what about that? We should be able to do this like adults.

I left the queue, placed a claret in the basket, rejoined at the tail.

This is not working, Yelena. I'm not saying I blame you. Not in so many words. But it's become painfully obvious, to both of us, that whatever it is you may think you feel for me, is… is what? Inadequate? Is inadequate. In what way inadequate, Willy? Humiliatingly so. Insultingly so. And therefore? And therefore I think it's better if we don't see each other any more. But my God, Willy, surely another chance…

'That's twenty-two forty, Mister.'

'Of course. Sorry.'

By the time I was setting down the bag of groceries beside the kitchen sink, the bottle of wine had expanded into a meal. A last supper. By God, I laughed, we'll show her royal highness there's more to Will Regan than one more simpering fool with a crooked leer. By God, we'll teach her to regret the… the *what*? The disdain, yes, disdain, that's the word. We'll teach her to regret the disdain with which she's tramped all over us.

It hardly needs to be said that she never called. All that night, a casserole simmered on the stovetop. I went to bed at one in the morning without any stomach to try it.

Father Ciarán was in when I called to Audoen's the following morning. He could only spare ten brief minutes. There was a funeral for a deceased colleague he was to concelebrate in some other parish. He served up two insipid coffees out of a huge catering vat.

'Your friend came, in the end. I have to say he was very late. I'd all but given up on him.'

Chester, unpunctual? Ha! 'He's not exactly having an easy time of it, Father.'

'No. I get the impression he's not.'

'As if things weren't bad enough as it is, the banks are threatening to repossess.'

'Surely,' the wise forehead frowned, 'he can get some sort of a stay of…?'

'Of execution? I don't know about that. From what I can make out, he's broke as a joke.'

The man remained reticent. Years of the confessional, no doubt. We both began to wonder why exactly I'd come. 'I understand he's written a play,' he tried, eyebrows raised. Damn it, he reminded me of someone! 'He has! That's to say, I haven't read it. I only got hold of the manuscript the day before yesterday. But I intend to read it. It's, eh… it's an autobiography. In part. At least, so I believe.' He was stoically resisting looking at his watch. 'In verse. So, how did you find him, Father?'

'In what way?'

'Only when I went out to his place there on Tuesday, it was as if someone had pulled the plug on him. Didn't react to a single thing I said or did.'

'I was very much afraid that might happen. When he was here with me on Sunday, it was the other extreme. Then there was nothing he couldn't do! He was all the time laughing. Making sly jokes about a Father Quinlan. Said we'd get along famously! He even offered to introduce me to the man.'

'But for God's sake! Father Quinlan is a character in his head.'

'In his head?'

'I meant to say in his play.' This was true. We both smiled at the slip.

'He takes his writing that seriously?'

'Oh God he does.'

'Tell me, has he anyone to look in on him?'

'No one I'm aware of. There's a wife, but sure she's half the trouble!' I decided on the spot to hold my fire in regard to the girl.

'Neighbours?'

'I get the impression the neighbours all think he's soft in the head.'

'And tell me, do you think there might be any thoughts of self-harm?'

Thoughts of self-harm? Was he having a laugh? Did he have a spare couple of hours? 'Listen, Father, if I'm detaining you...'

He had me promise, before he hurried away, that I'd get in touch with him immediately there was any change in Maher's condition. What he had in mind wasn't a change for the better.

The cold casserole squatted like an accusation on the stovetop. I'll say one thing for Yeats, he knew all about how a bird can fill your days with misery! Fuck her, I declared. Fuck her anyway! I was past hungry. It was about three o'clock, and I'd had nothing all day except the industrial coffee at the sacristy. I dug into the pot with a dessertspoon without bothering to reheat the contents, or even to skim off the scabs of grease. To complement the main, I tossed off wine in sour gulps out of a teacup. Then the scrape and rattle of a key at the inner door set me onto my feet with such haste that my thigh hit the handle of the pot. I watched it spin and bevel before it tipped over the table edge, bounced once on the floor, and then vomited stew across the kitchen tiles. 'Well fuck it five times anyway!'

'That's a charming greeting, Irishman! Where do you learn this?'

'From my mother,' I glowered. I was already down on all fours and streaking the gravy across the floor with the first dishcloth to hand.

I won't linger over the episode. Its dignity is self-evident. I wanted only for her to leave immediately, so that I could kick the pot across the room and then bludgeon myself unconscious with the half-empty wine bottle. Half-empty, not half-full. The price agreed to have her comply was that I'd go to a film with her later on that same evening. *That'll be your big chance,* Soul whispered, even before the door clicked shut. *That'll be the big chance to tell her exactly what you think of her. Don't say anything until after the film. Then suggest a drink or two. Gin and bitters. And then, goodnight Vienna!*

Some time after she'd gone I straightened up the place, showered, shaved, laid out my cleanest clothes, and even began to sing. I showed up twenty minutes early for our appointment. So I tossed off a double Cork Dry and tonic, slimline, to the memory of Mother and the dead generations.

Yelena was late. Okay. Nothing new there. But she'd put considerably less effort into her appearance. Still, she looked good enough to bring a heroic poignancy to the imminent parting scene. We'd have to scramble to make the cinema, and I downed a second Cork Dry with a flourish. All the while we ran, I felt its delicious flush in my complexion. We sank into two seats near the back.

But the film had barely begun when a light inside my pocket began to bicker and vibrate. I reacted as calmly as if it had been a venomous insect. I'd forgotten entirely about the mobile phone, and the possibility it might erupt at any minute. Surrounded by mutters and tut-tuts, I pulled it out, winced at Yelena, and pressed as many combinations of keys as I could find. One of them killed the jingle. Yelena frowned and dug a playful elbow into my side, and I slipped the animal back into my pocket. I sat back. The next thing, to my intense dismay, the beast sprang back to life! I was assaulted by curses, hisses and coughs, and from the back of the salon an usherette's torch swept like a lighthouse across the row. 'I'd better slip out for a minute,' I whispered, still struggling with the quibbling creature. But of course it had died for a second time before I'd run the gamut of knees and made the exit.

For several minutes I stood out in the hall, staring at the lifeless screen. I wasn't sure whether or not I wanted it to ring again. But I was aware of the cashier's ironic eyes, and they made me feel a prize tool. Then, for a third time, it erupted into melody. This time I hit immediately upon the right key.

'Don't you bucking hang up on me, pal!'

'Danger! I didn't. The phone did. Listen, I'm at a...'

'Don't you bucking hang up on me, d'you hear me? I swear to you, Regan...'

'What do you want, Danger?'

'What do I *want*? I want you to listen, carefully. Don't say anything, right? Just listen.' I just listened. 'I need you to get you-know-what out to me. Tonight.'

'But I don't know where you...'

'Shut up and listen. Take two buses. Don't take a taxi. Make sure when you're leaving your gaff that there's no one following you, right? The second bus you've to get is for Finglas West. You got that? Finglas West. Again you're on that bus, I'll have texted you the address. Now, as soon as ever you read that text, you wipe it the hell off your phone. Do you hear me, Regan? If you leave now...'

'I can't leave now.'

Pause.

'What did you say to me?'

'I said, I can't leave now. I'm in town.'

'In *town*?'

Pause.

'Well get your fat arse back to your flat, d'you hear me? I can't bucking risk sitting in the da's gaff a minute longer! I seen one of the cunts watching...' The voice broke off. He hadn't intended to let slip he was staying with the demented father.

'Danger? You there?'

Pause. I could hear the gears whirring under his baseball cap. 'You just get your fat arse home, Regan. Right this minute, d'you hear? And you get you know what out to me, right this bucking minute.' The phone clicked off and would not be resurrected.

By Jesus, Danaher, you've bothered me for the last time! I'll get you your famous holdall, and good riddance to it and to you.

I was surprised to find Yelena had followed me out of the cinema. 'You were gone a long time! You miss most important scene.'

'Yeah?' I waved the offending instrument. What scene was I about to step into? That's what I wanted to know.

'You never tell me you have a phone, Willy!'

'I wish the hell I didn't have a phone. Listen, Yelena, something's come up. I've got to run.'

'Okay, mister man. I see you maybe tomorrow.' She took me by the lapels and added coyly, 'but if I find is other woman, I strangle you.' Then she kissed me, lush and lingering.

The upper saloon of the Finglas bus was overgrown with brambles of graffiti, and the seats reeked of unlawful tobacco. To an inner-city mind that had barely strayed beyond the canals, it might have been heading into the Wild West, where ponies wandered unkempt reservations. What had Rakoczi's term been for the edge of the world?

It was already long past dark. Light beads of orange rain whipped across the windscreen. I'd be doing very well indeed to make the last bus home. But the edge was taken off any apprehension I felt by two considerations. Number one, I was ridding myself of the holdall, and with it any hold that Danaher had on me. He'd said himself he was skipping the country. Too risky, bro. Never again would his cheap cologne stink up the flat. And number two, I was giddy as a goat with the kiss Yelena had planted. All through the bus ride, Soul fondled the sad words we'd use at our imminent departure. 'Each man kills the thing he loves', isn't that what Chester had said? Because Mr William Regan was to make a clean sweep of things, at last. And Soul was intoxicated by the catastrophe we were rushing towards. I all but missed the stop.

There were few sinners out and about on account of the drizzle. I got directions from a couple, scarcely into their teenage years, who were devouring one another in the bus shelter opposite. The secrecy of bad weather must have been a boon to them. The journey then took me across an open green, mottled with old bonfires, past a deserted chipper, and down a concrete laneway that even the intensifying rain could not purge of its urinal stink. Two more left turns and I would at last be shot of Danaher.

I was halted by an intimation of danger. It slipped past my senses and sounded the alarm bell. Even now I can vouch for this much: my heart had begun to skip and caper before ever I made that last turn. I remember clearly I'd tightened the grip on the bag even as I lowered my head and picked up my pace.

Was I being forewarned? Was Fate, or Mother, sounding the scary mood music? Or was it that, unregistered, some reflective windowpane had flickered an intermittent alarm in blues and oranges? Whatever the physics of it, I crossed to the far footpath, and I sped past the lane on which Danger was staying.

I gave it the barest of glances. Hazard lights on assorted emergency vehicles were flashing their Morse into the nervous night rain.

By the following afternoon it was all over the city papers. I bought a late edition from a one-eyed immigrant at the lights on Charlemont Bridge. *Firebombing in North Dublin Feud.*

Back in the anonymity of the flat, I examined the grainy photo of a terraced house, its windows gouged and blackened. Some hand, it was hard to believe it was Russian, had daubed the walls with the lowest of all slurs: 'Grass' and 'Tout'.

At about ten o'clock last night, a number of masked men armed with petrol-bombs descended on the Finglas house. Witnesses speak of hearing a man's voice pleading with them that his father, who it seems suffers from Alzheimer's, was upstairs. He then ran back inside and slammed the front door on the masked men. Windows were heard to smash and, almost immediately, several motorbikes raced away into the night.

Seconds later, the man, who is 'known to the police', but whose name is at present being withheld, emerged from the doorway. A woman living opposite described the scene: 'His arms was flapping about like a lunatic's. He kept on screaming and racing about the place, bouncing off the walls of the garden. It was like watching a human torch. I left the window to call my husband, and the next I saw he was rolling about on the ground with most of the flames out.' The man was later rushed to the Serious Burns Unit of the Mater Hospital.

Hospital staff report that the man, who suffered burns to his face, chest and hands, is in an artificially induced coma. His injuries are not thought to be life-threatening. The man's father was released suffering only the effects of smoke inhalation. A Garda spokesman said it was too early to speculate on the motive for the attack.

I read the article through for the hundredth time.

I laid it out on the table, and then, in convulsive relief, I vomited across it.

PART THREE

XV

*O*ver half a lifetime, (supposing I am midway along life's path), I've come across any number of dark recesses in this city. Never mind the Liberties. Mother's candle guttered out in the lock-up ward of a madhouse, where inmates chomped their gums and chattered in some vague twilight of the mind. My own stint in the 'Joy was scarcely more merry. But nothing, nothing on this wide earth, could have prepared me for the horrors of the Serious Burns Unit of the Mater Hospital.

In particular, third-degree burns are a torture whose refinements I wouldn't wish on my worst enemy. A Filipino nurse explained the niceties as he accompanied me down ether-filled corridors to where Danaher lay mummified. In murder, as I'd come to learn, the nastiest degree is the first. It was natural to think the rule would hold for burns. Not so. It turns out the first-degree are the most superficial scars. What counts is the number of layers of skin that have been charred and flayed.

'Your friend has suffered such burns to thirty-five percent of his body.' To calm the jitters that had seized hold of me from the moment I'd crossed the portico of the Mater, I tried to imagine the figure, and how they calculated it. As I'd shortly see, the other sixty-five percent of him was no great shakes either. 'I wouldn't try to talk to Mr Danaher,' continued the nurse, grimly smiling. 'It would distress him.' Jaysus, he wouldn't be the only one distressed! 'You can go in, but don't be too close. In his condition there's a constant risk of infection.'

'You know,' chirped my cowardice merrily, 'I don't think I'll go in at all. Maybe I'll just stand at the doorway. I'll just nod to him like.' Ahead of us, a cotton-wool mannequin, female, in loose gown and slippers, appeared momentarily. She ducked clumsily inside a doorway as we approached, shy as a monster.

Christ, what a place!

'Is Joe Danaher in a lot of pain?' I slowed our pace to allow my guide the room to be expansive. He took to the suggestion with all the enthusiasm of a frustrated poet. In a voice that struck a fine balance between grimness and contentment, he began to divulge the exquisite torments of the Serious Burns Unit. 'I say nothing of the disfigurements that follow,' he grimaced, motioning to the gap where the mannequin had disappeared. 'That's a matter for the psychiatrists.' On raised fingers he began to tally the torments. 'To begin with, there's a shower. But this shower is so painful, it transforms all morphine into water. It's considered a great mercy to pass out under the nozzle.' He shook his head. 'And this shower's a mere curtain-raiser,' he moved to the middle finger, 'to the treatment to follow.' He paused. For effect, as they say. 'This they call debridement. Debridement,' he grimaced, with something approaching humour, 'is a curious word, to say the least. Would you agree? Debridement is exfoliation.' His fingers mimed how the victim is scrubbed down, to render away the dead rags of skin, layer after layer. 'But it's an exfoliation so agonizing it can only be performed under general anaesthetic. Maggots,' proposed his gallows grin, 'will do this job one day. They're so much more hygienic.'

'Maggots?' said I, stopping.

'Maggots.'

'Good God!'

We resumed our walk. 'Finally,' this on the ring finger, 'the patient, newly flayed, must be swathed in sterile gauze. But in this embrace, the perpetual pressure, however gentle, is more than most patients can bear. And to cap it all,' he tapped all three fingers and set to shaking his head triumphantly, 'the entire treatment is repeated every other day.'

My testicles by this juncture were at the base of my throat. Lord God above, Danger, what did you do to them to deserve such punishment?

Danger was in no position to answer, even if I'd given breath to the question. I watched mutely from the corridor. He was swaddled in bandages, far more than one would've thought the figure of thirty-five percent would warrant. He lay propped into a great stack of pillows. Two clumsily mittened hands dangled from wires, for all the world as though a puppet-master might at any moment animate the creature. The jaw was held fast by some manner of sling. Only the eyes were free to move. 'I'll leave you alone with him,' whispered my guide. In anguish, in dismay, I watched his diminutive figure recede down the corridor.

Mother, before her eclipse, had middling eyesight. I had thought I'd inherited the faculty. But now, as I watched the Filipino gaoler diminish, I had cause for doubt. Somewhere beyond him, a trolley laden with a bizarre human contortion trundled between doorways. The patient was sniffing at his own upraised arm! I rubbed my eyes. A trick of the distance conjured a trunk of flesh that tethered armpit to nose. But before I'd time to make certain of the vision, the trolley disappeared. Good Christ, what class of a freak show have they walled up inside this asylum?

Every square inch of my skin was pickled with goose bumps. It was in the grip of the horrors that I edged inside the ward. 'I, eh, I heard all about it on the news, Danger!' I called after a minute, when he hadn't spontaneously looked towards the door. Two ferocious eyes were instantly riveted upon me. 'So how are they treating you?'

His head motioned, the barest flick, demanding that I enter properly. An animal sound emanated from between the tightly clamped lips. The mouth had, as it seemed, been smeared liberally with axle grease. In fact the entire face was blurred under some kind of a gel. It was out of focus, as you might say. I took a few timid steps towards the cot. 'I was told I couldn't even come in, Danger,' I lied. 'Infection. You know how it is.'

I hadn't thought that eyes could have such power of expression in them. A nuance about the eyelids ratcheted up their intensity. Without allowing the wattage to diminish, they declared: 'I've something deadly serious to say to you, Regan. And no one else is to hear so much as a word of it, right?' So clear was this message that I actually looked about the ward, to be sure there wasn't a Garda lurking behind the curtains or under a bed.

He motioned, again with the subtlest of flicks, that I should place my ear next to his greased lips. I knelt beside the bed. I had to be careful not to get entangled in the wires that sustained his paws. Perhaps it was because his jaw was held in a sling, perhaps a result of scarring; in any event, when at last he spoke, his speech had the trick of a ventriloquist's dummy.

'The gag,' he muttered.

'What gag?'

'Get the gag the hell out of your gaff.'

'Oh, the bag!' I nodded, myself a puppet. 'I will, Danger.'

'And don't oaken it, to have a gawk inside. You do,' he paused for a moment, eyes shut, 'and I'll guckin' fix you so I will.'

'I won't, Danger. But where,' I wondered, shifting from one knee to the other, 'where is it you want me to put the bag?'

'Canal,' he panted. The nurse had explained his lungs had been scarred by the smoke. It was a great effort for him to speak. 'Cut stones in it, then guck it in the canal.'

'Right,' I said. 'I will.' I stood up. 'I'll do that!' He had sunk further into the pillows, and his eyes were shut fast. And how exactly do you want me to gut stones into it, Mr Einstein, if I'm not allowed to open the damned thing?

I turned only once as I stepped outside the chamber of horrors. 'There's nothing I can get you from the shop?'

He didn't answer. If he'd asked for twenty Caddles, I'd have been stumped.

There was no need at all for Joseph Mary Danaher to have concerned himself about his precious holdall. To understand why, we need to go back several days, several pages. Back to the night of the conflagration.

I'd hurried past the laneway of squabbling lights where his father lived, with head down and cargo clutched tightly to my chest. At every moment, I expected the black glove of a Garda on my shoulder. All I knew was that the authorities had surrounded his place, and that the bag was infected. So I tilted into the oblique rain, street lamp to street lamp, bus shelter to bus shelter, open space to open space. I pushed past feral ponies and the skeletons of burned, out cars. I walked until I was lost, shivering, soaked to the skin. When finally my motion stopped, the straps of the holdall had dug so relentlessly into my wrists that for minutes after I set it down my hands throbbed like lifeless things.

I looked over the deserted city, smouldering under a sky of iodine. Nearby, a humpbacked bridge cowered over a canal. It could only be the Royal. To follow it eastwards would lead inexorably passed Mountjoy and the North Circular Road, and then on to the Liffey. So I knew where I was.

The next thing was to know what to do. But this had me stumped entirely. For a while, staring into the stagnant water, it crossed my mind I should drown the bloody bag and be done with it. There's irony for you! With the gin and bitters earlier on, I'd all but put an end to one liaison. Damn it, I was on a roll! Surely the guards couldn't cheat me out of ending another? There was a heavy item in the holdall, an iron of some kind that persistently found the bag's bottom and would surely sink it. I swung my arm back. But I was too scared to do it. Months before, by a bridge on the other canal, I'd saved Danaher from a beating. But here and now my gut was in mortal fear the spirit of that man would rise out of these black waters to accuse me. Even if he were remanded in custody until convicted, say six months down the line, who knew what confederates might call on me one night, demanding that I deliver up what had never been mine?

But neither did I have the least appetite to return the bag's contamination to my flat. I'd connected neither the blue flashes to the fire brigade, nor the fire brigade to the faint spoor of smoke, nor the faint spoor of smoke to Danaher's father's address. I thought only that he'd been spectacularly arrested. It followed that, outside my place, there would already be a detachment of the Special Branch, warrants in hand. Even if the holdall was innocent, which I very much doubted, Danaher had killed that old woman. In an unguarded moment he'd told me as much. That alone made me an accomplice. With the evidence I was hauling through the streets like the afterbirth of a crime, it'd be impossible to deny that I knew the man.

Irresolution gripped me. So I walked on. At great length, I caught sight of the spire of St Peter's in Phibsboro. At that instant, with a snap of the fingers, I hit upon the rough expedient of Maher's place. I could neither drown the bloody animal nor bring it home. Far safer to bury the evidence at the back of a garden shed to the north of the river. I could always retrieve it if and when it was demanded. And in the state he was in, Chester was hardly likely to drag out the seven-inch reflector before I figured out my next move.

Everything in the vicinity of the Old Cabra Road was dead to the world. Everything but an ancient mongrel whose unconvinced bark was a car ignition that continually failed to engage. It idled into first gear only as I trundled over the wall and dropped into Maher's back yard. It then died with a yelp to the echo of a bottle breaking.

Of course I landed awkwardly, twisting my ankle. Destiny will have its little laugh! It was a full minute before I recovered the holdall and hobbled to the shed where the telescope was kennelled. I stopped short of it, and examined the peering windows to the far side of the street. But they were as blind as Mother.

In a trice I hobbled the remaining few steps. A moment later I dropped the bag and banged my forehead against the wood in dismay and rage. It was padlocked! Of course it was padlocked! Naturally it was padlocked! What class of fool are you, Will Regan? How could you not have realised it would be padlocked? Hadn't Maher himself told me he'd been broken into umpteen times? Hadn't he once found a junkie lying unconscious in his back yard with neither shirt nor shoes, the syringe still dangling like a parasite from his arm? I did further violence to my forehead with open palm as Soul laughed at my folly. Was it likely such a man would leave his hobbyhorse untethered?

I limped to the back window. This wasn't with any particular plan in mind. It was simply because I couldn't face the long march home at that moment. The long hobble home. Certainly not with the holdall, to which the faint reek of sweat and deodorant still clung. My mind vacant and fuming, I peered inside. But I could see nothing but abandonment, and that desolate sadness peculiar to deserted furniture. Christ, nothing for it, then! My eyes were so close to tears that I stumbled on turning, and grabbed onto the rear door handle.

It gave.

As I righted myself, it swung gloriously inwards. I tried it again, to be sure. Swollen ankle or no swollen ankle, it took me five seconds flat to recover the bag from where I'd dropped it, and to smuggle it into Maher's utility room, to the back of the kitchen. It took considerably longer to find a refuge wherein to conceal its bulk.

At last I manoeuvred the recalcitrant beast behind assorted buckets, staves, mops and rags in what must have been a broom cupboard. That done, I sneaked painfully out, eased the door shut, limped to the fence, hauled myself up, dropped in sweet agony onto the other pavement, and then hobbled in enormous discomfort through the dregs of the night all the way to Portobello, and to daybreak.

When I woke the following evening there was something moving about in the adjoining room. The fragments of the previous night came to me with the demolishing urgency of a bad dream. The arrest. The flashing lights. The feral ponies. The bridge. The cache in the closet and the barking mongrel.

But it was no dream. A sharp throb from my ankle confirmed the reality of these images. And now they were in the flat! They were ransacking the kitchen! I lay, still as a corpse. Maybe they haven't seen you! But that's too fantastic. Then deny everything! I'll deny everything. I'll deny I even know the man…

I levered myself in silence to the edge of the bed. I found I was still dressed. Would I be able to maybe sneak out? I reached a tiptoe to the ground. I barely breathed.

Cups could be heard clattering, and an insistent discharge of water from the tap. I flopped back onto the bed and exhaled.

'You were dead to the world, Mister.'

'How long've you been here?'

'Maybe for one hour.'

Yelena Zamorska followed her voice into the doorway. I tried to hoist myself, but my head, muzzy, dropped back towards the pillows, leading my entire body to subside. An arm jack-knifed over my eyes with the momentum of the fall.

'So I hope she was worth it.'

'Who?'

'The lady friend you abandon me to see.'

'Very funny.'

The smell of coffee and toast prised the arm from my eyes and I pivoted slowly onto my elbows. Yelena had set a tray by the bed, and now stood silhouetted against the seductive city dusk, her back to me. *Don't falter,* whispered Soul. Don't fall. *You've got rid of Danaher. Now see this whole damned thing through.* This must be the moment.

I tore into the toast, delicious with butter. Yelena, with strained patience, lit a cigarette.

'So do you not tell me where were you all of last night?' There was a tetchy edge to the question. That tetchiness settled my resolve.

'I think,' I said, sotto voce, 'that you'd better leave.'

'You want me to leave?'

I found neither words nor argument. But in any case my silence had all the eloquence required. She watched me take a mouthful of coffee, the firefly glowing and then dimming by her mouth. 'Okay, Mister.' She stubbed out the cigarette, fiddled in her bag until she found the key, tossed it beside me onto the bed, and marched to the door on clacking heels.

It snapped shut.

For a long time I watched a jet of smoke writhe about her absence. Then I laughed, darkly. Darkly.

XVI

*T*he notes are gathering to a head. Rushing towards their inexorable conclusion, as you might say. We're getting on. But am I any nearer to discovering the pattern of the trap?

There was a rhyme I always loved as a child; a relic from the days when Mother used to read to me. She did, really. 'All for the want of a horseshoe nail,' it ran. 'Because of the shoe, the horse was lost; because of the horse, the charge was lost.' Yesterday I scribbled seven words across a page: Providence, Destiny, Fate, Chance, Accident, Mishap, Hazard. Reading back through my notes, I still can't decide where along that spectrum the needle falls. If I hadn't gone to the Four Courts that day in April, I'd never have met Danaher. If I hadn't wandered off to the Magazine Fort, or if I'd left its battlements five minutes earlier or later, Chester Maher's belt buckle might never have given. If I'd dumped the holdall into the canal that night on the way back from the fire, maybe nobody would've been murdered.

Every one of these incidents now seems to share in that one guiding principle: all for the want of a horseshoe nail. When all is said and done, maybe that's the only law that governs the universe.

If I hadn't've had you, Will Regan. If Chester Maher had turned tattletale all those years ago and told my grandfather what he knew.

Back to the flat.

> *My love is like a red, red rose,*
> *Her every petal's whorl*
> *A profligate come-hithering,*
> *A maidenhead unfurled.*
> *The shadow in her damask bloom*
> *Teases the fumbling drone*
> *With intimate ingathering,*
> *Unravelling once he's flown.*
> *Her perfume hangs on every breeze,*
> *No scruple dare prevent her:*
> *My love is like a red, red rose*
> *All promise, and no centre.*

I set aside the pages and lay back on open palms. *My love is like a red, red rose, all promise and no centre.* For the second time in twenty-four hours, a dark laugh that appeared to originate inside my chest vibrated through the dusk-inhabited chamber. It was not a laugh I'd have recognised, up to this time, as my own.

All day, on and off, I'd been flipping at random through Maher's typescript. Maher's incomplete typescript, tattooed with unruly scribblings in red and with illegible marginalia. Yesterday's tray of cold coffee and toast crumbs still squatted by the bed. On the single occasion that I'd risen, I'd encountered the hull of a dirty casserole capsized in the kitchen sink. My guts were in turmoil. But I wasn't thinking of food. And Yelena's abrupt dismissal was only the half of it.

Part of me of course was on a high, fired by the drug of having finally made a decisive move. It might have taken Will Regan all of thirty-five years, but he'd done it, Mother! For real! The tray by the bed and the cigarette stubbed out on the windowsill proved it had happened. But my unruly guts were still anticipating the thump of a policeman's fist on the door at every turn. I hadn't as yet been to the hospital. I felt as sick as an anxious child who's done something unforgivable, and knows it can only be a matter of time before he's caught. Insecurity had filled me and the flat alike with unshakeable lassitude.

I hadn't gone outside since I'd bought that first newspaper. The radio, a relic of Mother's vintage with a dial the size of a saucer that dragged its needle across exotic-sounding cities, had been little help. I couldn't even be sure that Danaher was the 'tout' in question. Of course it had been the senile father's house they'd firebombed, but who knew? Might it not have been a brother, or even a crony, who was staying at the address?

If I understood the radio's whine correctly, the victim of the arson attack, the grass 'known to the police', had been taken out of an artificially induced coma, and was in a stable condition. But was it he? Mightn't the hooded monster's *kyak, kyak* resound on the landing at any minute? Or would it rather be the long arm of the law banging at the rickety door? I was living the unreal drift of hours of a man condemned.

Any memory of Chester Maher's manuscript is inextricably intertwined with that unreality. This remains true, even though I didn't attempt to read the damned thing in any concerted way until after I'd been witness to Danaher's injuries. Up to then it was, as you might say, a temporal unreality. Hours turned out to be minutes, minutes hours. It was a state of perpetual, protracted jitters, and it prevented the fragmented day from cohering. When I could endure it no longer, I precipitated to the Mater Hospital.

The relief was only partial. After my unforgettable passage through the Serious Burns Unit, I no longer feared the imminent arrival of the Special Branch. The holdall was safely stashed. Its unknown contents had become little more than a faint smell that lingered in the vicinity of its cupboard lair. But with that problem having flown the nest, as it were, the consequences of the rupture with Yelena began to creep and scurry from every cubbyhole of the flat.

You might say I'd simply exchanged one anxiety for another.

Maher's partial manuscript helped plug the gaps in the flat's defences. *Two down,* whispered Soul. *If you want to hold onto the third, you'd better understand the man.* So I searched the papers for any clue they might hold.

A drama in five acts, though the last act was missing. Written in verse. Why not? Think of it, he'd once said, as an opera without music. So the cuckold of the title is a man by the name of Kinsella. Or Kavanagh, as it's written throughout Act Four. I assume this was carelessness on the author's part. Second thoughts. In any case, characters on more intimate terms with the cuckold call him Chas, Charles or Charlie. I'd expected an anagram of Chester Maher, I'm unsure why. Maybe he'd been unable to come up with one.

There's no need to dawdle over the details of the plot, such as it is. The barest outline, then.

It scarcely comes as a surprise to find that middle-aged Charlie is married, unhappily, to a sensual Frenchwoman. In this case, though, the marriage is childless. No offspring to complicate the drama. No miniature vampire's grin, caught up in a tug of love. No wise child, scandalously aware, as Maher told me Stephie was, of the mother's instinctive infidelities.

There is a difficult father-in-law, but no sign at all of the harpy mother. So much for biographical parallels.

Maher's titular cuckold is bent upon writing a poetic masterpiece entitled (what else?) *The Cuckold.* After this detail, the resemblances with the author become less apparent. At the age of nineteen he had married Eveline de Claire, seven years his senior, and the only daughter of a French trucking magnate, whose game is exporting refrigerated meats. Irish branch of said French magnate's empire is based in Rosslare. Son-in-law has no talent for business. French magnate despises son-in-law. End of Act One.

Act Two is a flashback. The rhyme scheme is different. Years before, the pretext of the overhasty nuptials had been a phantom pregnancy of dubious paternity. This nuisance deflated almost immediately upon their return from the honeymoon. It is apparent that our young poet had been duped. Why the wild French girl's choice had fallen on his head is never made clear.

The remaining acts of the play return us to the present. Charles is bent on writing his masterpiece, and labours at it whenever he's alone in the office. Any time he writes, phantoms and faeries cavort backstage. His wife, who speaks in prose, or at least in lines that either don't rhyme or else rhyme in a half-assed manner, as when 'lover' rhymes with 'over', is unaware of his secret passion.

His only confederate is one Father Quinlan from Ardee. I'll be damned if said priest doesn't pray for the death of the Catholic Church! Charlie's father-in-law, having resigned himself to looking elsewhere for a business partner, is tearing his hair out for want of an heir. Eveline de Claire, always exasperated by her husband, has taken on a string of lovers, and flaunts them like a string of sausages in an effort to shame him into providing one. An heir, not a sausage.

Suspecting that his indifference must mean that he too has a lover, she marches into the office one day when he's away from it. She ransacks the place in search of a token, but turns up nothing beyond a series of copybooks. She is horrified by her discovery. Charlie's secret mistress lies between paper sheets! Finally, at the close of Act Four, in a fit of magnificent pique, Eveline destroys the manuscript. Years of torture and revision are burned in minutes while Charles is off-stage. This bonfire of the vanities is evidently the climax of the work.

Unfortunately, in the version that he'd given me, or to be accurate that I'd taken, Act Five is entirely missing. Fate again, you see! I recalled Chester's excitement when he was gripped by inspiration as to how the thing would end. This completed text was, no doubt, the version he'd sent to Longford. How would Charlie Kinsella react to the outrage? Depression? Suicide?

Exquisite revenge? If nothing else, the lack of an ending would give me a pretext to call back out to his house off the Old Cabra Road. No cloud without its silver lining.

I don't want to do Chester Maher a disservice. I am not, in any case, qualified to speak about the arts. I've never once set foot inside a theatre. Christmas panto, yes, when Mother still had her eyesight. But do characters really speak in rhyme there? I have to say I've my doubts. What I will give him is that, in parts, his fantasy amazed me. His opera without music. The stage directions were a revelation, with apparitions, gargoyles, monsters. The grotesque, the bizarre and the unprecedented rubbed shoulders with the mundane and the dull. I would not have thought Chester Maher so given to phantasms.

One scene in particular has stayed with me. It takes place at the end of Act Two. An early climax, always supposing a play can have two climaxes. On the last night of the honeymoon, the young Charlie Kinsella comes to realise the great progression of lovers in which he is nothing more than the latest term, if he's even that. Were the phantom pregnancy anything more than air, its authorship would likely have been down to a butcher's apprentice named O'Rourke. Charlie always speaks in rhyme. But like the French magnate de Claire and his harpy daughter, the butcher speaks only in prose. Later, we see O'Rourke rise in the firm until he has become the heir apparent.

Now, the honeymoon has taken the couple to Oslo, of all places. If there's a significance in the choice, it's beyond me. I should have asked Chester while I had the chance. But then, there are many things I should've asked Chester while I had the chance. Perhaps he'd visited the city in the salad days with Stephanie Dujardin. Perhaps, who knows, it's the very city my Norwegian sailor had sailed from.

In this most memorable scene, Kinsella leaves the hotel room in faultless *terza rima* and wanders the midnight streets. The instructions are particularly detailed in regard to the stage-set. At length he finds himself in a great park, filled not with trees but with stone sculptures. A petrifying moon looks down on every contortion of the human form. There are stone infants, stone women, old men in stone, family groups and solitaries. They form a marble chorus, singing to him, laughing at him. There are women wrestling men, men grappling with lizards, children screaming and raising tantrums.

Finally, he finds himself surrounded by an enchanted wood. Trees of stone, with figures cavorting through the branches, rise like great hands all around. As he circles them, the petrified wood becomes a life cycle. In the final tree lurks Death. The bones and branches are carved alike from granite. Or is it only the moonlight that makes them appear so? But far from frightening him, the figure of Death in the tree causes Charlie Kinsella to laugh, long and hard.

I could not read this scene without thinking of the winter copse in which I'd first found Chester Maher.

Later, musing on that Nordic vision of Purgatory, I recalled a visit I'd made with Yelena to the National Museum on Kildare Street. She had a fascination for what she called 'Celtic convolution', with its torcs and spirals and twisted beasts. Whereas I was struck by a display of bog bodies, and I left her to her coils.

Bog bodies. The term was buried somewhere at the back of my memory, but damned if I can remember where I'd come across it. It turns out these rough-hewn skeletons were cobbled together from leather and bone that had lain in the bogs for centuries. They'd been tanned there to the colour of tobacco by its juices. All showed the marks of having been tortured and sacrificed, thousands of years ago. But one detail I remember above all. The *fógra* said there was a theory that they'd been placed in the bog because they'd brought shame on the tribe. Here were the cowards and the sodomites, whose sins had to be covered up. The bog, being neither one thing nor another, would take them, but would never yield them up to an afterlife. It was an Irish limbo, as you might say.

It was in just such a limbo that I found Chester Maher submerged on the next day but one. I mean the next day but one after I'd entered the weird world of his drama. It was a dismal day. Wave upon wave of Atlantic rain swept the breadth of the country. The waves crossed the bogs and rivers, the towns and hinterlands and hills, until at last their monotony squatted over the housing estates of the city. A patch of sky would brighten a flicker, and then another thickening would raise hedgehog pricks along the gutter. Its quills would sweep the hooded people down the streets like so much refuse. The legs of my pants were so wet by the time I got to Cabra, I might just as well have been wading through that gutter.

There was no reply when I banged at the door. But the same intuition as before told me that Chester was inside. Besides, I had no intention of letting the soaking count for nothing. I tapped repeatedly at the window, and when that tattoo failed, I squatted down and hollered obscenities through the letterbox. Of course it was in the latter position that I attracted the stares of a passing nun.

There was nothing for it, then, but to try my athleticism around the back laneway. In the sodden daylight the lane was grey and forbidding, the wall at least a foot higher than it had been previously. I scrambled at it and skinned my arm against its coarseness. When I fell back down, the tedious bark of the mongrel began to turn over. I placed my back to the far wall, sprang across the divide, leapt, and pivoted upwards on my elbows until my nipples were level with the top of the wall. My legs were kicking wildly, but it was to no avail. Slowly, by agonising degrees, every inch that I had gained was conceded to gravity. I dropped back down, breathless, and with the report of a tear in my coat.

'Damn you to hell, Chester Maher!'

'Who are you looking for, son? Is it Jester Mare?' I recognised, from her glorious accent, the not-five-foot woman in the tea-cosy hat and the coat she'd knitted out of porridge. A grandmother now, she was pushing a stroller. The windfall visage pinched. 'He's not in.'

'Isn't he?'

'Well I don't know if he is or he isn't. Only the curtains is pulled across this three days.'

'He hasn't gone in or out in three days?'

'I couldn't tell you if he has or he hasn't; all I can tell you is that we haven't seen hide nor hair of him this three days. I said to Jacinta he must be gone away.'

'Yes,' I said. She was looking at me curiously, though not as yet suspiciously. A great hatpin skewered the tea cosy at the height of a child's eye. I had the urge to be rid of her so I could try again the wall. 'The way it is, missus, he asked me to keep an eye on the place. From time to time.'

'From around the back?'

'Only, you see,' I smiled effusively, 'I forgot my keys.'

She clucked. Then her hat made an odd, dismissive lurch and she set off on her way. I watched her waddle down the path and hesitate at the corner. But if a thought had come near the hatpin that skewered her tea cosy, it failed to perch.

The encounter lent a spring to my stride, so to speak. This time I levered myself painfully onto my thorax, shimmied forwards over the concrete until the fulcrum was closer to my hips, writhed through a half-turn, and then toppled into a bed of vegetable drills long gone to seed. I righted myself, and began to brush the clots of earth from my clothes. Then I surveyed the yard. My heart leapt. There was a face at the kitchen window, livid as a daytime moon. Two shadows where the eyes should have been had followed my fall.

'Jesus, Chester, you put the heart across me!' As I approached the window, the drowned head resolved itself into the familiar features, though for all that it lost none of its pallor. Neither did it respond. I smiled, saluted, and made my way to the back door. As before, it was unlocked.

'Chester! Would you not say hello to a man?' He was standing by the draining board, still as wax, with an open tin in one hand and a spoon clutched in the other. There was an ungirdled dressing gown about him, and his hair was as greasy as his complexion was listless. Only the stubble glistened like hoar on his jowl. But his personal state of neglect was as nothing to the state of the kitchen.

One thing I'll say about Mother, she could never abide a mess. With her bloodhound's nose, she'd know if I'd left the plates sit for even an hour after the evening meal. You'd live in a pigsty, Will Regan! Do you know what it is, it'd take one alone to straighten up after you. I don't know who's supposed to make you clear up after yourself when I'm dead and gone.

By God, she'd've had a stroke if I'd brought her into Chester Maher's that day, blind as she was. If I'd been shocked on my previous encounter, now I was overwhelmed. The entire kitchen was a battlefield. All over the table, tins stood or fell with spoons and forks still protruding from their innards. There were mugs in disarray, boxes ripped open, and the sink was a communal grave long since abandoned to the elements. But worse than these war-dead were the midges and flies that hung like apostrophes in the fetid air.

'Jesus Christ, Chester!' He set down the tin and made to leave the room. I was relieved to see that at least it hadn't been dog food he'd been eating. I'd read about such cases. I made after him and tapped his shoulder. He turned, the spoon still clutched in his hand like an impotent sceptre.

'Chester Maher, you'd better snap out of this fast! You'll die of typhoid poisoning so you will!' This detail I'd filched from Mother. It added plausibility. He turned away from me and continued his royal amble, as though what I'd just said had been in a foreign language. Too dangerous to ask him after his princess. You need to be bloody careful there. But Soul had already let slip the dart. 'What would social services have to say if they saw you now for God's sake? You'll never get custody of Stephie this way.' I've never found out if he heard either sentence.

I watched him shuffle into the sitting room and then, unable to watch any longer, I marched into the kitchen and thence to the broom cupboard. I'd intended in any case to throw an eye on the hiding-place, but now I had a new crusade. Opening the door, a cascade of broom handles tumbled to the floor, but that merely piqued my resolve. I looked briefly at the holdall, squat as an egg-sack in its cache, and then selected from the fallen staffs a bald broom and desiccated mop. There was a bucket in the yard, and this I scalded with a kettle that struggled asymptotically to the boil. I also tipped out a box filled with rags and made a coffin of it for the litter that cluttered every surface of the room. And before leaving, I attacked in mid air, with dampened tea towel, the torpor of the flies.

These efforts must have lasted a good half-hour, but they left me feeling energetic and virtuous. Even the dismal Atlantic rain failed to dampen my spirits as I made my way home along the South Circular. I believe I may have been singing. Then, when at last I arrived, I found a note squeezed into the jamb of the door.

Willy, this is no good. I know you are angry with me. I know you don't find me easy to understand. You are jealous. This is natural. Maybe I would be jealous if I was like you. But now please try to understand my point of view. This being apart is no good. I love you, Willy Regan. I did not expect this. I did not want it. It's crazy. But I think you like me very much too. This is second time I knock and you are not in. So maybe you will phone me? I write the number on the other side of page. I need talk to you Willy. Please phone.

And so, it starts again.

XVII

I slam the pencil to the table so hard that it snaps. That bitch's bastard of a dirty stupid tomcat is back, screeching like a soul in torment. His mewls tear across the fabric of the night. They destroy what peace I have. Ever since prison, the small hours have become my habitat, as you might say. The empty steppe over which memory prowls.

I clamber over the rickety bed and pull back the blind. There he is, the little shit, staring up at the window. Mrrgnaauu! It's enough to try the patience of a saint. Two days ago I slinked past the landlady palavering with a neighbour, an old biddy with whiskers on her chin who stared daggers at me. Seems Teddy, her Yorkshire terrier, had passed on, having spent all the previous night lapping up bowl after bowl of water and coughing up foam flecked with blood and powder. Vicious little tyke. Tut-tut isn't that terrible now it must've been something he swallowed the poor unfortunate d'you know what it is missus it's a bloody disgrace they don't clean up after them bins properly.

Teddy must've been partial to calf's liver. Tomorrow I'll leave out the balance of the rat poison. Only I'll sprinkle it over a bit of mackerel. That'll fix you once and for all, my feline friend.

Mrrgnaauu! The bitch of it is, I'm on a roll. I can sense the end. I can smell it! So much so that I ventured into the office stationers this morning, to pick up that famous typewriter. But the raven-haired girl behind the desk stared at me as if I was pulling her leg. Cheeky little vampire, a pin through her eyebrow like a hand-grenade. No, I don't mean a word-processor my miss. I mean a typewriter. 'Tak, tak.' A typewriter. Keys laid out where you can see them, like the bones of a ray out of Burdock's.

'You thought've having a look in an antique shop?' sneered the hussy. May she be seized with menstrual cramps.

'Now would you call that normal behaviour?' I was sitting opposite Father Ciarán Crowe, cradling a mug of clerical coffee. Its industrial powder, swept from the factory floor into huge tins, will forever be linked in my senses to the sacristy of St Audoen's. The sweet muck they served up in Mountjoy had infinitely more appeal.

I'd spent the last five minutes, as the mug went gradually tepid, setting out the most recent circumstances in which I'd found Chester Maher. The padre had told me that he too was a depressive. In and out of John of God's, wasn't that what he'd said? It seemed reasonable that he might know what was to be done.

'There's not a lot can be done.'

Beautiful!

'Not until he's ready to help himself.'

'There's nothing we can do for him?'

'Not a lot, except keep an eye out. It's like a great Atlantic depression. It has to be weathered, that's all there is to it.' We both looked through the net curtains at the glowering sky. 'One low pressure is as often as not followed by a second, and even a third.'

'And how long might this... *weather* take to clear, Father?'

'There's no way of telling. It might take weeks. But if it's more profound, he might be like that for months on end. Even years.'

'Years! But he hasn't got years! He hasn't even got weeks. The bank is threatening to put him out on the street...'

'Believe me, years. I've seen cases...'

I set down the mug, which courtesy alone had sipped. Behind him, the portraits of the Class of '64 looked on. Black and white men, each in his private oval. Crowe's photo was on the top row, third from the left. A young man, unbearded, with a collar like the top of a pint.

I set about examining his present features, as though the answer might be engraved there. It was what they call a lived-in face. If the furrows were lines of Braille, Mother's fingers would have had little difficulty in reading what time and concern had etched there. Should I tell him, I wondered, that the key to the whole thing might be Maher's girl? That Stephie, his princess, might be the one cause to make him snap out of his depression? That by his own lethargy he was in danger of losing her? *Keep your powder dry,* hissed Soul.

'Years, by God!'

'It could be.'

'Then do you think he should be, you know…' I wanted to say put into a funny farm, but the words stuck in my throat.

'Committed, is it? I'll tell you. There's one old lady that I sometimes talked to, in John of God's. I mean when I was doing my own time out there. We'll call her Kitty, God love her! Kitty had been in institutions ever since she was a teenager. Her own mother had had her committed at the age of thirteen, after she'd tried to set fire to the house. Now she's nearer sixty. And to talk to her, you'd think butter wouldn't melt in her mouth!'

His point, it seemed, had been made. 'And the mother?'

'The mother is long since dead, by all accounts.'

'So then, why is she still institutionalised?'

'I suppose, like the rest of us, Kitty is afraid. It's all the life she's known.'

'But that's not a life!'

'Isn't it?' Kitty cat. Kitty O'Shea. It came to me in a flash that Father Ciarán Crowe had the head of Charles Stewart Parnell! Parnell, with his gaze of a disappointed Christ. Our uncrowned king: a great dome of a forehead, sad eyes, and a beard that doubled the length of his face. Crowe also shared the politician's habit of gazing into space, as though contemplating a matter of great weight. A trick learned in the seminary, no doubt.

'How could you call it a life, Father, when every decision is taken for you? You might just as well be in prison.'

'Maybe,' he said, with a priestly pause, 'we're not as free as we like to think we are. There was a philosopher,' he went on, now looking directly at me, and with a spark of gallows' humour in his eyes, 'who said that all the freedom we have on this earth is that of the sailor who can cross from port to starboard on a ship that's sailing full speed due north.'

I thought at once of my own sailor, trapped in his circle of ten miles' radius. And if the voyage were circular, and the ship rudderless? 'Or due south?' I tried, when I found him looking at me.

'Or due south. The point would be largely the same.'

'It would be a different destination. The very opposite, in point of fact.'

'But with regard to freedom, the point would be largely the same.'

I lifted the mug, swilled the contents about, replaced it on the table untried. 'Except of course you'd have to cross from starboard to port, for the sake of symmetry. But tell me, Father, what do you think that destination might be?'

'I wish you'd call me Ciarán.'

'Everyone calls the priest Father,' I dragged out the old chestnut, 'except for his son. He calls him Uncle.'

'Well, I suppose as a Christian…' Now, I'd intended by my question Chester Maher's destination. It was obvious he was thinking of mankind. And I was supposed to *not* call the man Father?

'Spare me your Christianity! I don't want to hear about Shangri-La.'

He nodded, taking the interruption in his stride. 'There was a priest,' he began, looking deep into the air beyond me, 'by the name of Father Andrade. A Jesuit, on the Brazilian missions. He ended his days in a madhouse in Belém. I came

across his writings not long after I began in Clonliffe College.'
There followed a long silence, so long in fact that I thought his
story was finished. He sighed. 'He wrote, beautifully, about the
symbolism of the miracles. Naturally it was all in Portuguese.
But there was a Father Soares staying at Clonliffe at the
time who used to help me with the translation. He was also
something of a mathematician. Father Andrade, I mean. Have
you an interest in mathematics, Willy?'

'I have not. I never stayed on in school.'

'Oh?'

'On account of the mother.'

'Ah!'

Another of his pregnant pauses set in. Chester Maher's
monologues were studded with lengthy pauses, but their quality
was entirely different. Where Maher's were fitful and erratic, the
priest's bearded head sat like a brood-hen on the silence. We
waited for his next thought to hatch.

'There's a concept in mathematics called the asymptote. You
approach limits asymptotically. It's as much as to say, you can
never cross them. Do you know,' he looked again directly at
me, troubled eyes over gaunt cheekbones, 'it was contemplation
of that notion of the asymptote that drove Andrade to the
madhouse, in Belém?'

With Chester Maher I would have said 'I'm not with you'.
With Ciarán Crowe the remark was superfluous.

'He was considering that age-old conundrum of death and
consciousness. How can we experience our own death? From
the atheist's point of view, death is annihilation. Consciousness
ends, like a candle snuffed out. It follows that the atheist need
not fear death. It's only the fantasies of an afterlife that can hold
out any terrors.'

A candle snuffed out. Right.

'But Andrade had a different take on it. Almost diametrically
opposite, in point of fact.'

During the next pause, I found that my hand had already
raised the mug to my lips and had tipped half its contents into

my mouth. The mug was far lighter as it set it down, and there was an aftertaste of ashes on my tongue.

'For Andrade, you must make a distinction between absolute time and our perception of time. It's only the latter that has any validity, so far as our consciousness is concerned. Are you with me?'

I nodded, though the half of what he said might just as well have been Polish. All the same it seemed to me I'd heard this argument before. I'll be damned if his head, in the dimly lit sacristy, hadn't come to resemble the very skull of Parnell. 'Now, let's imagine that the atheist's span of life is fast approaching its end. You'll grant with me that it's impossible, for the atheist, to experience anything beyond death?'

'Always assuming that God doesn't believe in him either.' Not for the first time, my flippancy was out of place.

'From the point of view of consciousness,' the voice droned on in the darkening room, 'death is the line that cannot be crossed. Beyond it is a space where consciousness can never be found. For Andrade, it's a situation analogous, in mathematics, to the asymptote. The graph of one divided by one minus x cannot reach the value of x equals one. It can only approach it and approach it, ad infinitum. And since time is no more than the perception of time, it follows that in the approach to death, this perception slows down. It slows down infinitesimally and eternally, until we're caught in the last moment as surely as an insect is trapped in amber. The last agony. Our final second stretches to an eternity.'

When he talked of how time is no more than the perception of time and x is x minus one he might just as well have been speaking in tongues. But an insect trapped in amber, that was something a man could grasp. That was an image I could cling to, like the bodies drowned in the bog. 'Go on,' I prompted.

'Originally, he'd intended the argument would frighten atheists. But for Andrade, too, it led to a horror so dreadful that it finally drove him out of his wits.'

What price consciousness, if you're out of your wits? I wish, now, I'd asked the man.

'You don't believe that do you?'

'As a Christian…' he smiled. Then he stood up. 'I've been taking up too much of your time!'

'Not at all, Father. It's only my perception of time!'

I'd done, again, my schoolboy's trick of pulling a phrase out of thin air.

'Ciarán!' he laughed. 'I wish you'd call me Ciarán.' As he accompanied me out of the church and into the rain, he pressed an umbrella upon me. I reminded him of Chester Maher, that great fly trapped in amber.

'Oh God, I'd forgotten all about him! I'll tell you, next time you're to drop out to see your friend, call on me first. If I'm not otherwise engaged I'll accompany you.'

'Right,' I said, struggling with the recalcitrant umbrella, 'I'll do that. If nothing else I'll drop back this contraption!'

It wasn't an umbrella that either one of us was destined to see again. On the following evening, I left it behind in a Chinese restaurant somewhere off North Great George's Street. Pagodas and dragons, that sort of affair. Above our table was a print of a parti-coloured rooster, flanked on the left by a column of oriental characters. They might have been a reckoning, for all I knew.

My true love was treating me to a reconciliation dinner.

'It's not as if we haven't been down this road a hundred times. I told you, Yelena, I'm not putting up with it.'

'Putting up with what? I go to Athlone because Dónal help me with investment.'

'With investment.'

She'd informed me earlier that Rakoczi, at least, was out of the picture. Some complication in regard to the transfer of funds had forced his return to Odessa. 'You must close your offshore account,' she'd said, trying to sound offhand.

'Sure,' I'd shrugged. 'You do know there's a few thousand in there?'

Her eyes had opened. 'You don't move this already!'

'I was awaiting your instructions, ma'am,' I'd grinned. I'd enjoyed the literal truth of the statement.

'So move this money, then close account. Promise me this.'

I saluted. *Jawohl.*

'And Willy, don't do anything to draw attention from Revenue. Is important.'

'Such as what?'

'I don't know. But you are crazy man!' She cuffed my ear with her muff.

I'd already signed the last of her precious forms. She hadn't exactly brought up the subject of the forms, but I'd been feeling expansive. Now, in the restaurant, I regretted the gesture. Was O'Byrne, or O'Brien, really no more than another one of her dupes? 'You're not trying to tell me that investments is all you two got up to on his pleasure boat?'

The mood in the restaurant wasn't anything like as ugly as it reads. There was levity in our banter, though why this should have been so is beyond me. For someone who had again expressed her newfound love for me, Yelena appeared remarkably carefree. She'd lit up a cigarette, quite immune to the frowns of the parents at the table beside us. And I was amazed at how happy it felt to have her again across the table.

'Besides, I tell you already. It means nothing if I am with him.'

'Him, or anyone else!'

'Him or anyone else, yes! It means nothing.'

'It does. It means yours sincerely is in misery.' Through guarded eyes my soul peered at her. *You might just as well ask a leopard to change its spots*, it jeered.

'But we can't own one another, Willy. I tell you before, I never go back to this. And anyway, I don't stop you to have other girl.'

'So then it's back to the same old merry-go-round?'

It's no use. I can't transcribe this scene.

The notes lie mute on the table, next to the old Remington I picked up in a Barnardos charity shop. I've been putting the story to type. Tak taka tak ping! Zhit! Taka tak taka. Takes me right back to my time with Doherty and Fitzgibbon! The 'i' sticks, occasionally, when I'm too eager. Or it carries the key beside it. But when I get into my stride, it makes a sound like rain across the windowpane.

There's nothing wrong with the machine, it's the notes that are all wrong. Oh, I don't mean that they fabricate. There's nothing in them that I've invented. The words are the very words we used, so far as I can recall them. But somehow, their essence is missing. I haven't caught the music of the affair.

Was I anything more than a patsy, pure and simple? To read the notes with a detached eye, you might think so. But it had been me who'd invited her for that first drink, all those months ago. And if I was no more to her than an Irish name on a bank account, is it likely she'd have waited a full year before she asked me for it?

She paid the bill, we left, and it was precisely that: back to the same old merry-go-round. Would things have turned out any differently if I'd been more insistent? If I'd been more of a man, as they say? Idle question. But I have my doubts.

It was the same old merry-go-round, and yet there'd been a change in its balance. That was undeniable. But the leopard wasn't going to change her spots just like that, for all her purring. She mightn't see anybody else. But she wouldn't actually promise to be faithful either. She would on no account give up her old tricks. Or more precisely, she wouldn't give up her right to them.

But then, she'd no actual interest in anyone else.

We stayed in the flat for three days and nights, sending out only for pizzas and Chinese food that arrived in silver boxes. Once, we sent an awkward delivery boy out for cigarettes. We'd laid in a store of a half-dozen bottles of wine, and we dispatched them when the whim took, with no thought for the clock. And the flat was world enough for us.

XVIII

'Now the city draws near which is called Dis / With its great garrison and grave citizens'. Dismay, Discovery, Disaster. The jaunt out to Cabra took place one Saturday not long after this. Earlier in the week, Chester had failed our rendezvous. There was nothing unusual in this any more. Even at the best of times he'd failed a number of our trysts. The wonder would have been if he'd showed. But in the present circumstances, it gave the trip out a pretext it would otherwise have lacked. In any case, I was beginning to enjoy the company of Ciarán Crowe.

One last time, let me try to order my chronologies. To give the story rigour, as you might say. At the time we drove out to Cabra, I'd been back with Yelena about a fortnight. The arson attack must have been more than a month old. Danaher had discharged himself from the hospital ward, after the first of what would tally up, over the months and years, to an astonishing thirteen operations. Or interventions, as I've heard them called.

I know this date to be correct because, after the initial intervention, a photo that I still have somewhere in the shoebox had appeared on all the front pages. One tabloid version was folded up in my arse pocket as we rode out in the cab. I'd stared at it, a gerbil staring at a python, while I was waiting for the padre at the taxi rank. Danaher was being escorted down the steps, not of the Four Courts this time, but of the Mater Hospital.

From inside a hood pulled tight as any defendant's, the eyes stared straight back at me. There was an indistinct rage in that Hallowe'en portrait. It brought my tumour of anxiety straight out of remission. It seemed the very existence of the holdall had kept it malignant. Take hold of that bag you bloody fool and drown it in the canal, like you should've done weeks ago!

Crowe helped take my mind away from the blessed thing. He was in expansive form, joking from almost the moment I'd called at St Audoen's for him. At first he wouldn't divulge the cause of his jocularity. We sat into the taxi, and he quipped about the weather, the geography of our journey, and I know not what. There was a traffic diversion on the river – one of the bridges was under repair – and we had to cross its stinking lees by another, which was clotted with articulated lorries. Neither the stench rising from the riverbed nor the flippantly mounting fare bothered him. 'Want to know something funny?' I commented, to take my own mind off the meter's rapacity. 'It was just such a taxi ride that led to us two meeting.'

'How can that be?'

I went on to tell him of the unlicensed driver, with his bull neck and cowboy boots and his liberal Christian advice. 'I don't know what you think about coincidences,' says I, 'but if you ask me, there's something in it.'

'I think I've noticed that character at the meetings. He has a scar?'

'He has!'

'A little half-moon, here by the ear?'

'It's where a junky bit into him one night.' *Meetings*, he'd said. In the plural. 'You've been more than once to their sessions?'

'You'll think this odd of me,' he lowered his voice, as if afraid that today's Bosnian cabby might overhear, 'but for some time now I've felt compelled to attend every revelation and disclosure. To bear witness, if you like.'

'Witness, is it? You looked more like a persecuted rat the day I saw you, I'll tell you that much. But you hardly feel personally responsible for the shenanigans that went on?'

'We're all personally responsible, one way or another. A priest more so than the next man. That's a part of the cross he's asked to take up.'

Are you personally responsible, Will Regan? And if so, for whom? To whom? There's no mother any more to give you a clip around the ear for yourself. '*Personal* responsibility?' I doubted, aloud.

'Personal responsibility is the heart of the pastoral vocation. It goes with the territory I'm afraid.'

'But a vocation to act the scapegoat? If you didn't know…?'

'If I didn't know…' The echo was little more than a stage whisper, the meaning of which I've never managed to fathom. It's possible, of course, that the man had a propensity for martyrdom, plain and simple. Unless of course he'd been aware all along of something fishy. 'If the householder had known at what hour the thief was coming,' he started, as though he'd heard me, 'he'd never have let his house be broken into. Therefore be vigilant! For you know not the day nor the hour.'

'How about: "Therefore be wise as serpents"? Did you never hear, Father Crowe, that the Devil can cite scripture for his purpose? Besides everything else, citing scripture has a Protestant relish to it.'

'It has!' he laughed. 'It has all that!' He fell again to looking out the window. When he spoke, his good spirits had been restored. 'Did I tell you,' he rubbed his hands, 'I've had my reply from the bishop's office?'

'To what?'

'You didn't know? I put in for a year's sabbatical some months ago.'

'Do priests get sabbatical?'

'They do, on occasion.'

'But how can they afford to let you go for a year? I mean, when there's so few of you guys about?'

'To tell you the truth,' he leaned in towards me jauntily, 'I think they'll be glad to see the back of me.'

'And what will you do with this year's sabbatical?'

'I think I'll take the chance,' he stroked his beard, 'to visit the Holy Land. Ever since I was a boy, I've wanted to visit the Holy Land.'

'And when is this great vacation to happen?' I scoffed, to cover my dismay. I'd only met the man, and now he was going away on me.

'Oh, not for another thousand years!'

I stared at his eyes, lit with humour. 'Another…?'

'We'll have to wait for the new millennium!' he laughed.

'I daresay the Holy Land is the right place for a priest to go for the year that's in it.' The taxi pulled into the kerb and, as I settled the fare, I mentally jotted up the final cohort of months that separated us from millennium's end.

The front of the house presented the same aspect of neglect as on the previous two visits. 'You see the number, Father? Three, seven. Unless he is born again…'

'Now who's citing scripture?' he asked. It seemed to be a great day altogether for the scripture. The house had the same neglected look, and my knocking was equally ignored. 'If you'll wait here,' I winked, 'there's a little trick I know. I'll have us both inside in jig time.'

On this occasion I managed to take the rear wall in a single vault. No sign of the tea-cosy lady today with her 'Jester Mare' and her lethal hatpin. As I pivoted over its summit, it struck me that maybe it would've been better if I'd left the kitchen in the state that I'd found it. It would have given the priest an unedited view of the depths to which Maher had sunk. Still, I couldn't regret my efforts. Would it be too much to say that I was feeling virtuous about my Good Samaritan's deed?

The rear door was once again unlocked. Many days had gone by since I'd last been out there, and by all appearances he'd made at least some sort of a fist at keeping the place in order. There were unwashed dishes, it's true, but they were relatively few, and were submerged in the sink. Such cartons and tins as had been pillaged and sacked were wedged into my cardboard-box coffin by the door. But the smell had scarcely improved, and midges hung like spittle on the kitchen's sour breath.

'Chester!' I called. 'Where are you? You have visitors!'

He was not in the front room. Neither was there sign of him in the study to the side of the house. I peered up the stairs. 'Chester! Visitors!'

I'd already mounted the first several steps when a recollection paralysed me. The broom cupboard! In my mind's eye, I saw the door ajar.

I stood, one hand on the banister. I'd not the least doubt but that I'd secured it shut on my last visit. I'd leaned mop and bucket deliberately against the door, since the magnetic strip that held it was impotent. It would never have fallen open by a mere accident.

I began to retrace my steps. Of course, even if Maher had rummaged about in it, there was no certainty he'd have come across the holdall. I'd dug a pocket for it deep among rags and boxes. Perhaps he'd merely held the door open in a moment of idleness. Perhaps he'd wondered at the sorcerer's apprentice who'd straightened the place. But the anxiety dragged down my gut in proportion as I approached the accursed door. If the householder had known at what hour the thief was coming…

The bag was gone. Never have I been so fluent in my expletives, before or since. I slammed the door of the cupboard on the empty lair, I stormed back out to the hall, and I took the stairs three at a time. It wasn't anger that was driving me. With Danaher back on the streets, nausea was rapidly turning to cement inside my entrails.

The upper storey was as deserted as the ground floor, and with as many signs of neglect. There were so many clothes strewn about the floor of the master bedroom that for a while I failed to notice the bag. But a more frantic survey discovered it. It lay shrivelled in a corner, its belly ripped, emptied of its eggs.

I snatched it up. The unopened padlock dangled ponderously from one corner. It was the zipper that had been torn. Appalled, I rifled its innards. But it was quite empty. I fell back onto the edge of the bed. My emotions hovered between despair and disbelief. Disbelief won out. If it hadn't, I don't know how I could've been able to stand back up, replace the bag in the corner, remember the priest, and go down the stairs to open the door to him.

'The bird has flown the nest,' I shrugged.

'He's in the habit of leaving the back door unlocked?'

I nodded, not thinking how he knew that I didn't have a key. 'So what do you suggest we do now, Father?'

'Ciarán, please. We wait, I suppose. There's no reason to think he won't be back. He might have simply gone to the shops.'

The shops! A sick feeling congealed in my belly at his suggestion. 'In that case,' I said, steering him away from the front door, 'there's not much point in us waiting for him. What I mean is, if he's got enough go to him to go out shopping, he must be on the mend.'

'You make it sound as if he was entirely helpless before. But that's not the way it works. The affliction comes on you in cycles. One day you're down, but the next you might be up. Or one hour you're up, and then just as quick it all collapses again.' He'd resumed his trick of looking past me. 'Sometimes, I used to think it was like being in a pool with sides too steep or slippery to climb out. You scramble at them, but you never lift yourself much above the water. It's the whim of the tide alone that moves you.'

I'd got him as far as the gate.

'So how does it end? What's to stop you from drowning?'

'God's grace. Or, if you prefer a more mundane explanation, one day the chemistry of your brain begins to allow it to function again. The connections are re-established. The synapses begin to fire. I can tell you, a lot of factors have to come together for that to happen.'

'Come on, Father. We'll get a bus.'

I was again that child who's done something wrong and knows it's only a matter of time before he's caught. This conviction continued to poison my ease, even when several sleepless days had separated me from the crime scene. For Danaher, or an effigy of him, was out on the streets. He might at any time lay claim to my soul and demand his tribute. What made it worse, he had a key to the bloody flat! Every single time I mounted the stairs in those hectic days, my heart came close to packing it in entirely. And even if this monster didn't reappear, who knew what might come of that fool, Maher, who was wandering the city's byways with his illicit cargo. How long would it be now before the Gardaí came banging at my door with their handcuffs and warrants?

I could find ease only on such nights as I was able to stay over at Yelena Zamorska's place. On such nights as I was permitted to stay over. My star may have been in the ascendant so far as her affections were concerned, but liberty, or libertinism, was fighting a spirited rearguard action. One afternoon during this interlude I was standing at the doorway to her bedroom, one hand on the lintel, peering back over my shoulder to where she lay swaddled in a red and white quilt. It was her custom, the big cat, to linger in bed long past noon. 'What are you look at?'

'If you must know, I was considering how I might sketch you.' Odd as it sounds, this was true. She propped her head up on her palm, and the quilt dropped enchantingly from her bosom. 'It really is a pity that you gave up your drawing, Willy.'

'So you'd let me?' She angled her forehead, playing that she didn't understand. 'Would you let me draw you?'

She laughed. I assumed that that was the end of that. But she brought the matter up herself at the coffee table. For half the day, her metabolism survived on caffeine alone. 'So do you really want to draw me?' She fumbled about for the last of her cigarettes. For half the day, her metabolism survived on caffeine and nicotine.

'Certainly I do. Of course I'm a wee bit out of practice…'

'Naked, I suppose?'

Now it was my turn to laugh. 'Naked. Or draped in a quilt. It's how I see you most of the time.' She slapped me. But then it was 'Okay, Mister. Maybe I let you.'

The notion excited me to a fabulous extent, God knows why. I felt a tingling in my balls that was so strong she might have been cradling them. The sensation made me nervous. 'D'you mean it, then? Yelena? I'm not exactly Michelangelo. And besides everything else, I've never once tried to sketch cloth.'

'So then you do want to draw me naked! I knew this!' She cuffed me, and I carried her back like a newlywed into the bedroom.

Later that evening I brought over my charcoals, or what was left of them, and the last leaves of a pad which still bore the traces of previous efforts. No page was free of its little scattering of ash.

'So where do you want we do this?' There was a sweet smell of wine on her breath. So the little darling had been drinking while I'd been away getting the materials. Finding the courage, as they say.

'How about in the bedroom?'

'How about it?'

'It'll be boring for you, trying to hold a pose. At least in the bedroom you can lie down and maybe read.'

'And I can have a fag?'

'I wouldn't dream of drawing you any other way.'

Yelena had recently stepped from the shower, and was draped loosely in a drowsy gown. Her tendrils of hair were still damp and her complexion aglow. But there was something else, beyond the shower, that had brought up that pinkness. I'd noticed it, of late, the way one notices the first hints of spring. There was a bounce in her step. There was liveliness in her eye that wasn't unlike the spark of mischief. And her skin glowed as though she were out of breath; as though she were tubercular; as though she had been plated with some tincture of youth. I'll be damned if it wasn't…

But can she really be in love? scoffed Soul.

Many days had passed since Rakoczi had hastened back to Odessa. She'd never once since mentioned the affair, except to say she'd heard nothing from him. Nor had she looked for any new signatures. She'd never again insisted I keep a low profile for fear Revenue would be on top of us. I'd emptied out the offshore account, though it was still 'technically open', whatever they meant by their 'technically'. She'd never even asked about it.

Was it love, then?

Fondling this quandary was sufficient to distract my attention from the worm of guilt that was otherwise gnawing at my insides. All right, Soul. But let's suppose that she is. Can that glow be directed at Will Regan? Now I'd read, I don't know where, that women in love acquire a shine in the presence of the beloved. A dilation of the pupil. A quickening of the pulse. Adulteries have been proven on such flimsy evidence. Has the eye dilated this evening? Has the breath quickened? Folding over the first page of the clumsy pad, I determined to make full use of our sessions to observe her most intimate nuances.

We'd no sooner started than she lit up, and a moment later was taken by a fit of coughing. It was, I think, the first time I'd seen the smoke catch at her throat in that way. 'Oh I'm sorry, Willy. I spoil your picture.' Her eyes were watering and she was laughing. 'Not at all. I was just warming up.' In point of fact, I'd dispensed entirely with those indispensable warming-up exercises that had ruined so many pages during the life-drawing classes. 'Are you okay?' She coughed again, and laughed again. It was just as well. The strength of the swell of concern inside me had taken me by surprise.

We attempted three poses on this, our first and final session. The results were disastrous. I could no more foreshorten than I could dance a jig, and the sticks of charcoal crumbled and smudged like guilty things upon a fearful summons. Yelena looked kindly on the efforts, though, and in this, too, I sensed a sea-change in her. For my part, I discovered a pair of moles like twin stars in the small of her back, and an incomparable tenderness that I haven't felt, before or since. I'll be damned if the ersatz love I'd felt over the previous year hadn't been transformed, like a butterfly, into the real thing. Even Soul, that perennial cynic, was taken aback, and stuck for words.

Our idyll was short lived.

At ten minutes past six on the following evening, or perhaps the one after that, we dropped down to the pub at the corner, myself for a pint, herself a whiskey and Apollinaris. Curious, the details that cling, when so much has been forgotten. We were idling about the counter, waiting I suppose for the porter to settle, when something on the television screen caught my eye. There was a reporter standing outside a house. A familiar house. A terraced house. But the volume was turned low, and it was impossible to ascertain what he was saying.

Yelena had begun a humorous anecdote, but I laid a couple of fingers on her arm to stanch it. The reporter was now holding his microphone towards a woman in a tea-cosy hat and coat knitted out of porridge. It was as if I recognised the news report. It was as if I'd seen it before, and dreaded its logic. The accursed holdall! The police must be onto it.

'I know that woman!' I whispered in dismay.

XIX

I've done it! I've finally fixed that accursed cat. For three nights now there's been not so much as a whisper on the street. Not so much as a can being disturbed. The pavement, plated in neon, is deserted. It's been hours since the echo of a footfall rolled along it from the main drag. On my windowpane a few leaves cling to the wetness, like logos of November. It's been one hell of a year for leaves. The window opposite continues its white scrutiny, unperturbed.

It's nearly finished. One more effort, or perhaps two. Then I can pack away my notes. I can bury the Remington, with its dodgy key, to the back of the wardrobe. One more effort, perhaps two, and it'll be as if the comic opera I've been describing happened to somebody else entirely. Then maybe I'll discern its music.

Something had occurred at the Maher household. That much was obvious. Even before I'd seen the woman being interviewed, the hatpin-wielding grandmother who was a near neighbour of Jester Mare, and even before I'd registered the curtains drawn across the pebbledash front, I'd known it. The news story was merely the public acknowledgement, as you might say. I called to the barman to turn up the volume, and I stood before the TV like a hamster before a cobra, impatient at last for the strike.

214

By the time the reluctant barman had complied with my request to turn up the volume, the story was dealt with. The millwheel groaned on to fresher grist. I could hear all I wanted about the latest leaks from the Castle on the millions made and buried in land speculation. I could pick over the details of another Christian Brother whose past had been unearthed. But not another squeak about Maher.

All the same, in one sense at least, my dread had been appeased. Just before his story had been dispatched, a photo appeared behind the newscaster: a girl in convent uniform, maroon; a milk-tooth smile and ponytail. They might have been any elfin schoolgirl's, at a glance. But I knew those little fangs. I knew that trace of freckles running like daisies across the nose. It was young Stephie Maher, and no other.

Soul cavorted. Not the holdall, then! He hasn't done anything stupid with whatever contraband he'd dug out of its entrails! Not as yet... That was my first, and I admit it, shame-worthy thought. No bogeyman would rise up imminently from the floorboards, stinking of tracksuits and petrol and cheap deodorant.

Mercifully for my later self-esteem, the preoccupation with Danaher's bag was short-lived. There was the girl to worry about. For who knew what a melancholic fool like Maher might have got up to that her school photo was on the six o'clock news! Yelena and I went our separate ways, I to the dismal flat by Portobello, she to a rendezvous she swore was innocent. When she mentioned the name of Zbigniew, another Polish blow-in by all accounts with some class of legal expertise behind him, a part of me was about to let fly at her. But I held back. I was in no mood for a squabble.

I began instead to worry and wonder what exactly the depressive had done to earn a spot on national television. He'd violated Danaher's holdall, that much was certain. No doubt he'd found something in its contraband that was worth the taking. And he'd no sooner found it than he'd disappeared. So far, so good. But what contraband, precisely? As I'd heaved it out to Finglas West, half-full as it was, or half-empty, its innards felt like they were made of cardboard bricks, though with some heavier article that consistently tunnelled to the bottom. Was that the way drugs were bought and sold, in bricks? What did I know about it! But when it came to the drug trade, would Chester Maher really have any more nous than yours sincerely?

He was a desperate man, that much I did know. I'm sure Mother would've had some old adage for the genius of a man who's desperate.

Now, the photo on the evening news would suggest he'd taken the girl with him into hiding. It did not bode well. All sorts of sinister permutations kept me tossing and turning that night, with the result that I'd no time to be jealous of any big-shot solicitor by the name of Zbigniew.

The following day, the Maher story was hardly what you'd call all over the papers. All the broadsheets carried the report, it's true, but in modest single-column packages, tucked away on page four or five. I took advantage of the fact that the shop assistant was busy to have a good poke around inside them, and was dismayed at their reticence. The tabloids saw no such merit in restraint or discretion. Two bore, on their front pages, the familiar photo of Stephie Maher, though eclipsed in the one case by the corrupt smile of a politician, in the other by the grainy image of a drug baron named 'the Abbot', who'd recently been released from gaol. But the details of the Maher case stretched to barely a few lines in either one. Oddly, it was the third, which made no mention at all of the story before page seven, that was the most vociferous. Beneath an innocuous picture of a pebbledash terraced house, the headline stated it baldly: 'ABDUCTED WHILE MOTHER ON HOLS!'

The shop assistant was by now watching me. I paid for the last tabloid, along with the nearest to hand of the broadsheets. No discrimination between highbrow and lowbrow for Will Regan. But in any event, allowing for preferences in register, there was little to choose between them. There was a scarcity of fact about the case beyond what I already knew. Stephie

Maher (6) had been missing for two days. So too had Chester Maher (50), so far as anyone could ascertain. The mother (42) was abroad. Circumstances connecting the two disappearances were not described, though the tabloid was far more generous in its conjecture.

Where the papers did concur was in the hysteria of little Stephie's guardian. This unfortunate was a foreign national who begged to remain anonymous. She was frantically trying to contact Stephanie Dujardin about the abducted daughter. The mother was presumed to be in Martinique, if you please. A sober appeal for any information, from a Superintendent Purcell of Pearse Street, was carried only in the broadsheet. I read it again. Pearse Street? On the south side? It seemed a long trek from Cabra. I shrugged, having not the least knowledge of the topography of investigation. Stephanie Dujardin *mère's* abode might fall under that jurisdiction for all I knew.

I was restless. Against my better judgement I made my way out to Cabra. I hadn't the least idea of what I was going to do once I got there. But one thing is sure. Neither did I have any notion of the net that was already beginning to draw about my own darker activities. If I'd the least inkling of what song Rakoczi was singing at the time in distant Odessa, I'd have thought twice about it.

Maybe I should've paid more heed to that old story of the Greek lad who set out in search of his mother. Fate had already prepared one jaw of the trap for him when he was no more than an infant and his parents had banished him. There was precious little he could've done about that. But the other jaw of the trap, that was all his own doing. He should've stayed put in his foster city. It's like I said before every trouble on this earth is caused by a man's inability to stay quietly at home

I was nervous, naturally enough, but as to the snare I was about to fall into, I was in blissful ignorance. How else could I have walked up to the house, fully expecting to find a forensic team beavering away behind blue and white tape? How else, once the knocker had detonated into an empty hallway, could

I have skived around to the rear, clambered over the wall at the second attempt, set that bloody dog into his flat-battery bark, and then tried the handle of the back door? And all this in broad daylight? The gas thing is, I could've told the police neither why I'd come nor what I was hoping to find. I could've given them nothing at all that might account for my keyless presence in the house. But even though I was as jittery as a bag of cats, I scorned to take precautions. I've no way of accounting for that behaviour either. Bravado, or blind stupidity? I tried the light switches, both downstairs and up. The electricity had been disconnected. I saw there was a scattering of envelopes and spam at the foot of the hall door. There was a larger package wedged in the jaws of the letterbox. Then Superintendent Purcell hadn't even visited the place? It beggared belief!

I leafed through the envelopes. Bills. Reminders. Final demands. There was even one that bore the grim livery of the Bailiff's Office. I shook my head, and scattered the leaves back as I had found them. To cover my tracks, as the saying goes. I then knelt and extracted the package, which was folded once over on itself, from the door's maw. I was careful in no way to scratch the brown paper packaging. No doubt it was this operation that put me in mind of the holdall, discarded like an afterbirth in the room upstairs.

I leapt to my feet. I snapped my fingers triumphantly. That was what I'd come for! It was all I could do not to take the steps three at a time. Now I was eager to get away. I was frantic to get away. So frantic was I that I failed to recognise the carrier. I rifled through the tossed clothes and towels, and at first dismissed the bag, thinking what I found too small, too flimsy. A poor replica, in point of fact. But when futility returned me to it, I pressed my hands inside and pushed it to its full extent. The padlock dangled like an anchor, striking against my thigh. I stopped fast. Suddenly I was at the window, convinced I'd heard footsteps on the flags outside.

The path was deserted.

I made my descent, this time taking the steps three and even four at a time. I vacillated, snatched the package out of the jaws of the letterbox, rammed it into the belly of the holdall, then disappeared out the back door, too rash to think of wiping the guilty prints from the handle.

Where did I make for?

Isn't it obvious?

I retraced my steps, roughly speaking; those self-same steps of the accursed night in which I'd first deposited the bag in Maher's cupboard. That is to say, I retraced my steps past St Peter's of Phibsboro and on as far as the canal. This time, there would be neither hesitation nor remorse. This time, the fetid waters hissing through the lock would drown the murderous fabric. I stood by the water and drew out the package, almost surprised to find it in there. Before violating the brown paper, I weighed the manuscript. I'd already guessed the contents. Then I rummaged about for a brick or stone with which to replace it. I checked about me before dispatching the weighted bag into the torrent. What magnificent irony, if only I'd had the foresight to appreciate it! To the far side of the water rose the Victorian imperturbability of Mountjoy. I was as impervious as the walls as I waited for the holdall to struggle once to the surface, then disappear forever beneath the suds.

Late that afternoon I buried myself in the flat and began to consider what to do. I had no TV to keep abreast of the case as it unfolded. If it unfolded. So I made up my mind to visit the smoky pub downstairs in time for the late evening news. In order to kill the time between this and then, I took the manuscript from its packaging and laid it on the bed beside me.

Let me be quite clear on this. It was no longer fear that held me from going outside. With the holdall drowned like a bag of reluctant puppies, it was as if a great weight had been lifted from me. I'd grown so used to it that I wasn't entirely conscious of its oppression. But it had connected me to Danaher, and to his ninth circle of hell. Now it was gone, as if it had never existed. Even supposing I bumped into the man, I could tell him I'd carried out his instructions.

No. If I was reluctant to leave the flat, it was inertia that restrained me, not anxiety. I had nowhere to go, and no energy with which to go there.

I daresay I could've tried to track down this Zbigniew character. But there, too, there'd been a sea-change in my thinking. I knew that it was I who held the cards, provided it was Yelena who made contact with me. She'd said she loved me, well let her prove it. Let her sort out whatever financial anxieties were furrowing her brow, and let her come back to me.

So, with a clear conscience, as the saying goes, I put the chain on the door, poured a glass of wine and stretched on my bed with the typescript.

I have to hand it to Chester Maher, the final act of his *Cuckold* really takes the biscuit. For years, Charlie Kavanagh, or Kinsella, has been tolerating his philistine wife, with her shenanigans and her strings of lovers. For years he's been putting up with the jibes of his father-in-law, the prose-speaking French magnate, the baron of refrigerated beef. For years he's been enduring the rise and rise of O'Rourke, the butcher's apprentice. And he does all of this in strictest tercets.

In this newest version, towards the end of Act Four, Father Quinlan of Ardee comes on a visit and mentions a literary concourse that's soon to take place there. The cuckold is excited. After years, his labours may at last be vindicated. He begins to furiously revise the manuscript of his own *Cuckold*. Eveline de Claire, the inconstant wife, who has been curiously ignorant of his secret passion, has become convinced that his indifference to her infidelities can only be explained in terms of his own illicit liaison. This was familiar territory, unchanged from the previous draft. One day, when Charlie is out of the office, she ransacks his drawers looking for evidence of a mistress. Instead, she stumbles across the incontrovertible evidence that he has never loved her. She gathers up all the heretical papers and consigns them to a pyre. The curtain falls on the magnificent, maleficent auto da fe.

Act Five is written mostly in free verse. Or blank verse. Whatever. Some months have passed. This last act commences with Charlie Kinsella receiving first prize for his literary masterpiece, *The Cuckold*. Father Quinlan is in the audience. Asked to recite the winning entry, Charlie complies. He delivers the reading in what a marginal note identifies as 'alexandrines'. It's clear from the reaction of Father Quinlan that this is not the version of Charlie's poem that he's become familiar with. The new draft recounts the life of an artist who is so put upon by his wife's infidelities that one day he strangles her. Quinlan is shocked. What will Eveline de Claire say if she gets to hear of this version?

A chorus comprised of critics discusses the work. Is it a parable of Ireland, so long betrayed by perfidious Albion? Is it an allegory of the Civil War, if war can ever be said to be civil? Is it a rewriting of Bloom's eternal acceptance of Molly? The truth is far more simple. The truth is revealed only when the curtains are drawn aside on the final scene. The truth hangs frozen on a meat hook, to the rear of the continental depot of de Claire Refrigerated Meats PLC, Rosslare, Co. Wexford.

Curtain.

It was already past nine. I leapt from the bed, pulled on my boots and raced down to the pub. I was just in time to catch the end of the report. From a hotel foyer in Martinique, Stephanie Dujardin was being interviewed. Or more accurately, she was giving a prepared statement for the press. An appeal, I believe they term it. A striking mixed-race woman stood supportively behind her, stern and elegant. Stephanie, too, was stern and elegant, her coiffure as elaborate as a bird of paradise above a face that was only beginning to be lined. 'I would ask you, Chester, please, if you are watching this, please don't bring any more confusion to the child. Let her go, Chester, I am asking you.' *Chesteur.* Hints of Paris, stern and elegant. The mulatta leaned forward, whispered something in her ear. Stephanie nodded, rose, smiled gravely, and thanked the camera crew.

That night, I slept like a log.

On the following morning, returning to the flat with the entire gamut of morning papers, broadsheet and tabloid, I was surprised to find Ciarán Crowe waiting at the door for me. 'You're about the last man on this earth I was expecting to see here!'

'Your friend is in a degree of trouble.'

'My friend?' I fiddled about with the lock and key, the papers teetering between elbow and ribs. 'I daresay my friend knows exactly what he's doing. Come in, Father.' With the best will in the world, I seemed unable to drop the title.

'I'm not so sure that I share your confidence. Not if it's reached the pass where he's taken the girl. Did you by any chance see the news last night?'

'I saw the appeal of the distraught mother.'

'No,' he said. 'I mean before that.' Inside the flat, he went on to detail the concerns expressed by a psychiatric nurse who'd had considerable truck with Maher over the years. The priest had once asked me if Chester had thoughts of self-harm. It seems the copse in the Phoenix Park was far from being the first attempt he'd made on his own life. 'But what's all that got to do with young Stephie? I've seen them together. He's crazy about that girl!'

'I don't doubt that, not for a minute. A second detail emerged. It seems your friend hired a car. A Nissan Micra, red. It was due to be returned two days ago. Naturally, the guards are watching all the ports, but who knows where the bird has flown to by this time. There's always the North.' He'd pinched the bridge of his nose between the fingers of either hand, in an attitude not unlike prayer. 'You told me he was experiencing severe financial troubles.'

'And what about it? Haven't we all financial troubles? He's hardly going to do anything stupid on account of financial troubles!'

'There's no telling what a man will do when facing into the abyss of debt. Don't they say Pearse himself was driven to rebel on account of bad debts?'

'Do they, faith? I heard it was Nationalism.' I was hedging. In our verbal game of chess, there was a possible combination that I didn't want raised. 'Tell me,' he asked, his eyes in shadow, 'why do you suppose he's run away with her at this time? What made him wait until now to disappear with the child?'

Now that particular monkey-nut was one I was having the greatest difficulty in cracking. It was certainly true that his finances were crashing down about his ears. I'd seen the bailiff's letter, for God's sake! But what was new in that? He must've known for months that particular juggernaut was approaching. Yes, but he'd harped on the fear his daughter would be taken to live in France. For the first time? No, but still it was reasonable…

But that wasn't it! That wasn't the half of it. And boy did I know it! He'd absconded first and foremost with the contents of Danaher's bag. I felt physically sick as it rose once more above the surface of the canal. 'To tell you the truth, Father, I've been giving that one a lot of thought.' *Don't do it,* hissed Soul. *For God's sake, don't do anything stupid now! Do it, do it,* hissed conscience. For want of a better word.

'There's something else.' Fuck you, Conscience anyway! 'Something… out of the ordinary.' I felt giddy, surrendering to the combination; giddy, like someone who's about to resign his king; giddy like someone who's throwing his trouser-belt over the bough of a tree. 'Can I have your word that what I say won't go beyond the four walls of this room?'

'You have my word,' he said, and over a couple of non-industrial coffee cups I disclosed to the meddlesome priest all that I knew about the goings on of one Joseph Mary Danaher, his dodges, his intrigues, his burns, and his nefarious traffic.

'But what do you suppose was inside that bag?'

'That's the twenty thousand dollar question, isn't it? It felt like it was filled with bricks, only lighter. Cardboard bricks. I suppose it must've been drugs.'

'What makes you say drugs?'

'Why else would his accomplices have set fire to him?'

'I thought you told me he'd turned informer?'

'He had. I think he had. Damn it,' I cried, 'I wish the hell I'd never set eyes on the man!'

'We have to find him,' he declared, solemnly. He'd sat up, rigid, and his little eyes were boring straight into me. 'Find who?' I croaked. I was hoping he was referring to a depressive in a torn raincoat dragging his daughter around the country. Hoping against hope, as they say.

'Joseph Mary Danaher!' It boomed like an accusation ringing out in a cathedral.

I shook my head. 'How can we find him!'

'You say he's receiving treatment for his burns?'

'He's on a course of grafts. What they call interventions…' and so on and so forth until he had me standing in the very corridor that led to the Serious Burns Unit of the Mater Hospital. By a stroke of luck, good luck, ill luck, my grim Filipino was just on the point of knocking off his shift. I introduced the two men.

Crowe outlined for him the bones of the situation. He managed this without disclosing either the disappearance of the contraband nor my role in its trafficking. We were by this time standing on the hospital steps, out of earshot of curious authorities. 'But it's impossible,' smiled the nurse, his head swivelling. 'It's quite impossible. It goes against medical ethics you see. You're a man of God, and you must appreciate…'

The man of God touched me on the forearm. 'Would you mind leaving the two of us alone for a few minutes, William?'

To this day I don't know what precisely a priest says to convince a nurse to bend the rules. Filipinos are by and large Catholic, that much I do know. I've an idea the pope went there on a visit, after his Ireland jaunt. Was there a Cardinal Sin involved? But whether or not Catholicism had any bearing on the present conversation is more than I know. To cut a long story short, when he rejoined me several minutes afterwards, Father Crowe had a slip of paper containing an address not ten minutes' walk from the hospital.

It was a ten-minute walk that filled me with dread: the dread of the condemned man. The dread of the truant as he's dragged along to the headmaster's office.

There was no answer at the upstairs flat, although the meddling cleric insisted that we try the bell a number of times. But the curtains were wide open, and there was not the slightest evidence of anyone lurking about inside the place. We turned to make our way back down the stairwell, and for the first time in a while I joked with my companion. My levity was short-lived. It was beheaded by the visor of a baseball cap poking out from under a hoody the very minute we stepped out onto the street.

I was shocked at Danaher's appearance. It wasn't so much the scarring, the wax discolouration that had remoulded his face and stretched his eyes until they were mongoloid. Nor was it the threadbare hairs that bristled on his upper lip in imitation of a moustache. It was this: there was something new and unexpected in the pupils. His eyes looked craven. There's no other word for it. He looked craven, like a dog you're about to strike. At first I thought it was simply that he was being confronted on the street by two men, one of whom was unknown. But it persisted, even after he'd hurried us into the flat and out of the public eye.

I don't say he wasn't still all bluster. Far from it. But his movements, too, had lost their conviction. No longer did he walk with the strut of the rooster. Of course, he was physically constrained. The scarring extended to more than a third of his body. Both of his hands were gloved in gauze. And his voice, which was wont to rasp, had lost its powers of sarcasm. The lungs, too, had been scorched by the fire.

Even so, he tried to face us down with bluster and bravado. Crowe was having none of it. He demanded to be told what had been in the bag, and when the other replied with a colourful phrase or two, he declared boldly that he'd publish Danaher's new address abroad. On Tuesdays, he warned, he worked with the junkies down at Adam and Eve's. You'd be amazed who they were in touch with… I looked at the effigy of Danger Danaher, and I surprised myself feeling pity for him. On the wall behind him, a therapeutic mask hung from a nail, eyeless and translucent, something a snake might have sloughed off.

'Here! Here's your bucking evidence!' He'd suddenly begun to turn out his pockets, which caused him a deal of effort on account of the mittens, and to throw rolled up, coloured papers at us. 'Here's your bucking evidence! Go on, take it! Here yis are!' He was making quite a show of turning out each pocket, wincing if his fingers snagged, or if the pressure of the entry was excessive. It took a minute to realise what he was throwing at us was lucre. Ready cash. I picked up one of the balls, maroon, and unfurled a mincing Daniel O'Connell. I shrugged at Ciarán Crowe, but he was already on his feet. 'Come on,' he nodded, 'we'll leave him be.'

Outside, it dawned on me. The insipid smirks of Joyce and O'Connell were counterfeit. So that had been his game all along! All this time, while I'd been convinced his lark was peddling drugs, he'd been passing off false bills! It almost seemed quaint! But who knew on what lowlifes he'd tried to palm these notes off, to be repaid with sugared petrol? Was it that, or was it his treachery, which had the Russians, real and imagined, on his tail?

And then bad luck had prompted Chester Maher to stumble upon a bag still half-filled with golden bricks of counterfeit bills. In his downcast state, those smirks of Joyce and O'Connell must have appeared the very smiles of Fortune!

'So,' I exclaimed, 'what in God's name do we do now?'

'What do we do now? You can ask me that?'

I awaited the gavel of his judgement unflinchingly.

'We go and tell what we know to the police, that's what we do now. That man has to be found, and fast.'

Ha-ha! cried Soul, *see you round!* As Soul took flight, my heart fell into my boots. I knew full well I wouldn't have the strength to argue the toss with this goddamned… holier-than-thou!

I drew in short breaths. I'd begun to feel the trouser-belt tighten about my neck.

XX

*F*ate had concealed one jaw of its mantrap in distant Odessa. It was a place that Rakoczi had once referred to as the edge of the world. But if there was to be a second jaw to the trap, it would be in my own city and of my own fashioning.

I'd made a solemn promise to Father Ciarán Crowe of St Audoen's that I'd go down to Pearse Street Garda Station before the day was out. At the moment I'd said it to him, I meant it, every blessed word. When we'd shaken on it, I'd even begun to set off in the direction of Parnell's monument. But before ever I got as far as his *non plus ultra*, I stopped in my tracks. A few doubts had begun to weigh in, to say the least, the way that heavy iron I'd neglected to mention had a way of worming to the bottom of Danaher's bag. Foremost among them was this little horror: if Danger'd been so quick to give names to the cops the very minute they'd picked him up, was it likely the man would've been reticent to pass on the name of one William Regan to whatever hard-chaws he'd tried to buy off with those dud notes? And now, thanks to the same Will Regan, half the cache had gone walkabout! Damn it all, it was easy enough for a priesteen to say what was the right thing for a body to do, so long as it was somebody else. Wasn't that their job description?

And then there was Yelena to consider. Did she love me? It had been her word, after all. So could it be full-blown love, that uncertain fluttering our caterpillar liaison had developed into? Was Cupid's mischievous dart the cause of the glow I'd swear she'd begun to give off ever since our little breach and repair? If it was, who was I to put it in jeopardy? Hadn't she told me to be bloody careful? Hadn't she asked me to keep my head down, and not attract the attentions of the Revenue Commission? Hadn't she pleaded with me to keep my nose clean? And now I was supposed to walk into the guards like an eejit with a tale of false money? Oh by God there was nothing easier than for a priest to tell you what to do.

I took a little diversion. What was the rush? I soon found myself amidst the piebald bustle of Moore Street. Banks of flat amber eyes gawped back from atop the cart of a fishwife. Beneath it, a snot-nosed brat was firing caps at his snivelling baby sister. *I knew all along it'd end in tears.* All right, Mother. Maybe it was bound to. But what would you have me do? Would you have me turn snitch? Would you have me become the lowest of the low? What difference can it make, whether I go to see this Superintendent Purcell or whether I mind my own business? Mind your own business, cook your own fish, isn't that what you always used to say?

A couple of chuckaros in leather jackets bumped past me, speaking Russian. At least, I supposed it to be Russian. The urchin fired a shot after them, and then pointed his cap-gun at me just as a new thought took hold. A virtuous thought, as you might say. If Maher was leaving a trail of counterfeit notes behind him, would these same gangsters not also be able to track him down? Set fire to him too? I'd be a bloody fool to turn tattletale, but who else was there to give the guards a sporting chance of getting there first? Isn't that what Crowe had been driving at all along with his 'You can ask me that?'

Oh by Christ it was easy enough for a priesteen to say what was the right thing for a body to do, so long as it was somebody else.

I watched the fishwife fetch her brat a clatter with the back of her hand, and I saw her see me see the dig. 'Was there somethin' ye wanted or ere ye going to stand there gawking all day?' I pointed as if she'd cracked a great witticism, and pushed on. My indecision took me down Jervis Street, past Capel Street Bridge and the Four Courts, past the Croppy Acre and Kingsbridge and Walsh's of Parkgate Street, past Wellington's stern obelisk and on until I stood before the Magazine Fort. It'd been over a year since I'd been there. Some year! I looked at its irregular geometry, overgrown and dilapidated, and called to the abandoned nests in the battlements: 'The mother would never tell me: is it true I was conceived here? By a man called 'W'? Here, beneath these silent ramparts?' But like Soul, the swallows were long since departed.

In my gut, of course, I knew already what I was going to do. Well fuck you five times, Conscience! Across the valley, the street lights were beginning to flicker on. Soon the traffic would start its homeward flow. But from where I stood, to every point of the compass, a sense of abandon stretched as far as the eye could focus. I fully expected that this would be my last day of liberty. A delectable inevitability brooded over me. I could no more have escaped now than the nest could take wing and follow the migrating swallow.

I made my way slowly back along the north quay, past Collins Barracks and the Four Courts where I'd been contaminated by Danaher, past Capel Street Bridge and the Winding Stair. I paused only on top of the Ha'penny Bridge, its back arched like a cat over the bickering water. *Give it a minute*, whispered Soul. You're back? *I am.* So? *It was here*, sighed Soul, *that you first kissed her.* That *who* kissed *who*? Does it matter? Guess not. The first kiss returned so vividly, I'd swear I felt its wing brush my mouth. And now you're kissing her goodbye is it?

We passed from the Ha'penny Bridge to the Ha'penny Inn. There's a chess adage: sit on your hands before you make the decisive move. Pause for thought. I can't say the couple of pints and small ones had any great effect on the outcome of the game. I can say this. It was after closing time when I steered between Trinity College and the old wedding-cake Parliament, and crossed over towards the station, its stonework vivid and unreal as a stage set.

'I want to speak to Superintendent Purcell, please.'

D137 glanced briefly up and then returned to the ledger she'd been scribbling in. 'He's knocked off for the evening,' she said, without raising her eyes a second time. I watched her bun a moment, then looked about the walls of the place. A poster gave essential information for asylum seekers. Another warned of the dangers of drink driving. I turned to go.

'Was it anything in particular you wanted him for?'

'It's…' I croaked. A head like that of a starving Parnell swam up before me. Damn you, Father! Damn you, Conscience! Damn you, Mother, for ever having conceived me! 'It's connected with…the Maher case.' I turned about. The eyes of the ban-garda were now fixed upon me, mahogany, under tightly drawn auburn hair. As said, I've a head for trivialities. 'What did you say your name was, sir?' D137 poised her pen over the open ledger as if she were about to pin an insect there. 'Regan. Look, would I be able to leave a message for Superintendent Purcell?'

'Regan.'

'Will Regan.'

'Address?'

'Look, miss. I really would prefer to talk directly to the Superintendent.'

'Just a minute, Mr Regan,' she said, 'I'll see what I can do.'

I watched D137 step away from the desk, almost nonchalantly, and go back through the door to a rear office, where a male colleague was sitting by what looked like a switchboard. They didn't entirely close the door. She picked up a receiver, glancing once back in my direction, and I watched her profile talk into it. To this day, I'd swear I could read her lips as she pronounced my name, twice.

But there was a phone squatting by my elbow on the duty desk. Why hadn't she simply rung from here? Was it, in fact, Superintendent Purcell she was talking to? Had Danaher ever given them *my* name?

I grew increasingly agitated. The emptiness of the room might at any time be violated. I glanced behind me to the door that led out to the street. Then I looked back to the desk. The ledger lay open, the pen across it. I grabbed it up, pulled from my pocket the envelope in which I'd packed the counterfeit bills the gauzed hands had hurled at me, and scribbled a note for the Super on its reverse: 'Follow the trail of false notes. Like Hansel and Gretel, they'll lead you straight to Chester Maher.' I then lodged it in the spine of the ledger and hurried the hell out of the place.

Echoes of footfalls pursued me around the block and down Townsend Street. On Hanover Street, a cat leapt from a wall and put the heart across me. Then I ducked down Lime Street, followed by my own shadow, and had to double back up along the quay until I was able to cross the choppy river over the low span of Matt Talbot Bridge. At every moment I expected to be summoned back by a troop of guards.

I've no way of knowing what time it was when I banged on Yelena's door. But I do know this: there was no answer to my entreaty. To this day, I don't know for certain if she was inside and silent. Was she cowering, afraid to open it? Was she in Zbigniew's place, wherever that was? Or had she already taken flight?

Somehow, I walked away the rest of the night. As the lees gave way to the clear glass of morning, I slipped through the railings that are intended to keep vagabonds out of the Magazine Fort. There, in a crumbling building that smelled of piss and cobwebs, I shivered myself into a fitful sleep. God alone knows what visions came to me. I jerked awake at about eleven o'clock with a sensation of monstrous guilt.

I followed the low tide in as far as St Audoen's, my mind too numb to be bothered by the spasms of cold that still seized me. No, I'm afraid Father Crowe is out on a visit, mister... ahm...? But I was a familiar face by now, and was allowed into the sacristy to await his return. I'd never before appreciated so piteously the mug of ersatz coffee the housekeeper served up.

My eyes wandered about the walls, past the scrutiny of the Clonliffe Class of '64, and came to rest on the notice board. I was struck by a poster-sized photo that I hadn't seen there before: on a lake-isle, a building whose grey, regular geometry looked somewhere between a fortification and a prison. It struck me as familiar, even uncannily so. I, who had never once been outside the confines of the city.

'I didn't know you'd an interest in pilgrimage.'

'You're back!'

'You look like you've just come back yourself from Patrick's purgatory! Have you got wet?'

'I slept badly, that's all.' He was removing his gabardine, from the pocket of which a paper protruded. 'What news, Father?'

'Did you go and see your Inspector Purcell?'

'I did,' I lied. 'What news?'

'Take a look for yourself.' He extended the tabloid towards me. Crowe had a mischievous look about him that I hadn't seen before. I unfurled the paper, and was amazed to find a blurred photo of a topless bather on the cover. A tiny strip of black censored each nipple. My eyes flicked from the priest to the headline: 'STEPHANIE FROLICS WHILE SEARCH CONTINUES'.

'Good God!' I said.

'Perhaps,' he suggested, 'His hand is indeed to be seen in this.'

Stephanie Dujardin Maher was spotted frolicking topless on paradise beach with playmate and former pageant queen Desira Patel (28) early yesterday. This was at the very time when the search for her abducted daughter went nationwide (see page 7 for more pics).

'I don't think I follow you.' I placed the paper on the table between us and examined his arched eyebrows. 'God's hand?'

'What I mean to say is, all of this has to be good news for your friend.'

'How so?' That day, my head really was empty, or filled only with aches and cobwebs.

'I know little enough about the legal niceties, but that sort of carry-on,' he tapped the paper, 'has to have an impact in a custody case.'

'Do you think so?'

'I'm sure of it! How could it not? I only hope that he himself is aware of the developments. Oh,' he added, 'they found the car. The red Nissan.'

'Where?'

'Athlone. Did you tell your Inspector Purcell that the car was almost certainly hired on counterfeit money?' I felt my ears burn. 'I think he knew already,' I stammered. I think he knew I was telling fibs.

'And tell me, do you know of any friends or relatives who may live in the vicinity of Athlone?' I sucked in, repeated 'Athlone', forced my reluctant brain to concentrate. But the only bloody name I could think of in connection with Athlone was O'Byrne, or O'Brien. 'Nope. So far as I'm aware, Maher's an only child. A loner, too.'

'That's how his neighbour described him on the news. A loner. You know you look like death warmed up?'

I guffawed. 'That's something Mother would say! Even after she could no longer see what I looked like, she'd say that.'

'You really should go home and try to get some sleep.'

'Will you keep me posted about new developments in the case?'

'Certainly I will. Do you have a phone?'

I reached into my pocket and passed over the mobile that Danaher had given me. Damned if I knew how to extract my number from it.

'Do you realise you've three missed calls?' he asked.

'Do I?'

'And at least as many voice messages.' He looked at me, a supercilious lightness about the brow. 'Would you like me to dial them up for you?'

'By all means.'

He did so and, soul of discretion, he left the room while I attended to the apparatus. All three were from Yelena. She'd performed the same trick of extracting its number from it a couple of weeks earlier. But she'd not had call to use it. We were seeing each other most days by this time.

Each call was spaced by a couple of hours. There was a horrible progression in the voice, shredding itself by degrees into rags of exhaustion and despondency. The gist of what she had to say was that the Revenue was on to her. She'd had advance warning from a 'friend' of Adam Rakoczi. Rakoczi had been released, but then detained immediately upon his arrival at some airport. It may even have been Dublin. She felt too afraid to return to her flat. She was, she murmured, sort of passing over the words, staying over with this 'friend'.

A friend of Adam Rakoczi? Hearing her Eastern pronunciation of that hated name and the way she glossed over 'staying with a friend' made my instinct bolt towards jealousy. And where did Mr Zbigniew fit in? He at least hadn't been detained by any police immediately upon his arrival at Dublin Airport! I nodded my thanks to Ciarán Crowe. I then set off for my flat at a vigorous pace, guts in turmoil. Was the leopard changing back into her old spots so soon?

Of course, it was more than possible, likely in fact, that the Revenue had cottoned on to her shenanigans. *To your shenanigans,* Soul cried, in a voice of triumphant malice it could only have learned from Mother. And what of it? I growled. What have I to hide? There was never a penny of my own money in their accounts. *In your accounts!* Before I could answer, Soul handed the pitchfork back to the demon of jealousy. *Athlone?* he hissed. *Funny, that Maher should have gone precisely where Dónal O'Byrne keeps his love boat!* And so what? *Oh, nothing!* But all the way back to the flat the pitchfork prodded mercilessly, with scant regard to the etiquette of probabilities.

I lay with my head propped between open palms and stared up at the ceiling.

Once, there was a man named Chester Maher, who married a beautiful Parisian and who brought her to live with him in Cabra. For years he was tormented by her infidelities, but they had a child, and he loved this child more than the whole world.

The tributary of a long crack meandered lazily from right to left, and my eye followed it hither and thither, hither and thither. How would the story end?

Once, there was a depressive named Chester Maher who married a beautiful Parisian and who had a child by her. He loved that child more than he loved the world, and one day he stole her away to live with him in the west. But the police followed them there, because everywhere he went, Chester Maher left a trail of false notes behind him.

I stretched, yawned. This much at least had changed. So far as my talking to the guards was concerned, Yelena was out of the equation. If Revenue were on to her, Rakoczi was to blame for that. It freed my hand, as you might say. The only question was, had I drawn any unwanted attention to my own affairs?

Once, there was a suicide named Chester Maher who married a beautiful Frenchwoman who went with him to live in Cabra. She had many, many lovers. He had a child by her, on balance, and he loved that child more than he loved the world. One day, while she was out of the country, he stole her and fled to the west. He left a trail of false notes behind him. But when Social Services saw how little the Frenchwoman cared for her own child…

I sat up. But was Chester in a position to buy the tabloids? Did he even know about her high jinks on a paradise island in the Caribbean? Did the Gardaí know, as I knew, how critical it was that he should know this? There was nothing for it. Conscience, again! I swear, you give conscience an inch…

'Who is this, please?' Conscience had goaded me outside, and I was now standing on the canal bank, midway between two bridges, as far as possible from the clamour of the traffic. I was unused to phones, let alone mobiles. Still, the voice emerged fitfully from the crinkle of static.

'My name is Wi… Listen, I left in…hello? Can you hear me?'

'I can hear you.'

'I left you in an envelope. It was in connection with the Maher case. Did you get it?'

'Hansel and Gretel, is it? I was hoping that you'd ring, Mr Regan.'

'Oh?' So, they remembered my name was Regan!

'Perhaps you have something more to tell me?'

I looked about me. The canal bank was unpeopled. My eyes followed the water as far as the reflection of the bridge, the very bridge where once upon a time three thugs had set on Danaher. 'It's in connection with the Maher case. Are you still there?'

'I'm still here.'

'There's a couple of things you should know,' I said, all in a rush. I looked over the indifferent audience of mallards and moorhens. For the first time in my life, I felt important. 'Chester Maher is a manic depressive.' The phone remained silent. 'There's worse. On more than one occasion...'

'You're a friend of Mr Maher?'

'I am.' The connection really was appalling. There was a breeze gusting along the canal, wrinkling its water. Perhaps it was interfering with the signal. Carrying it away. 'The point is, it's absolutely critical that when you find him you let him know what's been happening with Stephanie Dujardin.' I waited. There was nothing but static coming from the other end. 'Can you hear me?' You bloody fool, Will Regan. Didn't Ciarán Crowe say his melancholia was all over the news? There was a noise like the crinkling of paper. 'You said there were a couple of things, Mr Regan?'

'The second relates to the money. You got the envelope I left in for you?' An indeterminate sound issued from the phone. I felt piqued at the lack of response. I imagine that's what made me continue so resolutely. So incautiously. Here goes, I thought, heart hammering. You're a damn fool, Will Regan! 'That money originated from Joseph Mary Danaher.'

Pause.

'You've heard of him!'

'Did it?'

'It did. So God alone knows who else might be after Chester Maher.'

'What do you mean by that?'

'You saw what they done to Danaher for Christ's sake!'

'And the money originated from that quarter?'

That *quarter*? 'That's what I'm telling you.'

'And you can vouch for that, Mr Regan?'

Now it was my turn to be silent. There followed what they call a pregnant pause. 'Are you still there?'

'I'm still here.'

'So you tell me that Chester Maher is an acquaintance of Joseph Danaher?'

'I didn't say that.' I held the phone away from me, appalled at its treachery. My treachery. 'I never said that!'

'Can you think,' crackled the phone, 'of any reason why Chester Maher might've gone to ground in Chapelizod?'

'I thought it was Athlone…' Suddenly, I sensed a trick. This plod was smarter than he was letting on. What was it he was trying to trap me into saying? 'Look, I've to go. I have to…' I shut down the phone that Danaher himself had pressed on me. I took three sharp breaths. Then, as though it were a thing contaminated, I hurled it as far as I could over the motionless water. It disappeared with a derogatory plop. What mess are you after getting yourself into, Will Regan?

XXI

*T*he mess I was after getting myself into was an interrogation room in Pearse Street Garda Station. This did not happen immediately upon my return to the flat, as I'd half-expected. But on the following night, a squad car parked itself on a double-yellow across the street from the window. I watched it, knowing well it had come for me, hoping against hope I was wrong. I watched the blue-clad officer stroll over to the building and then, after an infinite delay, my door vibrated before his knuckles. The knocks reverberated through my solar plexus. I was already dressed for outside. After I confirmed my details into a diminutive notebook, I was asked if I'd accompany the officer as far as the station. There was no question of being placed under arrest, sir. On this point he was quite insistent. I was merely being invited to assist the police in their enquiries. As the saying goes.

Something more had come to light in the Maher case, that much was obvious. There was a bustle about the station that I hadn't seen on my previous visit. But still I was left waiting in an anteroom for the better part of an hour, during which purgatory the very lettering of the posters opposite me became engraved on my soul. At a pinch, I could've recited the numbers for all sorts of confidential hotlines. I was mightily relieved when my name was called. 'First, I'd like you to tell us absolutely everything you know about Chester Maher, about his relations with Stephanie Dujardin Maher, and about the daughter, Stephie.' A white-faced, red-haired twenty-year-old with eyes set far too close together was sitting across the table from me. Behind my shoulder, to the left, by the door that remained conspicuously ajar, arms behind his back and mouth moving as though sucking on an Alka-Seltzer, stood Superintendent Purcell. I'd known since the phone call he was no Dub, and in his farmer's coat he looked quite the bogman.

'Something's happened, hasn't it?'

The seated officer looked up to Purcell, who shut his eyes and nodded.

'They've been located. They're in Chapelizod.'

'Chapelizod. I see.' Of course, I didn't see. Superintendent Purcell cleared his throat and edged into view. 'We followed your paper trail, Mr Regan, and it led us from Athlone to Chapelizod,' he confirmed, then added with forensic levity: 'there was a supermarket lodgement into a bank that the bank wasn't entirely happy to honour.'

'But you say they've been *located* in Chapelizod…'

'I say they've been *located* in Chapelizod.' Had I seen a wink, a twinkle, or a trick of the hurtingly bright light? 'We suspected as much when some of your bills showed up there.' Now, I didn't at all care for the way he said 'your bills', but I let it go. 'That was on the evening before last. The very evening of your phone call. Then another phone call came in early this morning. This, from a distraught woman who's doing her best to run a B&B by the name of The Salmon Leap.'

'The Salmon Leap.'

'This lady informed us there was a guest who'd been acting rather oddly.'

'Maher!' I exclaimed.

'Maher. He'd checked in some days ago with a little girl he'd informed her was his daughter. Nothing too unusual in that. But when they didn't put in an appearance at breakfast on the following morning, she tried his door. Locked, from the inside.

The key still in it. They failed to emerge at all that day nor the following morning either, and after she saw the story on the news, she put two and two together and so she rang us. She'd have had her suspicions about him earlier but that the child had seemed in fine fettle altogether.'

'And now?'

'And now we have the premises surrounded. He's barricaded himself into the room and the daughter in there with him. He's refusing to come out.'

'I see,' I said, beginning to see. I was surprised there was no stenographer, tapping away, 'tak-taka-tak'. I was surprised that the door was left ajar. Perhaps these were little signals to convince me that I was really there of my own free will. Assisting them with their enquiries. Purcell's hand invited me to return to the question in hand, and I summarised the domestic history of the Mahers, such as I knew it. They were patient with me. They had to be, for such help as I could give them had a tendency to ravel and repeat. Then Purcell cut it abruptly short. 'How does Maher know Joseph Mary Danaher?'

'But he doesn't!' I drew in a deep breath. The previous twenty minutes had been child's play in comparison to the melee we were now about to enter. 'He never met the man! In point of fact…' and away we went. How long this phase of the interview lasted I've no way of knowing. If I were to measure the time with coffee cups, the reckoning would run to three. Saucerless, they left a pattern of rings over the Formica surface. Occasionally Purcell left the room, but he never stayed away for more than five minutes at a time. Then he'd look straight at me. 'Tell me,' he finally interrupted my iterations, 'have you ever known your friend Maher to carry a firearm?'

'A firearm?!'

'A gun,' explained Foxy, as if I'd had difficulty with the term. 'Think carefully before you answer,' warned the Superintendent. 'No. Never.' He waited. Foxy waited. The interrogation cell filled with waiting. 'There was,' I sighed, after an interminable silence, 'a weight of some kind in that holdall of Danaher's I told you about.'

Here's the thing. They knew all about that gun. They must've done. But that's the police for you, more tricks than circus clowns. More than one bitter coffee had been drunk since I'd told them about the bloody denouement of Maher's *Cuckold*, with its fantasy of revenge, and only now did they mention he had a gun!

'So what next?'

'You're free to go. All the same I'd ask you to consider accompanying me to the scene of the abduction.' The *abduction*? Whatever else it was, it was no abduction. 'And what'll that achieve, d'you think?'

'You might be able to talk some sense into your pal,' supplied Foxy. I considered this. Could it be another of their damn tricks? Scarcely. Still, you never knew. 'We'd want to hurry,' interrupted the Super, now all bustle in the manner of the habitually indolent. I snapped my fingers and pointed. 'I'll tell you the very man who might well be able to talk sense into him!' So in the heel of the hunt, I found myself hurtling in the back of a squad car through the pre-dawn traffic in the direction of St Audeon's. The flippant single whoop of the siren as we sped through each red junction did nothing to calm my nerves. And of course the priest wasn't there. 'What day is it? Tuesday? I'll tell you where he is. It's his morning he does the drug clinic down at Adam and Eve's.' From the look Purcell fired at me, it was as well Adam and Eve's stood loosely on our path. But Crowe wasn't there either. He'd been summoned from Audeon's by an urgent message, though why they couldn't have told us that back at the church I do not know. It seemed that somewhere in Ranelagh or Harold's Cross a colleague of the cloth had been found dead. There were suspicious circumstances. 'Do you think we might…?' The Super looked hard at me and shook his grey head. Harold's Cross was a cross too far.

There was quite a collection of vehicles in Chapelizod village: vans with satellite dishes on their roofs and thick umbilical cables winding over the pavements, Garda cars parked at haphazard angles, even a great khaki army lorry. Purcell nodded to an officer in a luminous jacket and ushered me through the copses of onlookers and press-hounds and under the blue and white cordon. 'Keep up can't you,' he urged as he bore down on a squad car. But I'd frozen. My eyes were playing tricks. There was a face in the back-seat window that refused to come into focus. It was as if it had been smudged by a giant thumb. My heart hammered the base of my throat. 'Christ, what's he doing here?' Purcell turned to face me. 'We need him to give us a positive ID on that firearm.' So then, they'd known all along that it had been his? The smudge still refused to come into focus, but I resumed my walk, three paces behind Purcell's farmer's coat. 'Couldn't you have warned me he'd be here?' I hissed.

'And if I did, would you have come?'

He had me there! Danger was wearing his see-through pressure mask. I suppose it was on account of that that his appearance was so uncanny. The eyes were even more oriental than before, the lips pushed out in a manner that recalled Rakoczi. When I came into his field of vision, the eyes flitted first away, as though I'd caught him at something, and then back on me, all hatred and accusation. Then they flicked upwards to the Superintendent. 'I'm after telling yiz a hundred times, it's a Jaysus staaarting pistol!'

Purcell ignored him. He spoke instead to an officer who was peering through a giant telescopic lens in the direction of a house across the river. 'Any sign?'

'Nothing. Not a squeak.'

We left the car and made for the corner of a wall by the river where stood a pair of top brass in the company of a Garda in a flak jacket cradling an evil-looking automatic. Another, unmistakeably a cop in spite of the plain clothes, was training a more slender weapon on the upper-floor window of a house opposite, its blind down. Surely to God the comedy hadn't come to this pass! Purcell consulted his watch. 'You can inform the press that we'll lift all restrictions once this chap has tried his luck talking to the man. Tom, have you the bullhorn?'

I hadn't the foggiest what I was going to say. Something about the missus frolicking on a Caribbean beach, to be sure. But I dithered over the remainder. In any event, it wasn't a speech I was destined to make. Tom, a ridiculously young-looking sergeant, had returned with a loudspeaker, and now it lay idle in my hands as I hummed and hawed. Suddenly everyone cowered. Simultaneously, a report rang out. Seeing everyone on their hunkers, I realised it had been a shot. 'Get him out of here,' whispered Purcell. Bemused, bewildered, I found myself following Tom's ample policeman's backside on a crouch. When we got level with the bridge, I turned my head. Danger was straining out of the rear window as if the Garda car were trying to give birth to him: 'It's only a starting pistol!' he taunted apoplectically, 'a bucking staaarting pistol! Them's blanks he's firing for Jaysus' sake!'

We were now erect. 'Why the panic, if it's blanks?' I asked. Sergeant Tom weighed me up as if I were a prize fool. 'Sure you couldn't believe the Hail Mary out of that fella's mouth!' Then he looked over to the blind window. 'Besides, we haven't got sight of the piece as yet.' The 'piece'! As if it could've been any other 'piece'.

Twenty minutes later, we were ready for another go. They'd rigged up a sound system, which meant I could be kept out of harm's way. From a gun firing blanks? This time, I had no problems at all with fluency. 'Chester! Chester, can you hear me? This is Will, Moll Regan's boy…'

Purcell came up to us when I was finished. 'Would you run this man back into town, Tom? You're free to go, Mr Regan. But I'll give you a little word of advice. A file is being prepared for the DPP in relation to an international ring and their financial shenanigans, and one day soon you're like to be summoned in for questioning. It might be in your interest to anticipate that and volunteer what you know. I'll leave it with you. In any case,

Tom's the man can fill you in on any details as he drops you wherever you want.'

Next to the drama that was unfolding in Chapelizod village, my own private nightmare is bound to seem trivial. Yet we need to follow its logic. To round out the picture, as you might say. I had Tom pass by St Audeon's, but Father Crowe was still occupied with the affair up in Harold's Cross. I left a brief note for him in the sacristy, during which interlude I saw that the siege was getting what they call 'real time' TV coverage. Then I asked the Sergeant to take me to wherever it was that they were waiting to question me. I can't say for sure why I did that. Momentum, or the fear of being on my own. I can say that, blank or no, the sound of that shot had set a bag of kittens squirming in my stomach.

Once, there was a man named Chester Maher. He loved his daughter more than he loved the whole world. One day, he went to ground with her in a place called The Salmon Leap. Armed men surrounded them because he had a gun with him…

But was it a blank I'd heard? Of course it was a blank! The armed wing of the Garda Síochána knew bloody well it was a blank. Danaher had testified it was a blank. But then, you couldn't believe the Hail Mary out of his mouth.

This second interview was far less affable, far more an interrogation, during which the door remained resolutely closed. It continued well into the night, and when it was concluded there was no offer of a Garda car to drive me back to the flat.

Dark thoughts circled my footsteps with the doggedness of the shadows cast out by each successive street lamp. They were thieves after my tranquillity. There could no longer be any doubt. Irish Revenue, in cooperation with other far-flung jurisdictions, had unearthed a root system of money laundering in which, in however insignificant a capacity, the name William Regan featured. I was advised to cooperate, fully and openly, with the two interviewers. One, the greyer of the two, had a dour balance sheet of figures and names. From this he intoned, in foreign accents and precise grammar, a fiscal litany that I scarcely understood, but which included all sorts of exotic locations and currencies. I was shown photostats of documents in various alphabets, all of which I'd signed, apparently. The other, curly headed, effusive and obese, tossed off an odd threat in my direction as if it were the best joke in the world. I barely paid him heed, my ears still echoing with that shot I'd heard out in Chapelizod. I leafed through the photostats, unsure even now of what precisely I was being accused of. Yelena had been right. I was still a child.

Several things surprised me all the same. In the first place, neither of the two showed any interest in the goings on of one Joseph Mary Danaher. I began to wonder if the police could be so compartmentalised that they never looked beyond the blinkers of the particular case to hand. In the state I was in, all logic screamed of the relevance of Danaher's bogus bills to their lines of enquiry. In the second place, the jolly giant set before me a veritable beauty pageant of mugshots. He asked me whether I'd had intercourse with any of them. Intercourse. It was his word. No, I said, shaking my head at one after another of the unsmiling felons. I hesitated only over the slug lips and glasses of Adam Rakoczi. 'Let me see that one again,' I asked, finally, when I saw the two inquisitors exchange knowing looks. By this point I'd reviewed the entire portfolio. I'd been almost as baffled as I was relieved over the absence of Yelena Zamorska. Was this another of their accursed tricks? 'Yes,' I hummed, 'I think I may have seen this one before.'

'I'm bloody sure you may have seen this one before!' enthused Curly. 'I'm bloody sure we've sworn testimony you may have seen him before!' The dour one greeted this interjection with a look of repugnance. 'What's his name,' he delivered, more statement than question.

I looked to the mute walls. Was I turning snitch? Was I about to commit that most contemptible of underworld crimes? Would demons come to set fire to me in my own flat? The walls were blank and indifferent.

'His name is Rakoczi.' The two comedians exchanged a glance. 'Adam Rakoczi.'

I had no appetite to return to the flat and, though it was late, I allowed my feet to carry me to the sacristy. 'I'm afraid,' said Crowe, with no apparent irony, 'I'm not in a position to offer you a coffee. The fuse has gone in the canteen.'

'I've spent the entire day with the guards. I've coffee coming out of every pore.' We were both too weary to smile. 'So I told them everything. Just like you said. I even spilled the beans on a character named Rakoczi. Identified a photo for them. You'll say I was doing my duty. But I don't feel proud about it.'

'He was involved with your friend Danaher?'

'It's a long story,' and then I added, pointedly, '*Father*.' Did he even notice? 'Let's just say they're birds of a feather.' I inhaled, feeling very sorry for myself. 'So now I've turned grass.'

'You're being harsh on yourself, William. These men are criminals.'

'Jesus, they're nothing to the politicians and carpet-baggers has this town carved up between them.' I looked at my shoes and shook my head.

'You think you've let yourself down, is it?'

'I feel… a coward.'

'Sometimes,' he said, 'the more courageous choice can appear the more cowardly, and the cowardly, courageous. There's no honour in the so-called honour among thieves. It's just another way of passing the buck.'

'No pun intended,' I muttered sourly. But I welcomed the man's casuistry. It was a cud I'd be able to chew over, later on. 'Have you heard the latest on the Maher case?' He hadn't. 'They've tracked him back from Athlone to Chapelizod. That red Nissan must've been a decoy. He's holed up in a B&B with his daughter, Steph. Refuses to come out. We called around here for you this morning, only…'

'Only I wasn't here.'

Now I knew bloody well from the man's expression that whatever had taken him away had caused him unmitigated distress, but I wasn't ready as yet to face my demons alone. 'It seems he's got a gun.'

'A gun!'

'Danaher swears it's only a starting pistol, but...' I stopped. The man's gaunt expression put the fear of God in me. Suddenly, all concerns about Revenue and about turning tattletale had evaporated.

'He hasn't... threatened the girl?'

'Threatened the *girl*? Are you mad?' I searched his face for signs of madness. *Once, there was a man named Chester Maher...*

'But how do you know all this? Was it the police...?'

'I was out there, Father. I was supposed to calm him down.'

He consulted a wristwatch. 'The late news won't be on for another hour. Perhaps if you'd care to wait...' But things weren't to pan out that way. Fate had other ideas. At that very moment, the housekeeper entered, looking high and solitary and most stern. There was a telephone call from His Eminence. Ciarán Crowe nodded to her gravely, as though he'd been half expecting the summons. Left alone, my eyes moved around the sacristy and moved from the poster of the island monastery (was it?) to the class of Clonliffe. Was it on account of one of those faces, maybe, that he'd been whisked off to Harold's Cross that morning? When he came back in he looked as if every drop of blood had been drained from him. 'I'm afraid I'm going to have to leave you.' His eyes deflected, as though unready to meet mine. 'You may have heard, a colleague took his life this morning.' I felt a tickle of dread in my gut. This was symmetry, up to her tricks. *Once there was a man named Chester Maher...*

'A priest, was it?'

'They found him in the garage. He'd left the car engine running all night.' His eyes had withdrawn into shadow, and he'd fallen into contemplation. 'They say it's a painless way to go,' I supplied, feeling guilty I'd asked nothing before. 'Carbon monoxide,' I continued, 'they do say you're not even aware you're breathing it in.'

'Dear God!' he sighed, turning to the wall. Now he was looking at the heads in their constellation of black and white ovals. The class of '64. 'Was he…? Were the two of you very close?'

'I was in college with him. At one time, I suppose, we were close. Over the years we'd lost contact. It's the way of the world.'

'Was he…?' There seemed no word to round out the question.

'That was the Bishop on the phone. It seems he left a letter addressed to me. He'd been… oh dear God!' Crowe appeared to be suddenly startled by my presence. 'I'll have to go at once. We'll need to prepare a statement.'

'But why did he decide to…? Was it… you know…?'

'There were allegations. Allegations, no more than that.' He riveted his eyes upon me, imploring me not to ask him further. 'The press have been having quite the field day of late. I expect it finally drove him to despair.'

I'd drifted over to the portraits, but the turmoil in my gut was still howling: Chester Maher! Chester Maher! If I pick out the right photo, then he too has been finally driven to despair. My eyes ran over the ovals and were drawn irresistibly to a figure with glasses and heavy jowl.

'Is that the man?' I asked.

All the threads of the previous two years were weaving together. I passed my own front door, and on a whim I followed the South Circular until I was standing outside Yelena's flat. Here, the curtains of the bedroom were conspicuously ajar. But my sight could no more penetrate into the interior rooms than the television cameras could probe the recesses of Maher's barricaded bedroom. There was, for all that, an unmistakeable aura of abandonment about the place, far more profound than on my previous visit.

What is it about an empty room that exudes absence? The immobility? The melancholy of the furniture? I looked through the glass to the far wallpaper, upon which hung an emptied mirror, and I became certain that I'd looked for the last time on Yelena Zamorska.

No doubt it was this conviction that impelled me to hold a vigil. I leaned against a lamp post across the street as the invisible stars turned their slow cycle overhead. It ended only with the arrival of the mechanised street sweepers.

When Mother died, my thirty-year-old child's obduracy had tried to insist against all advice that she be brought back to the Liberties to be waked. But the common-sense view prevailed. Her open coffin sat all night in St Patrick's Mortuary, where toothless shades in slippers and cardigans shuffled in and out to pay their respects. I sat all night by the coffin, watching how the candles filled rock-pools of darkness in the tranquil wax of her face. They'd brushed her baby's hair, and dressed her in a smock that was embroidered with an image of the Virgin. No irony intended. Her hands were folded around her penny catechism. For whatever reason, the image of my dead mother haunted me all that night. It was as if her ghost had finally died.

How brief is the life of infamy. How soon does one disaster displace another from the fickle headlines. By the following morning, the papers all carried the suicide of the priest, of the suspect, of the monster. Of the balding man with glasses and a heavy jowl. I passed the newsagents and stood outside an electronics shop, where I watched his photo on the morning news. Various clerics spoke into various microphones. A bishop declined to comment. Then there was a report from the MacMurrough Tribunal. I recognised the sword and scales of justice tendered over the cobblestones of Dublin Castle. It all combined to knock the Chapelizod siege to third spot. From what I could make out through the glass, the standoff was continuing. There were a couple of tough-looking characters in body armour, and on the seat of an unmarked police car the camera picked out a gun. As for the B&B across the river, the cameras were unable to penetrate the drawn blind.

I don't know what time it was when I got back to my own flat. I fell into a profound slumber that was pierced by a sun already high. A spear of light stretched across the floor and into my pupils. My head was muzzy, my mouth sticky with mucous, as though I'd been drinking the night before. But I stood dizzily from the bed, gripped by the conviction that the standoff had already reached a cruel denouement.

I was not wrong.

Before I left the flat I scrambled together the price of a pint, just, and I hurried down to the local to catch the one o'clock bulletin. A news story was breaking, displacing both the suicide of the priest and the preliminary findings of the MacMurrough Tribunal. The first image was of a bulky figure with a coat covering the face being bundled into a squad car. There could be no mistaking who that character was. Then the camera went live to a correspondent across the river, standing at the front of The Salmon Leap. 'As the siege entered its third day, at eleven o'clock this morning the decision was taken by the authorities to force the door of the bedroom and to rush the assailant.' The assailant! 'But nothing could have alerted the Gardaí to what they would find inside that room.' The camera now jumped mistakenly back to the studio, then by another error to the church at Harold's Cross. At the third attempt, the grey head of a Garda Commissioner, not Purcell, came into prominence. '...that the tragedy could have been avoided. We'll have to await the coroner's report, but every indication is that the body had been lying there undisturbed for at least twenty-four hours...'

Once, there was a man named Chester Maher, who married a beautiful Parisian whom he brought to live in Cabra. For years he was tortured by her infidelities. But they had a child, a little girl, and he loved this child more than he loved the whole world. One day, tormented by debt, and by the fear that the child would be taken from him...

I stumbled as far as the canal. There, I collapsed into a squatting position, my eyes dry, burning, unable to focus.

Once, there was a depressive named Chester Maher, who married a beautiful Frenchwoman. She went to live with him in Cabra, where she had many lovers. He had a child by her, on balance, and he loved that child more than he loved the world. One day, while she was out of the country, he stole her and fled. But he left a trail of false notes behind him.

The police followed that trail of false notes and soon they had Chester Maher surrounded. He hid his child from them in a dark room. There, he tucked her up in bed, brushed the hair behind her ears, told her that she was his princess and, with ferocious tenderness, he smothered her beneath the red lamp of the Sacred Heart.

When, a full day later, they burst through the door, they found him still sitting on the bed, rocking backwards and forwards and laughing, soundlessly. There was a starting pistol on the floor beside him.

The rest of the story is easily told.

I was variously interviewed over the next few months by representatives of the Revenue, of Interpol, and of the Criminal Assets Bureau. During the course of one of these interviews I was informed that Yelena Zamorska had been deported. Whether they meant by this that she'd been extradited, I didn't ask. It was the first mention of her name, and although I felt my complexion burn, I maintained a respectful silence on the matter. I was amazed to find that the silence was reciprocated, though whether from ignorance, or from delicacy of feeling, I have never fathomed.

One afternoon, as the summer drew to a premature close, I was formally charged. I'd been in receipt of misappropriated funds and had acted as facilitator to a money laundering circle. If memory serves. My rights were read, and I was detained overnight in a cell. On the following morning I was brought into a large public building that smelt of antique wood and that displayed the various trappings of justice. I was amazed to find Purcell standing at the far corner of the huge desk before which I was led, for he'd taken no part in any of the financial interrogations. I was asked to confirm my name, and then the charges were again read out. Bail was set at a nominal amount. In keeping with my circumstances, as the magistrate put it. Purcell raised no objection. Legal counsel would be assigned, courtesy of the taxpayer. I was forbidden to apply for a passport, but was otherwise at liberty until such time as a date for the next hearing might be set. Adjourned!

Immediately outside the courtroom, in late sunshine, Ciarán Crowe stepped forward. He took me gravely by the arm and volunteered his services as character witness at the forthcoming trial. 'Whatever it takes', he promised. 'Even if I have to cut short my stint in the Holy Land.'

I shook my head. 'No need for that,' I smiled.

'Oh?'

'Not the slightest need, Father C. When the time comes, it's fully my intention to enter a plea of guilty as charged.'

And that is exactly what I did.

Postscript

*F*inita la commedia. My opera without music. But I feel I should add a few words. By way of postscript, as you might say.

The new millennium began for the author with the unparalleled drudgery of the penitentiary. He did not feel penitent, at least not in respect of financial irregularities. But he did soon feel the full weight of that interminable congealment of time. Time, whose infinitesimal trickle is the principal fact and experience in enclosures like the 'Joy. It'd be beyond my powers and purposes to describe the deadening routines, the nervous bravado, the fears and intimacies of the cell, where twenty-three hours out of twenty-four, the inmates breathe in each other's odours and prejudices.

I was lodged in the condemned wing. Oh, I don't mean that the prisoners there were condemned. They were petty felons like myself, for the most part. What I mean is that the wing had long since been condemned. Only the pressures of overcrowding had prolonged its dotage. Even buildings, it would seem, have their stays of execution.

It's no good. I can't continue to write it in this vein. The page refuses the ink. Ever since that gunshot, I was a changed man. Changed utterly. At blue o'clock in the morning, while the prison was resonant with slumbering, I'd be startled awake by that gunshot, or I'd find myself gasping for breath as though a pillow beneath a Sacred Heart lamp had been pressed over my face while I slept.

One day, one of the screws announced: 'Regan, visitor.' This was unexpected. I supposed it to be my legal counsel, for I couldn't think of a single person who knew I was in Mountjoy Gaol, let alone who might pay me a visit there. Crowe was in Jerusalem. Maher was on remand in the psychiatric wing of God-alone-knows what establishment, and undergoing all sorts of tests in tandem with his therapy. If the papers were to be believed, his trial mightn't take place for another year, pending the results of both of those. Yelena Zamorska was back in her native country, or was with Adam Rakoczi in his. I'd heard little since the deportation beyond a single postcard, which said *I will see you again Willy Regan*. There was no return address. In Ireland, they were *personae non gratae*, if that's the legal plural. And as for the possibility that Joseph Mary might bring his remoulded face within the confines of a prison, no, that was not to be countenanced.

I reflected dryly that none of my three acquaintances had fared particularly well in the two years that they'd known me.

Nevertheless, I had a caller. The screw stood by the open door, tapping it with idle truncheon so that it gave a low reverberation. Without having to accord him the satisfaction of a glance, I knew there would be an ironic malice in his eye. In all the months I'd been there, I'd not had a single visitor.

I made no particular effort to tidy myself before the improvised gong grew more insistent. There's a code of torpor that governs all motion in the 'Joy. But who in God's name could I be hurting with my non-compliance? Nor was this nice irony lost on Soul. I nodded to the indifferent guard as I stepped from the cell, and he allowed me to lead the way listlessly to the interview hall. He was hoping I'd lose my way along the labyrinth of cages and corridors. But I was up to him. I let instinct and hearsay guide my step, and unerringly

I arrived before my visitor. I had to look twice before I recognised him. Charles Stewart Parnell had shaved!

Of course I should've guessed it would be him, returned early from the Holy Land to visit me, the least of his brethren. The suntan suited him. It gave his skull a patina of health. So too the lack of beard. There was a smudge lodged between the eyes that wouldn't come into focus as I approached. Had he really grown so cavalier about his personal appearance? 'What happened your forehead?' I asked, sitting across from him, separated by the regulation two arms' length.

'Today is Ash Wednesday.' I squinted, and could just about make out in the charcoal thumbprints the trace of the crucifix. 'You didn't know?'

'There's not that much call for religion in a place like this.'

He smiled, ruefully. 'I'd have said that the opposite would be the case.' My eyes remained fixed upon the misshapen ashen cross. At the commencement of every Lent, Mother had worn those embers like a fading emblem of mortality. She'd never permitted me to wipe them from her brow before first confession on the following Saturday evening. 'I wasn't expecting you back so soon,' I said, when the silence extended between us. 'No.' I wondered for a while if that was all he was going to say on the subject. 'As you know, I'd intended to stay on until Easter. But things, as they say, have moved on since then.'

'One way or another, Father C., you're looking very well.'

'You still call me Father?'

'Old habits! Does it bother you?'

'It doesn't bother me.' He examined his fingernails. Then he looked directly at me. 'It's... no longer appropriate. You see I've come to a decision. I've decided to leave the priesthood.'

I sat back. This was a surprise.

'As you can imagine, it hasn't been an easy decision. But I decided in the end that I could no longer reconcile my position as a priest with the deep doubts that have been eating away at my belief.' He shifted about, momentarily ill at ease. 'What finally decided it for me was... do you remember my colleague?' An intensity in his eyes left me in no doubt he was referring to the suicide. I nodded. We all have our tipping points, it seems.

'He'd left me a letter, you see.'

'I remember.'

'But it wasn't so much the letter. It was this. He'd tried to get in touch with me beforehand. Twice, in point of fact, in the run up to that… dreadful night.' He sat up. 'Of course I was busy. I was dreadfully busy. His letter, too, set out to ease my conscience on that score. But still, I can't help but think, maybe if I'd made the time for him…'

'Maybe,' I said, fighting down the turbulence in my gut. 'There's no more dreadful word in the English language.' *If I hadn't've had you, Will Regan.* If I hadn't've pussy-footed about the city for hours on end… He shook his head. *Maybe,* said Soul, *there's more to it.* But I banished Soul from my company. When the silence grew prolonged, I looked again at the sooty badge between his eyes. 'You haven't said goodbye to religion entirely, though.' I wasn't ready yet for my own demons. 'To religion?' he smiled. Then he laughed, and so did I. Though I no more felt like laughing. Crying would be nearer the mark. 'I'd never equate religion with the Catholic Church! Do you know what the word actually means?' I shook my head. '*Religio* – I bind. It comes from the same root as the word ligature.'

'And so, you're bound to religion is it, like a bear to a stake?'

'I am tied to the stake and must stand its course.' I shrugged my ignorance of the quote, if quote it was. 'No,' he went on, 'it seemed to me that to stay on in the priesthood…' He shook his head and grunted. 'But tell me, how's your friend getting on?' Had thoughts of his colleague led to thoughts of my colleague? Thoughts of self-harm? Maybe. My guts were tumbling like a washing machine. Could I speak to the man? My eyes glancing to the warder, I played for time. 'You mean Chester Maher? The last I saw him was about a week before my own hearing…' I went on to describe the state of the man, still grinning and rocking himself in a catatonic other-world. Then, when I knew the session was about to be wound up, it came out: 'You know, they still haven't figured out the sequence of events? That shot. It's not clear if that was before or after he…' Words refused. 'I mean for God's sake, they don't even know for sure if it was his own head he was pointing it at!' And then a general bustle and words from the warder overtook us. Christ, I thought, yet again. Had he tried to shoot her? Had he tried to shoot himself, when he'd seen what his hands had done? Had that been part of his plan all along? Or, and this one always made me shudder, had he suddenly smothered his little girl, unable to face the future when the dud gun had failed to end his misery?

I'd avoided confiding in the priest. The ex-priest. But all that week I was in excruciating agony waiting for his next visit. I wasn't even sure he'd come. But I was sure only he could help me to get out of the pit I'd fallen into.

'I heard that gunshot! Don't you get it? I heard it!' But he didn't get it. 'All that day after I left you, instead of going straight to the guards like I said I would, I wandered around town, dithering.'

'But you did go.'

'Yes, but don't you see? By then it was too late. We could've been at that siege hours before we got there. For God's sake, even ten minutes might've made all the difference. If I hadn't been such a coward…'

He shook his head. 'Anyone can play that game.' His eyes bore into me. 'You went. That took courage.'

'And what good did it do?'

Eyes shut, he shook his head a second time. Perhaps he was thinking of the colleague that he'd let down. 'Anyone can play that game,' he repeated, his eyes shut fast. I glanced at the screw, standing vacantly in the corner. 'For God's sake,' I hissed, 'I shouldn't have interfered when that fool was hanging himself.'

I get the feeling he wanted to say something encouraging, something to take away my distress, my maybes and should'ves and shouldn't'ves. But he couldn't bring himself to do it. Not when it was so close to the bone.

On the third visit, he looked altogether more energetic. 'Tell me, when are you due to be released from this place?'

'With good behaviour, the earliest I can hope for is the end of August.'

'So soon?'

'The better half of my sentence was suspended. And then, there was the guilty plea to be taken into consideration.' I might've added, along with the fact I'd turned tattletale. I might've added, for all the good that did! 'I was never more than small beer in their investigations, Father.' Even without the beard, it seemed I couldn't leave off that Father.

'The end of August.' I could see he was calculating. 'Tell me, d'you remember you once asked me about a poster that was hanging up in the sacristy?' I made an indifferent gesture. 'It was a basilica, on a lake-isle. St Patrick's Purgatory.'

'Lough Derg?' The image of the octagonal building returned with unusual clarity. 'I remember,' I said, 'it looked like a prison.'

'It does, bedad! It does look like a prison! Well, I've come to invite you to go with me to that prison.'

'You're kidding me!'

'Not in the least. It's something I promised the Lord I'd do, when I was in Jerusalem. I'd like to invite you to accompany me there.'

'When are we talking about?'

'As soon as you're out. The pilgrimages run up until the first Sunday of September. So what do you say? Will you come?'

What can I say? I went. Isn't it obvious?

For the first time in my life, I broke out of the charmed circle of the city. I exchanged it for a mumbling circle of penitents, shivering with insomnia. But something on the lake-isle must have accorded well with the ascetic in me, because six weeks later I joined him on a pilgrimage up Croagh Patrick. It was on that windy summit, as we looked across the slant of Clew Bay with its three hundred and sixty-five islands, that Crowe first pressed me to set down all that had happened in writing.

'Is that to be my penance, Father?'

'Your *confessio*,' he corrected my quip. 'Maybe it'll help you make sense of it all.' Had he already foreseen the endless nights, spent before a desk in this misshapen room?

But it strikes me that all that is part of a different story.

We paid one visit only to Chester Maher. Crowe's idea. He'd finally been brought to trial for the murder of his daughter the month after I got out. By a unanimous verdict, he was found guilty, but insane. I understand we're the only visitors he ever received. We found him sitting by a bed in pyjamas and dressing gown, nodding and jabbering, and it wasn't clear he was even aware he had visitors. On the other hand, just as we were leaving, a trick of the light made me think there was something not altogether insane in his eye. I hope to Christ I'm mistaken.

Besides that single trip, I never again saw any of the three. For Yelena Zamorska, I had no return address, nor any way of knowing what country she was living in. My own addresses, too, became so uncertain I lost track of my own mail. As the first year wore into a second and the second into a third, she visited me less and less in my dreams until the time came when I had to make a conscious effort to remember her contours.

I met Purcell one day on the street. He informed me that Danaher's course of skin grafts, by which he meant interventions, was being continued in a hospital somewhere up North. A patchwork face for a patchwork jurisdiction. I don't know what sort of deal he'd cut with the DPP down here, but he was never prosecuted for possession of a firearm, for all that it was only a starting pistol, nor for fencing the counterfeit bills, nor charged with the death of the old woman.

Mother's ghost disappeared. Or she gave up on me. At any rate, she no longer dogs my steps down the side streets of this restless town, nor ghosts me as I read through what I've written. And what is it I've written? Chester Maher once told me they used to believe there was a music that governed the motion of the spheres. After four centuries, they still haven't heard it. But you have to ask: is that on account of silence, or deafness?